sammy KEYES

and the KILLER CRUISE

FAVORITES BY WENDELIN VAN DRAANEN

Sammy Keyes and the Hotel Thief
Sammy Keyes and the Skeleton Man
Sammy Keyes and the Sisters of Mercy
Sammy Keyes and the Runaway Elf
Sammy Keyes and the Curse of Moustache Mary
Sammy Keyes and the Hollywood Mummy
Sammy Keyes and the Search for Snake Eyes
Sammy Keyes and the Art of Deception
Sammy Keyes and the Psycho Kitty Queen
Sammy Keyes and the Dead Giveaway
Sammy Keyes and the Wild Things
Sammy Keyes and the Cold Hard Cash
Sammy Keyes and the Wedding Crasher
Sammy Keyes and the Night of Skulls
Sammy Keyes and the Power of Justice Jack
Sammy Keyes and the Showdown in Sin City
Sammy Keyes and the Killer Cruise
Sammy Keyes and the Kiss Goodbye

How I Survived Being a Girl
Flipped
Swear to Howdy
Runaway
Confessions of a Serial Kisser
The Running Dream

sammy KEYES
and the KILLER CRUISE

WENDELIN VAN DRAANEN

A YEARLING BOOK

Text copyright © 2013 by Wendelin Van Draanen Parsons
Cover art copyright © 2014 by Karl Edwards

All rights reserved. Published in the United States by Yearling, an imprint of Random House Children's Books, a division of Random House LLC, a Penguin Random House Company, New York. Originally published in hardcover in the United States by Alfred A. Knopf, an imprint of Random House Children's Books, New York, in 2013.

Yearling and the jumping horse design are registered trademarks of Random House LLC.

Visit us on the Web! randomhouse.com/kids

Educators and librarians, for a variety of teaching tools,
visit us at RHTeachersLibrarians.com

The Library of Congress has cataloged the hardcover edition of this work as follows:
Van Draanen, Wendelin.
Sammy Keyes and the killer cruise / Wendelin Van Draanen
p. cm.
Summary: Teen sleuth Sammy Keyes solves a classic locked-room mystery aboard a cruise ship.
ISBN 978-0-375-87054-5 (trade) — ISBN 978-0-375-97054-2 (lib. bdg.) —
ISBN 978-0-307-97409-9 (ebook) — ISBN 978-0-307-93062-0 (pbk.)
[1. Wealth—Fiction. 2. Family problems—Fiction. 3. Missing persons—Fiction.
4. Fathers and daughters—Fiction. 5. Cruise ships—Fiction. 6. Friendship—Fiction.
7. Mystery and detective stories.] I. Title.
PZ7.V2857Safm 2013 [Fic]—dc23 2012045296

Printed in the United States of America

10 9 8 7 6 5 4 3 2

First Yearling Edition 2014

Random House Children's Books supports the First Amendment and celebrates the right to read.

This book is dedicated to Sue Grafton, Margaret Maron,
and in memory of Joan Lowery Nixon.
Each provided encouragement to me in advance of the first
Sammy Keyes book, and each has been inspirational since.

Special thanks go to
Dr. Nanine Van Draanen, chemistry professor
and sister extraordinaire,
and to
Mark Parsons and Nancy Siscoe, my partners in crime for every
Sammy Keyes book, but especially this one!

sammy KEYES

and the KILLER CRUISE

PROLOGUE

I look back on things I've done and wonder . . . why didn't I see that coming?

Why didn't I know that was a bad idea?

Why didn't someone *warn* me?

Grams would tell you she *does* warn me and that the question should really be, Why don't I *listen*?

Which, yeah, I admit, is usually the case.

But not this time. This time, *I* thought it was a bad idea. This time, I warned Grams and my mother and Hudson and anyone else who told me it was a good idea that it was a bad idea.

This time, *they* didn't listen.

Which is how I wound up on a cruise ship with a dad I barely knew, an endless buffet of party animals, and a family of creepy millionaires.

Happy birthday to me.

ONE

I was allowed to bring one friend. And since Marissa McKenze has been my best friend since third grade, and since it looks like she'll be moving to Ohio in June because her mom's lined up a job there, and who knows how long it'll be before I'll get to do anything with her again after that, and since I wasn't allowed to bring Casey because he's my boyfriend and it would have been "inappropriate," and since my other good friend Holly thought cruising sounded like a nightmare, the choice was easy.

Marissa.

Even Mrs. McKenze was for it, and she's never for anything that has to do with her daughter spending time with me. According to her, I'm "hazardous."

And yet, there we were, at the Long Beach dock with our luggage and passports, about to cruise to Mexico.

Actually, I think Mrs. McKenze being okay with the trip had more to do with Darren Cole being my dad than her daughter having one last adventure with her best friend.

He seems to have that effect on middle-aged women.

Something about the shaggy hair and the guitar makes them lose their minds.

Or, at least, their common sense.

Him sending a car service to get us to the dock didn't hurt, either. Mrs. McKenze actually gasped when she heard it was how we were getting to Los Angeles, and I could tell I was suddenly a friend she *wanted* her daughter to hang with instead of the "hazard" I'd been before. Why a week away with a musician didn't register as a hazard to her was beyond me, but like I said, common sense didn't apply.

Marissa was over the moon about going on the cruise. She'd been on cruises before with her family, pre–financial meltdown/divorce. "It's awesome, Sammy. You have no idea! You can't even picture it, it's so amazing! It's like twenty stories of a Las Vegas resort steaming through the ocean!"

I've been to Las Vegas, so that didn't help sell me on the idea at *all*.

And since she hadn't actually met my dad in person yet, she'd blown the whole thing way out of proportion. People would ask us what we were doing over spring break, and she'd say, "Sammy and I are going on a celebrity cruise!"

"It's not a celebrity cruise!" I'd tell her through my teeth.

"Sure it is! Your dad's a celebrity and he's playing on the cruise!"

"He's playing one night. That's all!"

But it was like she couldn't help herself. She kept letting it slip out until finally I told her, "Knock it off or stay home!"

Her eyes had gotten huge. "You wouldn't do that to me!"

"Yes, I would! The whole situation is embarrassing enough without you doing this!"

Which it was. It had only been about six weeks since I'd found out that my dad was Darren Cole of Darren Cole and the Troublemakers, and I was still pretty weirded out by it. Partly because going from being poor to finding out you're the daughter of a rock star puts you smack-dab in the middle of some really strange territory, and partly because people at school love to gossip and Darren Cole being my father became Big News fast.

It was amazing to see how many new "friends" I suddenly had, too. People who'd made fun of me before were now kissing up to me.

Thanks, but no thanks.

And Darren had set me up with a cell phone—my first one ever, if you can believe that. At first I was like, Wow, this is so cool! But then my mother started calling. And texting. Like, constantly. It made me wish I *didn't* have a phone, because instead of just being able to come up with some excuse about where I was or why I was late, I was now on a buzzing leash.

What's weird was that she wasn't checking up on me or being, you know, *supervisorial*. Since she'd moved to Hollywood, we'd really grown apart, and now she was using the phone as a way to try to reconnect.

Either that or she was worried or jealous or whatever because Darren was texting me, too, trying to get to know me, asking me things that she was clueless about. I mean, how embarrassing is that? Keeping your daughter from her dad for almost fourteen years and then having her dad know things about her that you don't?

So between her being all, Come to L.A. for the week-end! Let's go shopping! and Darren texting things like, "Dream pet?" and "Favorite color?" and "Worst subject?" I was the one hiding and avoiding and "forgetting" to turn on my phone.

I was really relieved when Darren told me I couldn't use my phone on the cruise—something about "sky-high international rates." But I think it also had to do with the whole point of the cruise, which was us getting to know each other, not constantly texting.

I was also relieved when he told my mother that she couldn't come on the cruise with us. He didn't say it be-cause he didn't like her—they were obviously back to be-ing nuts about each other—but because with her around, there was no way I was going to relax and he knew it. So he told her no, even though that meant she was going to miss my fourteenth birthday.

I was secretly happy not to have her around on my birthday, seeing how she'd totally messed up the last one. Grams, I kind of felt bad about because she'd not only been at every one of my birthdays, but she'd also been there for me on all the days in between. But she was married to Hudson now, and the two of them were doing a slow tran-sition from the Senior Highrise, where Grams and I had been living for the past two and a half years, to Hudson's house on Cypress Street.

There was nothing slow about *my* transition out of the Highrise. Hudson invited me to live with them and, *boom,* I was gone. And my cat, Dorito, *loved* prowling around. So at first I didn't really get why Grams couldn't just abandon the Highrise and live happily ever after on Cypress Street, but Hudson explained that it was hard for Grams to give up her independence so spontaneously.

I guess Las Vegas weddings have their aftershocks, even when you're a senior citizen.

Grams and Hudson *had* thrown a little pre-birthday cake-and-ice-cream party for me, which was nice, but also sort of strange because thirteen wasn't actually over yet and my mother was trying too hard to make up for last year's fiasco. The best part of the party was definitely that Casey was there and had customized a pair of gray high-tops for me by writing on them with a black Sharpie. Both shoes were covered with things like "Shortcut Sammy Rides Again!" and "Holy Smokes!" and "Dive for the Bushes!" Plus he'd drawn little pictures that brought back funny memories. There was a pig labeled "Penny" and some skulls labeled "Not Candy!" and a headstone labeled "Sassypants."

And then there was the heart with "S+C Forever" in it.

It was the most amazing present ever.

My mother tried her diva best not to show it, but I know she was sort of miffed that I was way more excited over some "scribbled-on shoes" than I was about the dainty charm bracelet she'd given me.

The bottom line is, my mother doesn't get me, which is why I was glad Darren had told her she couldn't go on the cruise. I mean, birthday or not, and getting to know my rock star dad or not, sharing a cabin with Marissa was going to be a whole lot more fun than sharing one with a person who disapproves of everything from my high-tops to my attitude. And really, the fact that Darren seemed to understand that went a long way toward making me think that being trapped on a boat with him for six days might actually be all right.

Still. When we're at the Long Beach dock waiting for Darren to show up, and Marissa suddenly points and squeals, "There he *is*," I can tell she's going to be trouble. So I grab her and get right in her face. "No squealing. No fawning. No gushing or gawking or . . . or fainting! He is just a guy. Just. A. Guy."

There are masses of people swarming around and checking their luggage at different stations, but when I look over to where Marissa had pointed, I spot Darren right away. Maybe it's the Louis Vuitton sunglasses. Or the blazer he's wearing instead of the beachy clothes so many other people are wearing.

Or maybe it's the boots.

Who wears boots on a cruise?

"Sammy!" he calls, flashing a great big smile.

He's got no luggage. No suitcase, no guitar, no nothing.

And that's when it hits me—he's not coming.

Something's come up and he can't make it.

I can feel myself get mad and hurt and withdrawn all at once.

Like I haven't had enough cancellations and gushing apologies and pathetic excuses from my diva mother?

But, hey, just another reality check—I should be used to getting them handed to me by now.

"Sammy!" he calls again.

I do give him a nod, but Marissa doesn't catch it. "Why aren't you answering him?" she asks, and then does a big, dopey wave that people in Hawaii could have seen.

"We canceled?" I ask when he gets up to us.

He slips the Louis Vuittons down his nose and looks at me, eye to eye. "Canceled? Why would we be canceled?"

"Where's your stuff?" I ask, looking around like, Hello, stuff . . . ?

"It's being loaded in with the band's gear." He has a quick conversation with our driver/escort and signs some papers, and then all of a sudden he calls out, "Marko! Marko, over here!"

Marissa whips around to look, then whips back and whispers, "Who's Marko?"

"The drummer," I tell her, and before you know it, he's standing right there, in board shorts and a cool gray T, with his shaved head and a little piratey earring, smiling from ear to ear, going, "Dude! The ship is *huge*."

Darren slaps his shoulder and checks him over with a grin. "You goin' on a cruise or something?"

"Dude, I am so ready!" Then Marko smiles at me and says, "Hey-yo, Sammy!"

Darren pulls out a big envelope of paperwork from inside his sports coat. "Let the adventure begin!"

"Uh, I'm Marissa?" Marissa says, putting a hand out.

Darren pumps it. "Darren." He turns to Marko. "And this is my best friend and troublemakin' timekeeper, Marko."

Marko shakes her hand and says, "Nice to meet you, Marissa," but as Darren starts to walk, she looks around a little and asks, "Aren't we waiting for the others?"

Darren looks over his shoulder at her. "The others?"

"The rest of the band?"

Darren smiles at her. "Glad you're on the lookout for trouble, but Drew and Cardillo aren't meeting up with us until later."

"Wow," Marissa whispers as Darren leads us to a line where we're supposed to turn over our luggage. "Is he your dad or what?"

"Shh!" Then I ask, "What do you mean?"

"His eyes, the way he smiles, the way he—"

"Shh!"

"How can you be so matter-of-fact about this? This is awesome!"

And I know she's right.

I know that it is.

And the truth is, I have butterflies.

Not nervous butterflies.

Happy butterflies.

I can't quite believe we're here, doing this. I can't quite believe that nothing's "come up," that nobody's flaked, and that I'm going on a cruise with . . . with my dad.

"Why are you crying?" Marissa whispers.

I shake it off. "I'm okay."

"You sure?"

I nod and roll my luggage up closer to Darren and Marko.

Let the adventure begin!

TWO

After we turned in our luggage, Darren and Marko led us inside a big metal building where we went down some corridors, passed through security, and wound up in a warehouse where we got in a long, zigzagging line.

I did a lot of gawking because it was all new to me, but the only thing Marissa seemed to be impressed by was Darren.

"Knock it off!" I finally told her, because she was watching his every move. And she did knock it off for a whole minute, but then went back to staring. *"Marissa,"* I said through my teeth.

"Sorry!"

And since I knew that wouldn't last, I decided to make up a distraction. "If you'd quit staring and look around a little, you'd notice *you're* being watched."

That made her eyes fly open. "I am?"

"Those guys?" I whispered, nodding at the backs of two boys in the zag ahead of our zig. "They were definitely checking you out."

Now, since the line is snaking back and forth, it doesn't take too long for those same two boys to be facing us instead of walking away from us. And since Marissa is now on high alert, she starts checking *them* out, and before you know it, they're noticing that the cute girl in the line behind them is watching them. So then they *do* start checking her out and pretty soon my little lie has become reality.

Amazing.

Anyway, while we're zigging and zagging and scooting forward in line, Darren and Marko are oblivious because they're all intent on filling out forms. Darren seems really *serious* about it, too, checking and double-checking paperwork and passports and birth certificates, shuffling stuff around until it's in some special order.

"Did she give you my forged birth certificate?" I finally ask, and really, I meant it as a joke because I figured my mom had, you know, confessed her sins. And since the paternity test had come back saying I was his kid, it wasn't like a birth certificate that had the wrong year on it was going to mess that up.

But the minute it's out of my mouth I know that it's a stupid thing to joke about. His eyebrows go flying. "There's a *forged* one?"

"Uh, never mind." I try to wave it off. "It had to do with getting me into school early."

"Why would she . . . ?"

He's obviously still clueless about my mother's sneaky ways. So I just shrug and say, "It was cheaper than paying for day care? But I wound up being a 'behavioral problem' and got held back."

"So . . . you did kindergarten twice?"

"Mm-hmm." I grin at him. "Scarred me for life."

Marko chuckles. "Troublemaker."

And I eye Darren and tell him, "I did thirteen twice, too."

"Thirteen . . . ?"

Darren's voice trails off again, but Marko figures out what I'm saying. "So Lana didn't tell you that she'd enrolled you in school early until last year?"

I nod and give a little snort. "It was some birthday, let me tell you." I mock my mom's voice, going, "Terribly sorry to break it to you, darling, but you're going to be thirteen all over again." I look at Darren. "You have no idea how happy I am to be leaving that number behind."

Darren stares for a minute while it all sinks in, and I have to laugh because Mr. Cool Rocker Dude is not looking cool at all. He's looking flustered. And worried. Like he's just realized he's in the deep dark woods without any weapons.

Marko laughs, too. "Take a breath, bro. It'll be okay."

Right then Marissa grabs me and whispers, "The blond one has *gorgeous* eyes," and that's when I realize that the whole time I've been talking about doctored birth certificates, Marissa's been checking out the boys I'd told her had been checking *her* out.

I roll my eyes.

"What?" she says, all defensively.

"You're such a butterfly."

"A butterfly?"

"Yeah."

"Like a *social* butterfly?"

"No. Just a butterfly. You know, pretty, fluttering around, checking things out but not quite landing . . . ?"

"I am not fluttering around!"

I laugh. "But you're definitely checking things out!"

She backhands me and whispers, "Shh! Here they come!"

Which is true. They're facing us again, and as they scoot forward in their zag line, we do the same in our zig. The guys look like they're our age or maybe a little older and they're with three adults—two women and a man. Two of the grown-ups are obviously a couple because they're the same shade of tan, and with their matchy polo shirts and sun visors, they look like they've just stepped off the golf course.

The other woman looks, well, *diagonal*. Like she's been spun through a giant apple peeler or something. Her hair is cut in a spiral that starts at the top of one ear and swoops around the back of her head to the bottom of her other ear. And her sundress has only one shoulder and it sort of spirals down to the hem, which angles from about mid-thigh on one leg to below the knee on the other.

Anyway, all of them are some variety of extreme blond except for one of the boys, who is African American. And as they scoot closer, I can see what Marissa means about the blond boy's eyes—they're incredibly blue.

"What did I tell you?" Marissa gasps when they're safely past us.

I give a little nod. "Like beacons of light in a dark, troubled world."

"Shut up!" she laughs, and backhands me again.

Now, the whole time we're scooting away from them

and then turning and moving *toward* them again, Marissa's fluttering. To the point where Marko notices and nudges Darren, who finally tunes in to what's going on. "No!" he says, looking from us to the boys and back again. He turns to Marko. "I don't know if I'm equipped for this!"

Marko just laughs.

We all scoot forward again and now Marissa and Beacon Eyes are not even hiding the fact that they're fluttering around.

"Hey," Beacon Eyes says with a grin, "I'm JT."

"And I'm his cousin, Kip," the other boy says.

Kip's voice has a little accent to it, and since there's nothing blue-eyed or blond-haired about him, Marissa's looking back and forth at them, obviously thinking, You're *cousins?*

JT totally calls her on it, saying, "Yes, he's adopted."

Awkward!

Marissa blushes and since everyone's scooting forward again and it feels like we're trapped in Awkwardville, I smile at Kip and try an escape hatch. "Well, her name's Marissa and she was raised by wolves."

Kip gives me a smile back. "And you?"

I grin at him. "Wolves, too. But my name is Sammy."

Kip laughs. It's a kind of tittering laugh. You know, sort of a guy giggle? And something about it makes me turn around and grin at him again—this time bigger.

He's looking over his shoulder, too. Grinning, too. "See you on the flip side," he calls, and moves on.

And then Darren's hovering over us going, "I should probably lay down ground rules?"

15

He says it like it's something he knows he should do, but isn't really sure how to. So I ask him, "About . . . ?"

His face gets a little contorted. "Boys?"

"All we did was say hi to them."

"You call that just saying hi?" He pops his sunglasses on top of his head. "That was way more than just saying hi!" He stares at me, then starts blinking in a very un-rock-star-like fashion before he turns to Marko and mouths, "What am I going to do?" which Marissa and I can both totally see.

"Look," I tell him, "you've got nothing to worry about."

Marko chuckles. "Famous last words."

So Darren put his rock star foot down. "Here's the deal: no boys in your cabin, no visiting boys in their cabins. Boys and you stay in public areas. Are we clear?"

Marissa and I nod.

"I want you to have fun, but please don't go wild on me."

Part of me wants to act insulted that he would even *imply* that we're that kind of teenager, but he's obviously stressed, and really, how would he know?

So I just give him a simple "Got it." But even after I've given him zero argument, he's still looking . . . bottled up. Like there are pressures inside that need to come out. So I finally go, "What else."

He looks right at me for a minute, then kind of shakes his head and looks down. "When I was a teenager, I wanted to get away from my parents so bad. I honestly have no idea what I'm doing with this dad thing. I don't want to be the heavy, but I know it's a mistake to try and be your friend. . . ." He gives a little shrug, then looks at me. "So expect me to screw up, and when I do, don't cop an attitude or play head games with me—just tell me."

This was so different from any conversation I'd ever had with my mother. Instead of trying to cover up or hide, he was just laying it all out there.

Which sort of stunned me.

But was also really . . . nice.

So I give him a little smile and tell him, "I can do that."

He laughs. "I bet you can!"

"And really," I add, "you can trust us—we won't cause you that kind of trouble."

He takes a deep breath, holds it a minute, then lets it out. "Okay. Thanks. I think I can handle the other kinds."

I felt weirdly happy after that. Then we passed by JT and Kip again, and Marissa let it slip that we were with Darren Cole. "You know, the musician?"

I give Marissa a dark look and say, "Do not do that!" but it's too late. All of a sudden, the Diagonal Dame and the Golf Team are reaching across the aisle, shaking hands with Darren and Marko, going, "I'm Teresa, Kip's mom!" and "We're JT's parents, Lucas and LuAnn!" and then spouting off about how they're doing the trip as a "Kensington family reunion" and throwing around information about themselves like they're long-lost friends. "I'm a fashion designer!" the Diagonal Dame says, rummaging through her purse for a business card. "I could do some really interesting pieces for your next tour!"

"We've got villas all over!" Tan Man says, handing Darren a business card, too. "Be our guest anytime!"

Darren takes the cards but I can tell he doesn't want them, and somewhere along the line, the sunglasses have come back down.

"I can't believe they make you slog through this line!" the Fashionista says to Darren, and then the Tan Man adds, "That's right—isn't there some VIP entrance somewhere?"

Darren says, "Normally, they'd have us come in through the crew entrance, but I'm here with my daughter for the full experience." Then he slings an arm across my shoulders and grins at me.

I don't know how to explain it other than to say that the theory of a dad—or even knowing who he is—is not the same thing as feeling like you have one. I mean, everyone's got a dad. Or, you know, a father. But just because you know he exists in your head doesn't mean he's also in your heart. And the truth is, I'd sort of quarantined Darren Cole to my head. I mean, the situation was strange and awkward and bizarre, and I was having so much trouble wrapping my head around finally knowing who he was that I didn't see how he could ever actually become a "real" dad.

But something about his little sling over my shoulders, something about the grin and the way he'd said I was his daughter like he was actually *stoked* about it—it was the first time I felt a little hiccup in my heart about him.

And then his arm was off and we were moving forward, and Darren was talking to Marko, and Marissa was talking to me, and my head was putting Darren back in quarantine, where a dad you barely know belongs.

THREE

Darren did ask Marissa not to point them out to people again, and then casually kept his back to the cluster of Kensingtons for the last zig and zag of the line.

After we'd made it through check-in, we went out of the giant warehouse through a wide corridor room, where a cheesy photographer made us stand in front of a cheesy backdrop and say, "Cheese!"

Then, finally, we went outside.

"Holy smokes!" I gasp, and stop dead in my tracks.

"Big, huh?" Marissa says, like this floating city in front of us is no big deal.

She keeps on trucking, following Darren and Marko along a covered walkway that parallels the cruise ship, but I just can't stop gawking. The ship is really long and really white, and there are, like, fifteen stories of little windows going up, up, up. And it's *right there,* with only a narrow channel of water between us and it.

"Sammy! Come on!"

Marissa's waving me up the walkway, and ladies wearing sundresses are passing me by, so I race to catch up. "I can't believe how *big* it is!"

"I know, right?" Darren says, and since he's sounding pretty amazed, too, I ask him, "Is this your first cruise?"

He nods. "Cruising was not exactly on my bucket list."

"Mine, either," Marko says as we turn onto the gangway and head across the channel toward an opening in the ship. "But I'm thinkin' maybe it shoulda been."

The gangway's not a couple of funky planks like you see in old movies and cartoons. It's wide and long and has safety siding and an arched blue canopy over it. Like something you might see outside a fancy hotel or restaurant, only much longer and bridging over deep water.

"So wait," Marissa says. "I'm the only one of us who's cruised before?"

Marko eyes her over his shoulder, then announces, "Overboard with the wench! No repeat offenders allowed."

I laugh 'cause, really, who needs been-here-done-this when you're amped about something new?

At the end of the gangway there's a man announcing, "Have your sea pass out. Remove hats and sunglasses. Welcome aboard!"

Darren shuffles through all the check-in stuff and hands around what look like credit cards. Mine has my name and a bunch of other stuff printed on the front, and on the back it tells me that I should carry it with me at all times.

"What is this thing?"

I was asking Darren, but Marissa pipes up with, "That's your sea-pass card. It's your stateroom key, your extras charge card, and you need it when you disembark and reboard."

I look at Darren for help but he just sort of shrugs and laughs, "I think she's saying, 'Don't lose it.'"

Marissa nods. "Exactly!" She starts pointing to stuff printed on my card. "This is our formal dining room and the table number, this is our seating time. . . ." She looks at me all twinkly-eyed. "The dining rooms are *amazing*."

I blink at her. "You're not talking seven-silver-forks amazing, are you?"

She laughs. "Maybe only five?"

I look at Darren. "I cannot do five-fork dining!"

But we're at the head of the line now, and one by one we hand our cards over to a woman behind a podium, get mug shots taken, then get our sea-pass cards back.

"What was that for?" I ask, because I have no idea what just happened.

"They sync up your card to your face," Marissa tells me, "so if you leave the ship, they know it's you when you get back on."

"Wait. When am I getting off the ship?"

She looks at me like she can't quite believe how green I am about this. "At the ports?"

Now, the truth is, there was all this stuff Darren had told me to read about online, but my head hadn't been in the cruise. I'd been trying to get my schoolwork done so I wouldn't have to worry about *it* on the cruise. To make a long story short, I really want to get on the college track when I move up to high school next year, which means that I've had to buckle down. I didn't used to care, but now I do, and let's just say it's not easy to catch up when you're as far behind as I was. But I'd managed to finish all my makeup work, plus everything assigned over spring break . . . *except* for Ms. Rothhammer's science assignment, which was brutal. We were on a chemistry section, and the work sheet had gnarly word problems that made you do confusing calculations of chemical reactions. There was a time I would have blown it off, but Ms. Rothhammer is my favorite teacher, so I'd brought the assignment with me, thinking that if I did only three problems a day, I'd have it done on time.

Anyway, the *point* is, I never went online to check out the ship or the ports or the food or the cabins or the dining rooms. I just collected most of what was on the list Darren had sent me, threw it in a suitcase, and got in the town car when it showed up at Hudson's house. So I wasn't, you know, *prepared* for any of this, and I sure wasn't expecting what we saw after we left the mug-shot zone and stepped around the corner.

It was like entering an air-conditioned palace. The room was huge and ritzy, with marble and glass and brass everywhere. There were wide, swooping staircases that went up one flight, and glass elevators that went up for *miles.* And as we walked along, we passed by a whole *feast* of food, complete with a chef slicing meat off a giant roast.

I guess Marko hadn't done his homework, either. "Dude!" he said, about bursting with excitement. "This is killer!"

And Marissa was right—it did feel like we were in some ritzy resort in Las Vegas instead of on a ship. "Can we eat?"

I ask, because the food looks *amazing* and suddenly I'm starving.

Darren's shuffling through paperwork. "How about we find our rooms first?" Marko catches my eye, and I can tell he'd like to chow down now, too, but Darren's already heading for the elevators, going, "Our rooms are on Deck 9," so we wind up following him instead.

The back wall of the elevator is glass and bowed out, and once the doors close, Marissa and I stand looking outward as we start going up. We can see people inside the elevators that are across a big open area from us, everything below, and even above, which is so cool. It's like being in a glass pod flying through space. I get this urge to wave at the people going down in the elevator across from us, but I know it's dorky, so I hold back.

But then I realize that I *know* people in the elevator across from us.

So I cut loose!

"Hey! That's JT and Kip!" Marissa says, and waves, too. And we're acting like such doofs, jumping up and down and waving real big, that they *do* notice us, but it's at the last minute, and then they've zoomed out of view.

"Oh, maaaan," Darren says, and he's shaking his head.

I give him a little shove. "Don't *worry* so much."

We're at Deck 9 now, and when we step off the elevator, Marissa asks, "What are our stateroom numbers?"

I squint at her. "Why are they called *state*rooms?"

Marissa shrugs. "Cabins, staterooms, whatever."

Darren's checked the paperwork, and the minute he

says, "We're in 9606 and 9608," Marissa checks a plaque that's mounted on the wall and announces, "Port side!" and starts toward the other side of the ship.

"Whoa, whoa!" Darren says, calling her back.

It takes a few steps, but Marissa does stop and come back. "They're over here, really!"

"I'm sure they are," Darren tells her, "but legally, you two can't have a room together. You have to be with someone twenty-one or older, so the travel agent signed Sammy up with me and Marissa up with Marko in rooms right next door to each other. So Sammy and Marko will just switch."

Marissa nods. "That's what my mom and dad did with me and my brother. That's what everyone does." She looks at me and Marko. "You need to switch cards so you can get in the right room, but you can't get off or back on the ship without trading back."

Marko's not looking too convinced. "Sounds . . . complicated."

But Marissa snatches his card and my card and switches them. "It's easy, really," she says. "You'll catch on."

"Marissa," I tell her through my teeth. "You're being kinda bossy."

Which makes her totally back down. "Oh!" She looks around at all of us. "I'm sorry. I'm sorry, sorry, sorry! I'm just excited. I'll shut up now."

Both the guys tell her it's all right, and then Darren says, "Port side, huh?"

"As opposed to what?" I ask.

"Uh, starboard side?" Marissa says.

"Wait. So the port will always be on *that* side," I say,

pointing to where she'd headed, "and the stars are always on the other side? How can that be? Stars are everywhere. And what happens when the boat goes the other direction?"

"Silly," she laughs. "When you're facing the bow, the left is always port and the right is always starboard. Doesn't matter which way you're going."

"Well, that's confusing. Why would they call it the port side when the port is on the other side?"

"Can we just find the rooms?" Darren asks, and I can tell we're already giving him a headache.

But Marko's grinning. "I wonder if our rooms are fore or aft."

"I'm guessing forward of here," Marissa says. "Since we're closer to the stern than the bow."

I shake my head. "Please. This is already too hard. I can't memorize a whole vocabulary list just to know where I'm going! My brain is full up with Avogadro's number and the stupid periodic table!"

Marissa's eyes get huge. "Tell me you didn't bring homework!"

"I had to, and my brain's already full of stuff I don't understand, so can we please just use simple English? Forward, backward, left, right, up, and down?"

Darren laughs. "Amen."

"Whatever," Marissa says. "But you're gonna get turned around because the signs all say *fore* and *aft,* and when the captain makes his announcements, he'll say *starboard* and *port,* and how will you know where to dash to see the dolphins if you don't know what he's saying?"

I give her a little squint. "I'll follow everyone else?"

We go by a big balcony view of the open area between the sets of glass elevators, and looking down makes me kinda dizzy. "Whoa."

"Yeah, don't fall," Darren says, pulling me away.

Not that I could fall.

Well, unless I did some climbing first, but why would I do that?

"They're right here!" Marko says, diagonaling to the right. And sure enough, "staterooms" 9606 and 9608 are at the very beginning of a hallway right by the elevator area.

"Whoa," I say again, 'cause now I can see that the hallway goes off in both directions and seems to go on *forever*. Suddenly the layout is feeling very disorienting. Like you *could* be walking down one of these long hallways and forget which direction you're going. I look at Marissa. "Uh . . . which way's the front of the ship?"

"Forward, or *fore*, is that way," Marissa says, pointing to the right.

I nod, 'cause she's made that easy to remember.

"It takes you to the *bow*," she says. "You *bow* forward, right?"

I give her a little bow and smile because I know she's trying super-hard to be nice about this.

She points to the left. "That way is *aft*. It's *aft*er everything else. Like your back end, right? Which on a ship is called the stern." She rolls her eyes a little. "Don't ask me why."

"So are we on the port side?"

"Yes!" she cries.

Like I'm her star pupil.

Which actually makes me feel pretty good until I remember that she had *said* earlier that we were on the port side.

Marko gives me a piratey look. "Arrrg! What's this mutiny of simple English?"

I laugh. "Don't worry. I still know how to speak it."

Darren's already opened 9608 with his sea-pass card and tells Marissa and me, "Go check out your room, then let's eat!"

Darren and Marko's door is in the very corner of the elevator area, but ours is definitely *in* the hallway. Marissa nods at the doors across the hallway from us. "Those are interior cabins," she whispers. "No windows. I'm glad your dad got us one with a balcony."

"Call him Darren," I tell her, and it kinda bugs me that she already knows what our room is like when we're not even inside it yet.

Anyway, we go in and pass by a little bathroom on the left and a closet on the right, and then enter the main part of the cabin, which has two beds, a little couch, a TV, a compact armchair, and a built-in desk.

"Check it out," I laugh, 'cause there are white towels folded into the shape of turtles on the beds.

"They do a different animal every day," Marissa tells me.

"Who does?"

"Our steward."

"What's a steward?"

"Like a maid? Only they come in and tidy up two or three times a day."

"Two or three times a day?"

"Yeah. They usually time it so you don't see them." She picks up a card by her towel turtle and says, "Ours is named Ellery and is from the Philippines." She puts the card down. "A lot of them are from the Philippines. They're away from their families for, like, a *year*, doing back-to-back cruises and sending their money home."

Now, the room has lots of mirrors that make it feel bigger than it really is, but our luggage has already been delivered and is standing in the middle of the walkway, making it feel kind of cramped.

"Hey," Marissa says, taking charge of the luggage, "this is Marko's. I'm going to go swap it for yours."

Before I can say, Wait—I'll get my own darn luggage! she's on her way out the door. And since I'm feeling pretty bugged by her and cramped by her big ol' suitcase, I escape out the sliding glass door to the balcony and, *aaaah*— instant relief.

The balcony isn't big—it's only got a small table and two small chairs—but it's open to the world and that changes the feel of everything.

I take in a few deep, salty breaths, then lean over the railing just a little and check out the harbor and the seagulls and the cargo ships and giant cranes unloading seatrains. And I'm thinking how *awesome* it is when I hear, "Don't fall!"

I look to my left, and there's Darren, peeking around the barrier between our balconies.

The barriers between balconies are more for marking boundaries than they are for privacy. They're frosted glass in metal frames, mounted about a foot off the ground, so they're easy to see around and under. And since the guard-rail between me and the deep blue sea comes up to my armpits, I laugh and go, "Fall? I'd have to climb on one of these chairs and—"

"Don't!" he says, because I'm grabbing a chair like I'm going to drag it forward.

"I won't!" I tell him with a laugh.

He's looking straight down at the water. "Don't even joke about it." He looks back at me. "No clowning around. You would not survive that drop, you understand that?"

"You are way too worried!" I tell him.

"I've heard stories," he grumbles.

"About me?"

"Yes, about you!"

"From?"

"Your grandmother."

I think about that a minute. "Well, maybe I've gotten into some scrapes, but I do not have a death wish, okay?"

Marissa's joined me outside and throws in, "It's not like *we're* rock 'n' rollers who are notorious for throwing things off balconies and jumping into pools from them."

"Yeah," I tell him. "Maybe *you're* the one we should be worried about."

"Come on," he says, ducking out of view. "Let's all unpack and explore the ship."

"Explore?" I call after him. "First we eat!"

I start to follow Marissa inside, but right then I see something fluttering in the corner of my eye, and when I turn, I see something drifting down from above. It's a deep, dark blue, and when it gets closer, I realize it's a small scarf. I lean out and can see the bottoms of white pants on a balcony to my left, one deck up, turning to go inside. "Hey, wait!" I call as I stretch way over the railing to try and catch the scarf.

I manage to snag it, and it turns out to be a fancy handkerchief. You know—the kind men stuff in their suit coat pocket?

"Hey!" I call again, but the person in the white pants is gone.

Like they didn't even care about the scarf.

Which is strange, 'cause it's silk.

And obviously expensive.

And, I realize as I turn it over, monogrammed.

FOUR

When I go back inside the cabin, I find Marissa reading a blue-and-white sheet of paper. "This is the Cruzer Calendar," she says without looking up. "There's a new one delivered every day, and it tells you what activities are happening when." Then she sees the handkerchief in my hand. "What's that?" she asks, forgetting all about the Cruzer Calendar.

"It fell down from a balcony above us." I hand it to her. "It's monogrammed."

"Wow," she says, rubbing it between her fingers. "That's really nice." Then she holds it up to her nose and says, "It smells good, too!"

I take it back and sniff, and it does have a definite scent to it. Sort of musky, but with an edge of . . . spice?

The monogram is a small capital *J,* then a big capital *K,* then a small capital *T.* "Is the big letter for the last name?" I ask.

She nods. "When it's like that, yeah. When they're all the same size—"

Then she gets why I'm asking, and grabs it. "You're kidding!"

I laugh. "It's gotta be a coincidence, right?"

Her eyes are all wide. "But he goes by JT, and his parents said it was the Kensington family reunion!"

I shake my head and grin. "You were hanging on every word, weren't you?"

"Me? What about you?"

"I was annoyed with how they went on and on about themselves and were falling all over Darren."

But I can see that the wheels in her brain are gaining traction in a different direction. "This," she says, waving the handkerchief a little, "is a great excuse to go find JT!"

"Marissa, there's no way a teenager has his own monogrammed handkerchief."

"I know." She gives me a sly smile. "I said it's just an excuse."

I laughed, because it was so Marissa. And I could tell she was excited about seeing JT again, because as she moved around the room, putting things away, she was all chatty, talking about every little thing that crossed her mind. Like about how the captain was sure to have some suave accent and about the orange life vests in the closet and how the rails on the shelves in the bathroom were there so things didn't slide off when we started pitching around at sea.

I'm sure I could have learned a lot if I'd completely tuned in to the Marissa Channel, but she was being so random and something about the whole scarf thing was causing major static. It felt like a kind of eerie omen. I mean, what were the odds? Like, how many people on this ship had *my* initials? I would be flipping out if I found a handkerchief with *SJK* embroidered on it.

Or sKJ.

Whatever.

But maybe it was like birthdays, where you grow up thinking the day is *yours* and then discover that not only is it not just yours, but that you share your "special day" with about twenty million other people around the world.

Including your boyfriend's sister.

Anyway, when Darren and Marko knock on the door and ask, "Ready?" I'm definitely ready to think about something else.

Like food!

"Yes! Starving!"

Darren laughs, "Then let's go!" and we grab our seapass cards and head out.

Lots of people are using the elevators now, so we decide to take the stairs, which are just a few yards away. They're not like the swoopy stairs we'd seen when we'd first gotten on board. Nobody's going to be posing for any glamour shots on these. Basically, there are two sets of wide, rectangular stairs—one on the left side of the elevator area and one on the right. They go down half a flight to share a long, wide landing, then U-turn toward each other and join into a set of double-wide steps for another half flight.

From the stairs there are places where you can see the glass elevator pods going up and down, so of course Marissa and I start flying down the stairs, trying to stay ahead of the elevators, which actually turns out to be easy because the elevators are stopping at almost every floor.

Marko's keeping up with us, but Darren's lagging.

"You need to dump those boots!" I call up at him. "Get in some high-tops!"

"I've been telling him that for years," Marko says.

Marko's in Vans, but okay. He's got the right idea.

And then we're on Deck 4, at the monster spread of food, where people are still streaming onto the ship from the mug-shot zone. "How does this work?" I ask when we've got plates and silverware.

Marissa cocks her head a little. "What do you mean?"

I whisper, "How do we pay?" and she whispers back, "Everything's free."

"What?"

"Take anything you want. It's all included."

"Are you sure?"

"Positive."

So I load up!

Darren laughs at what I've got. "You're too skinny to eat that much."

"Watch me!" I tell him.

Trouble is, it turns out this monster spread is just supposed to be a little welcome snack and there aren't many places to sit. So we wind up following Marissa up a level to an outside deck, where there are lots of chairs and a great view of the harbor with all the big industrial boats and cranes. We chow down for a while, but it's kind of weird to be on a boat and be just parked in the water, looking at big industrial boats and cranes. So I finally ask, "When do we take off?"

Darren chuckles. "We set sail at five-thirty."

Now, the way he chuckles is like he's finding my "take

off" a little, you know, bumpkin-like. So I look square at him and say, "Set sail? Do you see any sails? Do I see any sails? You'd need sails as big as Los Angeles to move this monster through the water, so don't get all hoity-toity on me with your setting sail stuff."

Marko eyes Darren. "Dude. Stop with the hoity-toity."

"I wasn't being hoity-toity!"

"Pardon me," I say in a phony British accent. "Perchance, are you aware of when we set sail?"

"Now *that's* hoity-toity," Darren says, like he can't believe Marko and I are ganging up on him.

"*Anyway,*" Marko says. "Does anyone else want to check out the ship?" He turns to Marissa. "Is there really an ice-skating rink?"

"I think it's on Deck 2."

I blink at her. "Are you serious?"

But Marko keeps going. "And I want to check out the venue where we're playing Thursday night."

Darren nods. "The Poseidon Theater. Right. And I'm supposed to get with the entertainment director—"

"That Archie Wolfe dude?" Marko asks.

"That's him."

"I wonder if he's hairy," Marko muses. "Dude, how cool would it be if he looked like the Wolfman?"

"Hairy or not," Darren tells him, "he wants us to check in with him before we"—he zooms in on me—"set sail!"

"Sorry!" I laugh, 'cause he's obviously having a little trouble letting it go.

"Hoity-toity," he mutters.

"Uh . . . so what's the plan?" Marissa asks.

Darren looks at her. "The plan?"

"Are we sticking together the whole time?" Everybody just kind of stares at each other, so she adds, "Usually . . . and I'm not saying we have to do this or anything . . . but usually the kids check in with the adults every few hours or whatever. Or everyone has breakfast together at a certain time and then meets up again for dinner." Then, real fast, she adds, "But of course this is a . . . a *different* kind of situation, so . . . well, it's up to you. I'm just saying you don't have to worry about leaving us on our own while you take care of business or whatever."

We all look at each other like, Well? And since I don't want Darren to feel like he has to babysit or like he's being ditched, I shrug and say, "I'm good either way."

Darren doesn't seem sure, but when Marko says, "She knows what she's doing a lot better than we do," he makes up his mind. "How about Marko and I take care of some band business and we meet you back at the rooms before dinner?"

"What time?" I ask.

"We've got the late seating for dinner, so how about be dressed and ready to go at quarter to eight?"

"Dressed?" I ask, 'cause I'm not liking the way that sounded.

"You dress up for dinners, Sammy," Marissa tells me. "Just deal."

"Hoity-toity," I grumble, which for some reason makes everyone bust up.

So Darren and Marko go off to find the Wolfman, and Marissa leads me on a tour of the ship, taking the stairs down as far as they go, and then checking out each deck all the way back up to Deck 14.

And I have to admit, I would have gotten completely turned around and lost if it wasn't for Marissa. For one thing, there were *two* sets of those double stairs on the ship—one about a third of the way back and the other about two-thirds of the way back. So we'd go up the "fore" stairs, walk around the deck for a while, then continue up via the "aft" stairs, only I'd think they were the opposite of what they actually were and get all confused.

Plus, I wouldn't have known that I could go up to Deck 11 and serve myself frozen yogurt anytime.

Yum!

There was also so much to take in, and really, a lot of it was unbelievable. Outside, on the upper decks, there was a full basketball court, a rock-climbing wall, a minia-ture golf course, a roller rink, Ping-Pong tables, swimming pools with miles of loungers, Jacuzzis, and a jogging track. Inside, mostly on Decks 3, 4, and 5, there were theaters, game rooms, a huge arcade, a casino, a bunch of loungey places with different themes, including a karaoke lounge, and an entire *mall* of stores.

I was actually kinda sore and tired from going up and down so many stairs and racing around each deck, and I was looking around for a place where we could maybe rest for a minute, when all of a sudden an announcement blasts from a speaker right above us.

"Good afternoon! This is Captain Harald. We are look-ing forward to setting sail shortly, but first we must con-duct our muster drill!"

"Oh!" Marissa says. "I forgot!"

"What's a mustard drill?"

"It's *muster*," she tells me. "No *D*."

Then Captain Harald's voice gives me an actual answer: "We are required by law to conduct this safe-evacuation drill before departure, so please, follow along with the instructions you will be given. We will begin momentarily, so at this time proceed to your staterooms and await further instruction."

"Come on," Marissa says. "There's no getting out of this."

"What do we do?"

"Make like lemmings." She looks over her shoulder at me. "It's like a fire drill."

We're barely back at our cabin when announcements start about getting to the muster stations. I knock on Darren's door, but no one answers, and when a really loud air horn blasts, Marissa shouts, "Come on! Let's go!" and we head out toward the stairwells.

Marissa's right about the lemming thing. People are flooding in from all the hallways, and they're all funneling toward the stairs. "Hey!" we hear from behind us. "Sammy! Marissa!" And when we turn around, there's Kip, sort of jostling around people to get to us.

"Hey!" I call back, and then something clicks in my head. "Wait—your cabin's on this floor?"

"Yeah." He points down our hallway. "We're in 9584. About midship."

As we merge in with other people going down the

steps, Marissa asks, "Where's JT?" and then real quick she adds, "We have something that might belong to him."

"To JT? What is it?"

"I'll show you later," she says, which she pulls off okay because we're hurrying downstairs, and who says she has the handkerchief on her anyway? But I know that she does and that she wants to show JT, not Kip.

And maybe he's just being helpful or maybe he's got good intuition, but he volunteers, "He'll be here."

"Where?" Marissa asks a little too fast.

He gives her a little smile. "At the muster station. His family's in 9582, right next to us."

All of a sudden, I can tell Marissa's wishing she'd brushed her hair.

And checked her teeth.

And changed her clothes.

JT and his golfy parents and Kip's fashionista mom are already at our muster station—which turns out to be just some random deck space under life rafts. "There you are!" Kip's mom says, and she's not looking too happy with him.

"Sorry!" Kip tells her, then we all file into the little rows that have formed.

JT greets Marissa with a kinda sly grin, which makes Marissa totally blush. And since we're supposed to stay quiet during the drill, she waits until the all-clear horn blasts before pulling out the monogrammed handkerchief. "Hey," she says to JT. "Check it out."

"Whoa," JT says, taking it. "How'd you get this?"

Marissa turns to me, so I give a little shrug and say, "I was on our balcony and saw it fluttering down, so I reached out and snagged it." I kinda squint at him and ask, "It's not actually yours, is it?" because he's looking like he recognizes it, but if his cabin is on the same deck as ours, how can it be his?

Then Kip's spiral-cut mom says, "How on earth . . . ?" and she turns to JT's dad and says, "Lucas, that's Daddy's pocket square."

JT's dad takes it in his super-tan hand and zeroes his blue eyes in on me. "Where did you say you got this?"

So I explain all over again, and this time I add, "We're not trying to keep it. We just recognized the initials and thought—"

"Oh, sweetheart, no," he says. "I'm not accusing you of anything. Thank you *very* much for making the connection." Then he turns to Kip's mom, who also has those amazing blue eyes. "Why would . . . ?"

His voice just trails off, but apparently his sister understands what he's asking. "Maybe it was symbolic of letting him go?" she says. "You know how attached they were."

JT's dad frowns. "Or maybe Bradley had it. Mom said they're in the suite next to her."

"Of course they are," the Fashionista grumbles.

"It's just a room," JT's dad tells her quietly.

"I *hate* the way he works her!" she says through her teeth.

JT's dad can tell we're listening, so he clears his throat and says, "You know . . ."

Now, you can practically see his thoughts jumping on

a turbo golf cart and racing around in his head. And after some silent conversation with Kip's mom, which involves blue eyeballs, blond eyebrows, and little shoulder shrugs, he turns to Marissa and me and says, "How would you two like to see the sail from the Royal Suite? That's where the boys' grandmother is staying, and I'm sure she would love to meet her grandsons' new friends."

Then JT's mother says, "Grandma Kate is very nice."

"And she'd be fascinated to hear the story of your daring rescue!" JT's dad adds with a super-sparkly smile.

I blink at them. "My daring . . . it wasn't *daring*."

JT's dad gives me a wink and a grin. "I'm sure you could make it *sound* daring, hmm?"

So okay. Going up to some granny's "Royal Suite" with a bunch of people I don't know and turning a simple hanky snatch into some wild, daring rescue was not what I wanted to do.

What was the big deal anyway?

But Marissa's giving me a wild-eyed look, which is a combination of Please, please, please, and I can't believe this is happening! so I finally give in and say, "Sure."

And that was the turning point.

We'd just been sucked into the mad, mad world of Kensingtons.

FIVE

The "Royal Suite" turned out to be a stateroom even Marissa didn't know existed. It was on Deck 10, very near the elevators and on the same side of the ship as our room, and instead of a room number, there was a brass plaque with a crown that said ROYAL SUITE.

It was *huge*. I'm talking grand-piano huge. It had a big sitting area with white couches and a black marble wet bar and Roman pillars and gold-plated fixtures and . . . space. Even with all the Kensingtons gathering inside it, there was *space*.

The minute we walked in, I felt totally awkward. Let's just say scribbled-on high-tops and worn jeans totally clash with Royal Suite décor.

"Grandma Kate," on the other hand, definitely belonged. She was wearing a coral-colored top, a string of pearls, an *enormous* diamond ring, and . . . white slacks.

My mind flashed back to catching the handkerchief, and I tried to picture where our room was compared to the Royal Suite. We were one deck down, and basing on where the elevators were, about two doors closer to the front of the ship.

Or maybe just one, seeing how the room sizes were so different.

What that meant was that I was probably looking at the same white pants I'd seen earlier, which for some reason made me feel even more uncomfortable.

But Marissa was too impressed with the suite to worry about not belonging in it. "A grand piano?" she whispers. "This is unbelievable!" But in between taking in the ritz of the suite, her eyes keep flicking back to JT.

"What are we *doing* here?" I whisper back, because I'm starting to feel like I've been sucked onto some alien ship and that any minute all these blond-haired, blue-eyed people will transform into fangy monsters and I'll never outlive being thirteen.

Marissa's obviously not feeling the alien vibe. "We're here because we were invited!" she gushes.

"But why?" I eye Grandma Kate as she's hugging JT and Kip. "They're having a family reunion—we don't belong here!"

A voice behind me whispers, "Please stay," and when I whip around, there's JT's mom. Her mouth twitches to one side like she's either trying to smile or hide the pain of a toothache, and I'm clueless about why she's whispering or twitching or wanting us to stay. Her eyes are *brown*, though, and for some reason that makes me feel a little less weirded out. Like, okay, I'm trapped in a room with a bunch of blond-haired, blue-eyed aliens, but one of them's an imposter who *also* might be looking for a way out.

And then all of a sudden we're being waved over by

JT's dad. "Sammy! Marissa! Come meet Kate and tell her about the pocket square."

I hesitate, but JT's mother gives us a little nudge and says, "Kate loves kids. Go on."

So we go over to the sitting area, where nobody's sitting.

Well, except Kip, who's off by himself on a stool at the wet bar.

Now, JT's golfy parents and Kip's spiral-cut mother look like they're forty-five or fifty, so Kate has to be older than Grams, but while Grams' face looks soft and has wrinkles, Kate's looks very . . . polished. Like someone buffed her cheeks smooth and anchored the corners of her mouth up a little into a permanent, pleasant smile.

Her hair's also very *styled*. It's thick and blond and swooped back with a dramatic gray streak in the bangs. And even though her eyes aren't that same brilliant blue as JT's or his dad's or Kip's mom's, they're still blue.

Standing next to her is a woman who looks a lot like her, only not as swooped or polished. She seems nice enough, too, giving us a little don't-be-afraid wave over.

"Hello, girls," Kate says, flashing a pearly smile. Her voice is low and warm and not at all old-lady-like. "I'm Kate and this is my sister, Ginger. So glad you could join us!"

Marissa's all of a sudden tongue-tied—probably because JT's watching—so I say, "I'm Sammy and this is my friend Marissa."

"So what's this I hear about you rescuing my husband's

pocket square?" Kate asks as she holds it in her manicured hand.

And that's when I notice that on the coffee table in front of her is a framed picture of a smiling older man. It's beside a fairly large, squatty silver-and-gold vase that has a beautiful diamond pattern going around it. And I'm wondering why the vase has a *lid*, when it hits me that it's *not* a vase.

It's an urn.

All of a sudden, my stomach goes topsy-turvy because I know what's inside the urn.

JT Kensington.

Well, the *original* JT Kensington.

What's left of him anyway.

Now, having old JT in an urn on the coffee table is better than having him laid out in a casket—which, believe me, could definitely have fit inside the Royal Suite. But still. The whole time I'm telling my little story about snagging the handkerchief out of the air, I'm thinking that this situation is just *weird*. Why would the High Priestess of Blond Aliens take her dead husband's ashes with her on a cruise? Or to a family reunion? What are they going to do—sit around and talk to the urn? And how can she be standing there so pleasantly, listening to me so intently? Actually, why is everyone listening to me like they had never heard the story before?

Why are these crazy, blue-eyed aliens acting so *interested*?

Well, except JT, who's obviously only interested in Marissa.

Anyway, when I'm all done talking, Kate has a sort of sweet, sentimental smile on her face as she says, "Perhaps John wasn't ready to leave us."

Kip's mother scowls. "He had a heart attack, Mother. Of course he wasn't ready."

"Teresa . . . ," Kate warns.

"Well, it's true!" Teresa snaps. "John Tyler Kensington never voluntarily relinquished control of anything!"

JT's dad shakes his head. "Are we talking about Dad or the handkerchief?"

"She's the one connecting the two," Teresa grumbles.

There's a moment of awkward silence, and then JT's dad says, "So it was you, Mother? You let the handkerchief go?"

"Of course," she says. "And it was pure joy to watch it fly." She sniffs the hanky and smiles like it's a bouquet of roses. "And I think it's very symbolic that fate has brought it back to me."

Well, *no*, I'm thinking, *I* brought it back to you. And it's a hanky, lady, not your husband!

And then, *ding-dong*, I'm saved by the bell.

That's right, the Royal Suite is so big, it's equipped with a doorbell.

"That must be Bradley and the girls," Kate says, her blue eyes twinkling. "The reunion is complete!"

Still, for all her twinkling, no one moves a muscle to get the door. And since this seems like the perfect time to make our escape, I grab Marissa and say, "Well! It was nice meeting all of you and—"

"No, wait!" JT's dad says, and JT's mom actually steps in front of us, blocking our way. "Please stay," she says softly.

And that's when it all becomes clear.

We *have* been abducted by aliens!

"Please?" she whispers, and something about those brown eyes makes me back down. Plus Ginger's already heading for the door, so my beautiful, smooth exit is completely messed up.

And then another blond is joining the alien hive. This one's older and his hair is definitely abandoning ship. And even though he's paunchy and not at all tan and there's nothing much fashionable about his businessman clothes, he's definitely got those Kensington eyes.

Kate gushes, "Bradley!" like he's a dashing prince there to rescue her. And after a kiss-kiss she asks, "Where are Brooke and the girls?"

"The flu!" he says. "First it was the girls, then Brooke caught it."

Kate's jaw drops. "So they're not coming?"

He shakes his head. "I barely made it myself. They're miserable, and very disappointed."

"Well, at least you're here," she says, giving him another kiss-kiss. "Now say hello to your brother and sister."

"Like they said hello to me?" he asks, loud enough for everyone to hear.

Kate gives him a stern look. "Bradley . . ."

He turns and seems a little thrown to see me and Marissa, but he gets over that quick and puts on a diplomatic smile as he looks at his blue-eyed, alien siblings. "Hello, Lucas, hello, Teresa." Then he turns to JT's mom and says, "LuAnn," and then says, "Johnny," to JT.

Everyone nods and says some version of hi, and then Kip calls out, "Hey, Uncle Bradley," from his bar stool.

"Oh, Kipchoge. Didn't see you there."

Kip hops off the bar stool and moves in. "And this is Sammy and Marissa."

I give Bradley a kind of awkward smile and wave, then say, "And Sammy and Marissa have got to get going. . . ."

Trouble is, before I've had the chance to move one step, there's a really loud, long horn blast from outside.

"The sail!" Kate cries. "Let's all go out to the deck!"

Now, what I'm thinking is, That was no sail! That was a huge, farty *foghorn*! And there's no way I'm going out on a deck with these scary blond aliens!

But JT swoops in and grabs Marissa's elbow and says, "Come on," and off they go.

Which leaves me stuck.

"Sorry," Kip tells me as everyone's filing out to the suite's enormous private deck. He says it under his breath, and when I look at him, I can tell he totally gets that I'm feeling trapped.

The foghorn blasts again.

Loud and long.

"Why do they want us to stay?" I whisper.

"Kensingtons won't fight in public," he whispers back.

"We're not *public*."

He eyes me. "You're as close as they could get."

"But . . . what's there to fight about?"

He laughs. "A lifetime of resentments?" Then he lowers his voice even more and says, "But mostly money. Should be interesting when Grandmother does the big reveal tonight."

I whisper louder over another foghorn blast. "What big reveal?"

"Oh, you know—what's going to happen with the company now that Grandfather is gone."

"What company?" I whisper.

He stares at me for a minute, like he can't quite believe I'm asking. "Kensington colognes? Perfumes? Creams?" He grins. "Haven't you noticed how good we all smell?" Then he adds, "I thought for sure your friend had figured it out."

I blink at him a minute as all this sinks in. I'd seen ads on billboards and in magazines and on TV . . . their regal, script *K* had been around since I could remember.

No wonder they were in the Royal Suite!

I shake my head. "Marissa hasn't made it past the blue eyes."

He snorts and kinda rolls his brown eyes. "Yeah. And then there's that."

We'd been sort of hanging back as we'd talked, so we were the last ones to reach the deck doors, but just as we're about to join the rest of the alien hive, the doorbell rings again.

"I hope that's Noah," Kip says, doing a quick U-turn toward the front door.

I do a U-turn, too. "Who's Noah?"

"Ginger's son. He's my mom's cousin, although *uncle* is a better description." He tosses me a look over his shoulder. "He's also the ship's cruise director."

"What's a cruise director?"

"He's like the cruise MC. He makes it look easy, but it's actually a really big job. If the captain's like the president, Noah's the vice president." Kip laughs. "And he's *way* more fun then the rest of my family combined." He whips open the door, and there's a middle-aged man with kind of kinky, ginger-colored hair and a great big smile. "Kip, m'man!" the guy says as he comes inside. "How's the fam? Everyone comfy?"

"With the place? Sure. With each other? Never." He closes the door and says, "This is my friend Sammy."

Noah sticks out a hand for me to shake. "The name's Bond. Ionic Bond. Taken, not shared."

I kind of blink at him like, What? but he turns to Kip and says, "You think they'll like that one?"

"Nope."

"Darn. And here I've been rehearsing it all day." Noah drops his voice. "How about . . . What do you do with dead chemists?"

"Not a good idea," Kip warns.

Noah's eyes pop. "You barium!"

Kip busts up but then stops laughing quick. "You can't do it, Noah. It's tacky."

Noah slaps his arm. "Oh, I know that. And I wouldn't. I liked your grandfather." He grins. "But it's a good one, don't you think?"

"Compared to some of the others?" Kip nods. "Definitely."

"Everyone out watching the sail?" Noah asks, heading for the deck doors.

"Of course," Kip tells him.

"Well, let's go!"

So we follow Noah outside, and the first thing he says to everyone is, "If H_2O is the formula for water, what is the formula for ice?" and before anyone can say a thing, he cries, "H_2O cubed!"

"Noah has arrived," Bradley mutters, and turns his attention back to the water. Everyone else shakes Noah's hand or gives him a kiss-kiss—or in JT's case, a little wave.

"Why chemistry jokes?" I whisper to Kip.

"Because of the business," he says back. I give him a kind of blank look, so he adds, "You know, fragrance formulas? Grandfather was an amazing chemist."

I'd never thought of perfumes and colognes as having anything to do with chemistry, but now that he's said it, it makes sense. "Oh." Then I kinda laugh. "Noah's jokes are the closest I've come to liking chemistry."

Now, I didn't exactly *whisper* this. And Kip eyes me but doesn't say anything, so it flashes through my mind that I've probably just insulted the entire Kensington clan.

Like telling the broccoli farmer that you don't like vegetables.

Then Marissa waves us over to the railing where she and JT are standing, and once we're looking over the deck, I forget about fragrance fanatics and start to get into "the sail." We're moving out, leaving the port behind, and people onshore are waving, and little security boats are putting alongside, and seagulls are gliding beside us, and the breeze feels wonderful.

"See?" Marissa whispers, 'cause she can tell that I'm really liking it.

For a little while nobody says anything. We all just look out across the water at the port as we move farther and farther out to sea, and I actually forget that I've been abducted by aliens. Then Kate says, "I think this calls for champagne!"

"Not for me," Noah says. "Time for me to kick into gear out there. Lots planned for tonight." He gives his mom a kiss and says, "Glad the room worked out. Swanky, isn't it?"

Ginger holds his cheeks and says, "You're a gem, son." And then he's off, calling, "Welcome aboard, everybody!"

When he's gone, Bradley moves away from the railing and says, "Are we having our meeting, Mother?"

"How about a toast first?"

"No champagne for me, you know that," Bradley says with a dark look.

"Of course, dear. I have your favorite sparkling water."

I cut in with, "Uh, we *really* need to get going. But thank you for having us over."

Kip's mom tries to protest, but Kate levels a look at her and says, "Enough. Let them go." Then she looks at Kip and JT and says, "Actually, why don't the four of you explore the ship together?"

Apparently, what Kate Kensington wants, she gets,

because Kip and JT followed us out. And I was so relieved to escape the alien hive that I didn't even care that the boys were with us. I just wanted to get away from there as fast as I could. Maybe Marissa was too wrapped up in JT to notice, but it was more than clear to me.

The Royal Suite was about to blow.

SIX

The four of us wound up outside on Deck 11, where we played some doubles Ping-Pong. We didn't follow any complicated rules. If the ball came your way, you hit it. That's all. And that was just fine with me, seeing how I'd only played Ping-Pong, like, four times in my entire life.

Marissa wanted to be on JT's team, so I wound up on Kip's, which was fine with me, too, because he didn't make fun of how awful I was and took the time to give me some pointers.

Mostly "You don't have to hit it so hard!"

Plus he didn't hit me back when I accidentally whacked him in the hand.

Or the arm.

Or the head.

I was going for the ball, okay?

Anyway, even though I was pretty awful at first, we made a great comeback, and I *was* having fun, so it took a while for me to notice that Marissa was not.

Marissa's a good athlete. She's an awesome softball pitcher, but she's good at anything athletic that involves a ball.

Ball *bearings* don't count.

She's a terrible with a skateboard.

And never, ever hitch a ride from her on a bike.

But when there's an actual ball involved? Watch out. Marissa will dig in and dominate.

Unless, it turns out, there's a blue-eyed alien on her team hogging the shots. It got so bad that after the third game, I put down my paddle and said, "Isn't that frozen-yogurt dispenser around here somewhere?"

"Good idea," Marissa says, sliding her paddle across the table.

JT looks shocked. "Already? I was just warming up!"

"You and Kip can keep playing," I tell him, but Kip puts his paddle down, too, and says, "Frozen yogurt sounds great!"

So we all wind up getting yogurts, but the whole time we're hanging out, JT seems like he's not real happy. Like he's thinking about something else, or wishing he were somewhere else, or . . . I don't know what. And then Marissa's in the middle of telling a very funny story, about the time she got stuck on top of a chain-link fence thanks to you-know-who, when he actually gets up in the middle of a sentence and says, "I'm gonna head back." He looks at Kip and says, "See you at dinner," and takes off.

Marissa's jaw drops and just dangles, but mine's still working fine. "Wow, what a jerk."

Kip snickers.

That's all.

Just snickers.

Finally, Marissa asks, "Was I talking too much?"

Kip shakes his head. "The story's great. Go ahead and finish it."

"Uh, no," she tells him.

I move over next to her. "Hey, it was totally not you."

"Totally not," Kip says.

"So what's his problem?" I ask Kip. "He was acting like a jerk when we were playing Ping-Pong, too."

Kip looks from me to Marissa and back. And finally he says, "Kensingtons don't talk bad about each other in public."

My eyes bug out at him. "But they can act bad and that's okay?"

He gives a shrug. "Look, I don't like the way he acted, either, but those are the rules and I'm a Kensington."

I can tell he's thinking something else because he gets kinda cloudy, but he doesn't actually *say* anything else. So finally I stand up and yank Marissa along. "Well, good luck with that."

"Yeah," Marissa says. "Good luck with that."

Neither of us even looks back. And as we're marching along, I'm thinking how it took Marissa *forever* to get over this jerk named Danny Urbanski, and if she's going to be whining and pining over another jerk on this cruise, I'm going to *throttle* her, when she says, "You have nothing to worry about."

"What?"

"I don't care if I never talk to him again."

We're at the stairs now, and as I start down them, I grumble, "Famous last words."

She grabs me by the arm and yanks me back. "He may be cute, but I'm done with jerks."

I just stare at her a minute, then break into a smile. "Hallelujah."

When we get down to the Deck 10 landing, I nod over at the Royal Suite and say, "I know you were all hypnotized by JT, but I was kinda freaking out when we were in there. I felt really trapped."

"It *was* a little weird."

And then the Royal Suite starts to open.

I grab Marissa and duck out of view.

"What?" she whispers with her eyes bugged out.

I couldn't really explain it. Something about the door opening freaked me out. Like the alien hive sensed we were there and was going to try and suck us back inside.

"What?" Marissa whispers again. She looks up and around the corner, back at the hive, and then all of a sudden she's yanking me down the steps. "Quick!" she whispers. "It's JT's parents!"

Well, obviously, she didn't want it to seem like she was spying or on the lookout for JT. So I barrel down the steps to the ninth floor with her, but there's a slight problem with our escape plan.

JT's family is staying in a cabin down our same hallway.

"Quick!" Marissa says again as she swipes her sea-pass card in our door lock and swoops us inside. But since I can't stand being inside and not knowing what's going on outside, I leave the door open enough that I can hide behind it and peek through the slit by the hinges.

"What are you doing?" Marissa whispers.

"Shh! Hide!"

So she ducks into the bathroom while I keep watch.

I can hear them coming before I can see them, which is funny because their voices sound like they're trying to whisper, but they're so mad that it's like a yelling whisper. JT's dad says, "There's no *way* Dad said he wanted him to take over the company! After the way he crippled it with his overseas deal? It took years to recover from that! And I don't care if he's been sober for five years now, nobody should trust him! He's the same arrogant liar he's always been, and he'll make the same damn mistakes!"

I can see them now, and JT's dad isn't the only one flushed and angry. "The nerve of him calling us trust-fund tourists!" JT's mom says as they march by. "And Teresa, a dilettante? At least we've built lives of our own!"

"And we never crippled Dad's business with reckless blunders!"

They're past the door now, so I swoop around, and as I watch them storm down the hallway, I can hear JT's mom say, "She won't make him CEO, Lucas," and JT's dad answer, "My mom's a sucker for him, LuAnn. Leave those two alone and he'll talk her into anything!"

I can't hear much after that, but I keep watching until they disappear inside a room about ten doors down.

"Well?" Marissa asks, peeking out of the bathroom.

So I shut the door and catch her up on what I'd overheard. "Whatever," she grumbles. "Who cares? I'm going to avoid all of them." Then she starts going through her clothes. "Now let's get dressed for dinner!"

Turns out what that meant was putting on a stupid dress, which I *had* packed because it was on the list, but it was wrinkled, and let's just say irons and I don't get along. So I'm holding it up, trying to figure out if I can get by with it the way it is, when Marissa stops what she's doing and says, "No."

"No what?"

"You either need to iron it or wear another dress."

"I don't have another dress."

She blinks at me. "You only brought *one*? For six nights?"

"I have to wear a dress *every night*?"

"Well, you can't show up in the dining room in jeans and high-tops! And you can't wear *that* to formal night."

"Formal night? What's formal night?"

"Didn't you read *anything*?"

I plop down on my bed. "Maybe I should have, because then I'd have known not to come!"

Marissa sits next to me. "Sorry. Look, formal night's not until Friday, so you have plenty of time. And you *do* want to go, Sammy. They set up places where you can get your picture taken and—"

"I don't want my picture taken!"

She cocks her head a little. "You have *no* pictures of you and your dad. Zero. Wouldn't you like to have a really nice one?"

I look down.

"See?" She snatches my dress and stands up. "I'll go iron it."

I reach for it and tell her, "I can do it."

"You'll burn it. Besides, they don't have irons in the rooms, so we have to go down to laundry and—" And then she sees the time. "Forget it. You can wear one of mine tonight."

It turned out she'd brought eight.

Eight.

And as we're getting dressed, she says, "I tell you what—we'll go shopping tomorrow. They have some great stores in the promenade. And since tomorrow's your birthday . . ."

I squint at her. "So for my birthday you're going to force me to shop for a stupid fancy dress in a ridiculous *promenade?* Sounds like another extension of unlucky thirteen."

"I'll make it fun, I promise! And we're at sea all day tomorrow, so we'll have plenty of time."

All of a sudden, I'm feeling really claustrophobic.

I'm stuck on this boat for a *week?*

I have to wear a dress every night for a *week?*

What a nightmare!

Just then there's a little tap on the door, which makes me jump, 'cause I'm not *even* ready to go to dinner.

Marissa, though, is cool as can be. "Don't worry. That can't be your dad—"

"Darren," I snap.

She rolls her eyes. "Well, it can't be him because rock stars are *always* late and we still have seven minutes."

Still, I zip up quick and slip into my dress flats and head for the door.

Only Marissa's right.

It's not Darren.

Or Marko.

It's nobody.

I look up and down the hall, but there's nobody near our door. And I'm starting to wonder if what we'd heard was something besides a knock on the door when I notice a small, folded piece of paper down by my feet.

So I pick it up.

And open it.

SEVEN

The note is short.

And written in neat, unusual handwriting.

And it's definitely not from housekeeping.

"What is that?" Marissa asks.

I hand it over. "An apology. I think."

He doesn't like to lose. Especially not to me.

She squints at me. "You call that an apology?"

"Well, it's not signed, and he must have run away after he slipped it under the door, so I think he thinks he's taking a big risk telling us this much." I give a little shrug. "So he must feel bad, right?"

Marissa frowns at the note. "This is not an apology. An apology includes the words *I'm* and *sorry*. This is an explanation. And a pretty lame one."

I take the note back. "You're right. And JT's actually the one who should apologize."

"How'd Kip even know which room was ours?"

"He must've seen us come out during that muster drill. He caught up to us, remember?"

"Or maybe he's been spying on us."

Just then there's another knock on the door, so I brush my hair quick and hurry to open it.

"Hey, don't you look nice!" Darren says.

So I attack him. "You didn't tell me I had to wear a dress every night for a week!"

Marko's right behind him, nodding. "I informed your dad that I'm not wearin' a tie after tonight. The buffet is good enough for me."

My eyes pop. "The buffet's open?"

He nods. "Round the clock."

"So why don't we just eat there?"

Marko looks at Marissa. "Come on, join the rebellion!"

Marissa's eyes get all big with worry. "But the dining room food is *amazing*."

"We'll talk about tomorrow later," Darren says, scooping an arm around my shoulders. "Tonight, we are dining in style."

So we head down the stairs to Deck 5 and go toward the back of the ship, then stand in line outside a glitzy dining room until Darren's greeted by a guy in a maroon coat with *tails* and white gloves. Darren shows him his sea-pass card and Glove Guy hands us over to a short guy in a short coat that has about fifty brass buttons and no buttonholes. "Right this way," Button Man says, and snakes us through a whole sea of white tablecloths, shiny silverware, and sparkly glasses.

The dining room is shaped like a giant donut, and you can see down a big open center section into the sparkling dining rooms on Decks 4 and 3 below. "Holy smokes," I say, sort of under my breath.

Marko hears it, though, and goes, "Dude. I'm feeling very *Titanic*."

"Great," I tell him, giving him my best disgruntled-teenager eye roll, which for some reason makes him laugh.

"Here we are, sir," Button Man says with a little bow, putting one hand out toward a U-shaped booth. Marissa scoots in from one side and I scoot in from the other, then Darren sits next to me and Marko sits next to Marissa.

The booth is padded and comfortable and has a high back, and it opens out to a big area of the dining room, so it feels like we're in our own little zone with a front-row-center view.

"See? Not so bad," Marissa says, straightening her already straight silverware. "Only three forks."

"And three glasses. Why do I need three glasses?" And then I see the group of people being seated at the large table right in front of us and gasp, "No!"

Darren looks over and sees JT and Kip and the whole Kensington colony, then kind of eyes me and says, "Something happen this evening?"

Now, from the way I'd gasped and the fact that the last time he'd seen Kip and JT, we were waving like idiots across elevators, it made sense that he'd picked up on the fact that something had changed.

But still, it surprised me.

I mean, I'm not used to adults noticing.

Or asking.

And it threw me enough to actually say something

instead of my usual "nothing." "We had a super-weird, blue-eyed-alien kind of evening."

Marko laughs, "A what?" And when Marissa growls, "I can't believe their table is *right there*," Darren says, "So what happened?"

"Well, let's see. Where to begin?" I look at Marissa. "The Royal Suite?"

"As good a place as any," she grumbles.

I look at Darren. "Actually, you don't even know about the handkerchief, do you?"

"The handkerchief? What handkerchief?"

I take a deep breath. "Well!" So I back up to snagging the handkerchief out of the air and realizing the initials were the same as JT's, and then meeting up with JT and Kip's family at the muster drill and getting snookered into going with them to the Royal Suite, where we discovered we were dealing with *the* Kensington empire, including the dead dad in an urn.

Now, while I'm talking, a dark-haired man with a big nose comes to our table and introduces himself. "I am Doyle, your waiter," he says in an odd sort of British accent, "and this is my assistant, Arthur." They bring us bread and water, and explain the menu and take our orders. So there are lots of interruptions, and I can tell that Darren's losing track of the story, but instead of telling me to cut to the punch line like most people do, he says, "Back up a minute. I know we met some of these people in line, but I don't remember their names."

Marissa leans in and keeps her voice low. "Kip's the

African American. He's the adopted son of Teresa, who's the woman with the angled haircut."

I throw in, "The one who wants to design your next tour wardrobe, remember?"

Darren pulls a little face. "Oh, right."

Marissa goes on, saying, "JT's the boy with blond hair, and he's the son of Lucas and LuAnn," and I tack on, "The Tan Twins with the villas you're welcome to use anytime."

Darren cringes and Marko asks, "You're talking about the dude in the salmon-colored shirt?"

I nod. "Him and his wife."

Marko butters a roll and says, "I don't trust men who wear salmon."

Darren nods. "They're definitely fishy."

They give each other bro grins, then Darren tells Marissa, "Continue with the lineup."

"Okay," she says, looking back at the alien table. "Bradley's the paunchy guy sitting next to Kate—"

"The dame in diamonds?" Marko asks. "Or the one without?"

Marissa laughs. "The dame in diamonds. She's the family matriarch and wife of JT senior—"

"—whose ashes are in an urn in the Royal Suite, which is why he couldn't tux up for dinner tonight." I look at Marissa and shake my head. "I can't believe you remember all their names."

She shrugs. "I was paying attention." She gives a haughty little look at a bread roll and rips it in two, saying, "And now I'm not."

"So who's the diamondless dame?" Marko asks.

And since I actually remember her name, I jump in with, "That's Ginger." I grin at him. "And she's the dame *in* diamonds' sister."

"Who also happens to be the cruise director's mother," Marissa adds.

"Wait," Darren says. "The diamondless dame is the mother of the cruise director?"

"Right," she tells him. "And the cruise director's name is Noah."

Marko's sipping from his water glass, but stops to sputter, *"Noah?"*

I grin at him. "Some ark he's got, huh?"

"No kidding!"

Darren shakes his head. "Expect me to need reminders, but go on with your story."

"Where was I?"

"In the alien hive."

"Oh, right!" So I go back to being in the Royal Suite and Bradley walking in and how awkward that was, and then Noah's chemistry jokes and the sail and finally escaping the hive and going to play Ping-Pong.

And the whole time I'm talking, Doyle the waiter and Arthur the assistant bring us drinks and salads and soups, and clear all those dishes away and deliver our main courses.

I'd ordered the scallops, and they turn out to be so delicious that I just shut up for a minute and eat. And I guess everyone else's food is delicious, too, because our table goes totally quiet.

And while we're quiet, the Kensington clan starts getting loud.

It's not a happy loud. Or a family-reunion loud. Or even a drunk loud.

It's a *harsh* loud.

Like a drill, boring into a cement wall, buzzy and sharp.

Now, JT has his back to us, but Kip is on the opposite side of their table and had spotted us somewhere around our salad delivery. And since I was in the middle of talking about his family, it was kind of embarrassing to not nod back when he nodded hi across the room.

Especially since he'd left the non-apology note.

So I *had* nodded, but I'd avoided looking at his table since. But now I look again and see that he's tearing little chunks off a roll and putting them on his plate while sharp, buzzy voices zoom all around him.

Then Kate's eyes flash and she stands up and commands, "Stop it. All of you." When they all fall quiet, she forces a smile and raises a martini glass that has some kind of pale blue liquid in it and says, "To John Tyler Kensington, a brilliant man, humanitarian, and visionary."

Ginger lifts her wineglass high, and Kip and JT lift their water glasses about halfway, but the other glasses stay put.

"Is that actually *in* his will?" Bradley asks. "He never said a word about it! And I can't believe he'd *do* that to us!"

"Your father had become convinced that his children cared more for money than family."

Bradley gets even redder. "He's accusing *us* of that? We grew up in boarding schools so you two could travel the world in search of *fragrances*."

"Bradley . . . ," Kate warns. "Your father was *extremely* generous with all of you. And he always made time for our annual cruise, so *you* traveled the world, too!"

Bradley crosses his arms. "I demand to see the will."

"You demand," Kate says, and she's sounding pretty steely all of a sudden. "Are you calling me a liar?"

That shuts him up quick.

"These were your father's wishes and we *will* respect them," Kate says. Then she shoots eye daggers at JT's mom and says, "LuAnn? He was your father-in-law for almost twenty-five years, and he made it possible for you and Lucas to enjoy a very comfortable lifestyle. You don't have the courtesy to raise a glass in his honor?"

JT's mom picks up her wineglass and says, "It's just a shock, Kate."

"Yes, Mother, a shock," Kip's mom says, but she picks up her wineglass, too.

"Bradley? Lucas?" the queen asks her pouting princes, but neither of them join the toast. Instead, Bradley pushes back from the table, throws down his napkin, and storms out.

"Well!" Queen Kate says, watching him go. "So much for Kensington class. And he hasn't heard the half of it."

"There's more?" Kip's mom gasps.

Kate eyes her. "We'll discuss the rest after Bradley cools down." Then she turns to JT's dad, her arm still hoisted to toast. "Do my eyes deceive me, Lucas? Or are you breaking form and siding with your brother?"

"Dad was a lot of things, Mother, but a humanitarian? And selling the business to build a hospital? In *Africa*?"

"Lucas! Raise. Your. Glass," Kate snarls through her smile. "My arm is getting tired."

So Lucas frowns, picks up his wineglass, and clinks it with everyone else's.

"There," Kate says, sitting down. Then she gives them all a pinched smile and sips from her blue martini.

"A hospital in Africa?" Marissa whispers. "That would cost a fortune!"

"I think that's the point," I whisper back. "They're not getting the fortune; a hospital in Africa is."

We're all quiet a minute, then Darren says to me, "Don't worry, I don't have enough to build a hospital in Africa."

I blink at him. "Why would I be worried? And a hospital seems like a *good* thing."

He just stares at me a minute, then looks at Marko. So *I* look at Marko and see him give Darren a little shrug. And since I don't get what's going on, I turn to Marissa.

She gives me a hello-idiot look and says, "Uh . . . you're Darren Cole's *daughter*?"

I blink at her, and when it finally sinks in, I whip around and look at Darren. "I don't want your money!"

"Well, you didn't exactly get my *time* growing up, did you? And look how bitter they are over that."

"That wasn't your fault. You didn't even know I existed!"

"But *you* knew *I* did." He gives a little shrug. "I just feel bad about it."

"Stop it! And don't even think about me wanting your money, 'cause I don't!"

70

We're quiet a minute, and then Marko says, "Dude, I don't want your money, but your pork medallions?" Then he skewers some of Darren's dinner with his fork and announces, "Trade time!"

Suddenly Darren's stealing one of my scallops, and Marko's swiping food from Marissa, and she's going, "Hey!" and he's saying, "You're hanging with rock 'n' rollers, baby, there is no safe zone," and Marissa's retaliating, snagging something from his plate, and Darren's going, "Ladies and gentlemen, this is not suitable dining room behavior," like a hoity-toity old lady, and we're all busting up.

Until we notice the Kensingtons watching us.

And just like that, we all stop laughing.

EIGHT

They were *all* staring at us, so you know what I did?

I waved.

Waving has gotten me in more trouble than I like to think about. It's a reflex, and sometimes after I've done it, I want to kick myself and go, Why did you *wave*?

But in this case it turned out to be the perfect thing to do, because apparently Kensingtons don't *stare* in public, either. After I waved, all the ones who'd turned around to look at the rowdy rocker table turned back, and all the ones facing us looked away.

And since the desserts were also amazing and people were no longer staring at us, we wound up swiping from each other again, which somehow turned into us telling food-fight stories. Marissa and I had lots of them, but so did Marko and Darren.

Which was kind of strange.

I mean, picturing the two of them as fourth graders in a school cafeteria?

Hearing about "the perfect fling technique for cata-pulting mashed potatoes"?

Having them say they'd demonstrate, "except the spoons here are all wrong"?

It was . . . surreal.

And after learning that "the only spoon for serious spud flingers is a Quick Serve Seven" because it has a "wide mouth and barely bendy neck," I look at Darren and say, "You've been faking it."

"Faking it?"

"Yeah. You don't belong in this dining room any more than I do."

Marko scrapes up the last lick of some raspberry chocolate drizzle on his plate and laughs, "Dude, your cover has just been blown."

Darren tosses down his napkin. "So let's get out of here, huh?"

"Wait!" Marissa says as we all start to scoot out. "Does that mean we're not coming back? Not even for formal night?"

"Especially not for formal night," I tell her.

"You can't be serious!" she cries, chasing after us as we beat feet across the dining room.

I look over my shoulder to tell her, You bet I'm serious! but then I notice Kip watching us go. He's looking all bummed, and, I don't know—I forget about telling Marissa anything and just turn around quick.

"We *are* going to the show, right?" Marissa asks when we're outside the dining room.

"What show?" I ask

"They have a show every night?" Her forehead's all

wrinkly. "Variety shows, comedians, Darren Cole and the Troublemakers . . ."

"Hold up," Marko says. "We are *not* to be put in the same sentence or even *paragraph* as *variety show*, got it?"

"But you're entertainment on the same cruise ship!" Marissa says.

The rest of us just stare at her.

She gives me a desperate look. "But they are!" Then she turns to Marko and Darren and says, "Which means the other acts must be great, too, right? So all I'm saying is, we should check them out."

We keep staring at her until Darren finally says, "Fine. Let's go."

Marko hangs back. "Maybe I'll just—"

But Darren yanks him along and growls, "You're coming, man."

So Marissa leads us through the promenade, past jewelry and clothes and souvenir shops, and when we get to the fore stairs, we go down them to Deck 3. "Here it is," she says, and we merge into a sea of people flooding into the Poseidon Theater.

Now, I don't know what I was expecting, but from everything else on the ship, I should have known that the theater would be big. And ritzy. With velvet seats and upper-level lounges and little couples tables and a huge stage with swoopy velvet curtains.

But I was still surprised.

"Wow," I gasp as we move forward toward the stage.

"It's cool, right?" Darren asks, like he's not sure that it is.

I laugh. "Seems a little clean for a rock band."

Marko grumbles, "I tell you, bro, they're going to make us turn down."

"Look," Darren says. "It is what it is. I get to spend time with Sammy, you get a free cruise—no, no, wait. You get *paid* to cruise, with me springing for an upgrade."

"Not complaining, dude. Seriously."

So we find four seats fairly close to the stage, and when the lights dim, there's an announcement over the PA welcoming us and then telling us to "Put your hands together for the Seafarer Association's cruise director of the year, *No-ah Mar-lowe!*"

Noah bounds out of the wings, holding a microphone, smiling like he's the happiest guy on earth. And when the applause dies down, he says, "A neutron walks into a bar and asks, 'How much for a drink?' The bartender replies, 'For you, no charge.'"

Behind the curtain, there's a *ka-thump* on a drum.

And nobody in the audience laughs.

"Okay, then . . . What do you call a tooth in a glass of water?"

Silence.

"A one molar solution!"

Ka-thump.

"Hmm," Noah says, looking out at the filled theater. "I told a chemistry joke today and there was no reaction."

Ka-thump.

"Get it? *Reaction?*"

This time there are a few chuckles.

"Forgive me, please," Noah says, "but these jokes are

a tribute to my brilliant uncle, Dr. John Tyler Kensington, who loved them. And they're meant to lift the spirits of his widow, my fabulous aunt Kate, who is aboard our fair vessel along with her children." He looks around the crowd. "Any Kensingtons here tonight?"

Silence.

He keeps his smile plastered on. "Well, then! Let's get on with the show!"

"So *that's* the alien nephew?" Darren whispers while Noah's introducing the act.

"Yup," I whisper back.

He slouches a little. "That is one strange family."

I slouch a little, too. "No kidding."

The show turns out to be a lot of singing and dancing and costume changes with crazy wigs and props galore.

Not my thing.

Or Darren's.

Or Marko's.

But Marissa thinks it's "amazing!" and keeps grabbing me to tell me that the main guy in the show is "so talented!"

When it's over, Noah comes back onstage and announces all the things that are still going on around the ship, because "It's only eleven p.m., people! Time to get out there and boogie!" Then he launches into what's on the agenda for "our fun-filled day at sea tomorrow!" including bingo, an art auction, and a jewelry sale. "You won't want to miss any of it!"

As we're filing out, Darren's kind of watching me, and I can tell he's worried. "So what do you want to do tomorrow?" he asks. "Bingo in the Poseidon Theater does not seem like the way you'd want to spend your birthday."

"True. . . ." I think a minute and say, "Actually, anything's okay. As long as it doesn't involve me turning thirteen *again*."

"As far as I know, you're moving on to the big one-four."

"As far as you know? So there *is* the possibility?!" I look around. "Are you saying my mother's onboard somewhere?"

"Not that I know of!" Then he adds, "And I sure can't picture Lana as a stowaway."

I blink at him, 'cause that's so true. "Okay, then, see? Anything else is fine with me."

But apparently he can't think of anything to suggest, so after a long, awkward pause, he says, "Well . . . have you had enough for one day?"

I tell him, "Yeah," and Marissa says, "If we're going back to our staterooms, can we take the elevator? I'm sore from all the stairs."

"Good idea," I tell her, because all of a sudden I want to escape to my room the quickest way possible. Trouble is, people from the theater are swarming around the elevators and it's taking forever, so we finally give up and head for the stairs. Only they're really packed, too, and some of the people are both slooooooow and impossible to pass.

I guess Marissa can tell I'm dying, because we've only gone up two flights when she cuts out of the crowd and says, "Let's go up the aft stairs."

So she leads us toward the back of the ship, through

the promenade and all its shops, and we're just getting to the swoopy stairs, which are located a little before the glamour-free stairs, when she comes skidding to a halt and cries, "The boarding pictures are out!"

"Boarding pictures?" And then I see the racks of cheesy say-cheese pictures.

Aisles and aisles and *aisles* of cheesy say-cheese pictures.

"Marissa, no. I do not want a cheesy say-cheese picture!"

"Oh, let's just find ours and then you can decide."

Darren says, "Sure, let's do that," and follows her into the Forest of Cheesy Smiles.

I give Marko a pleading look, but he distracts me with a little head nod. "Uh . . . aliens on aisle two?" And when I look to where he'd nodded, I see Kate and Ginger scanning the wall of pictures in front of them.

I grab Marko and we duck down the back side of the same aisle, which is also covered with pictures. "We avoiding the Diamond Dame or spying on her?" he whispers.

Now, the truth is, I hadn't even thought about spying until he mentioned it. But since the walls are just metal mesh covered by racks of pictures and not exactly *soundproof,* I figure it won't hurt to, you know, move down the aisle and pretend to be looking at cheesy say-cheese pictures, too.

So I give Marko a little grin, and he gives me a piratey one back, and before you know it, we're down the aisle with our ears perked. We can barely see Kate and Ginger through the mesh—just little squares of them here and there. But it doesn't take too long for us to tune in and hear, "So what are you going to do?"

There's a sigh, and then, "It has certainly not gone well so far. And it's much harder than I'd imagined. Their reaction was . . . well, frankly, it was a shock."

Marko leans in and whispers, "That's Diamonds?" so I give him a quick nod and listen as Ginger says, "I haven't seen a lot of tears, that's for sure. And I couldn't believe they wouldn't toast him."

"I'm telling you, as their mother—as the one who was sure they would rise to the occasion and support their father's wishes—this is *extremely* upsetting."

"Are you saying John was right?"

"I'm saying I don't like the direction this has taken."

They're quiet for a minute, then Ginger says, "It's hard to believe they've all blown through their trust funds."

"I'm sure they always counted on there being more."

"But how do you go through that much money?"

"Well, Bradley was convinced he had great business acumen and made some bad deals; Lucas borrowed heavily against some of his properties to buy others and is upside down on all of them. And Teresa?" Another sigh. "She refused to come up through the ranks and learn from a legitimate designer, and then self-distributed her artistic delusions with disastrous results. Did you see that blouse she was wearing tonight? No wonder nothing sold."

We can see them moving slowly down the aisle, apparently looking at everybody's pictures. Then they stop and Kate says, "I am not looking forward to breaking the rest of the news to them, though. They are going to be furious. I wish John could be at my side!"

"I can't believe none of them gave it any thought. Especially Teresa. It's ironic, really."

"Yes, it is. And Bradley will almost certainly try to do something about it, but he'll get nowhere. Hammett Spade was very thorough in preparing the documents."

"Is Hammett up to speed on . . . everything?"

"Oh, yes." There's a moment of silence as they move farther down the aisle, and then Kate says, "Look here!"

Through the mesh we can sort of see a picture move and then hear Ginger's voice say, "Oh! That's cute, actually." She chuckles. "But what a motley crew, huh?"

"They were being rather wild tonight, weren't they?"

"JT told me that that one is somebody famous. A musician?"

"Oh, well, that would explain that. The girls were polite enough up in the suite, though, did you notice?"

"I did."

"And they're both darling, but why those shoes?"

"Maybe Teresa could help?"

Kate chuckles. "I take it back. The shoes are perfect."

They both bust up and then Kate says, "I could use another martini. Shall we?"

"You're avoiding."

Kate sighs and we can sort of see the picture slide back into place. "It's eleven-thirty. Haven't we had enough for one day?"

"Rip off the bandage, Kate. Get this over with."

Another sigh. "You're right. They're all still up. Let's call a meeting."

I look at Marko like, A meeting? Now? and he looks back like, I know, huh?

Then we both beat it farther down the aisle before we get caught snooping.

NINE

I'm not sure that I'd ever snooped with an adult before. For one thing, it's just not natural. And adults are the ones who are always telling you to mind your manners. To sit up straight and fly right.

Or whatever.

But the weird thing was that it *wasn't* weird to be listening through a wall of pictures with Marko. Maybe because we were listening in on people way older than both of us. Or maybe because I knew that under all those years of adulthood, Marko was a spud flinger.

Or maybe because rock 'n' rollers get old, but they never really become adults.

Whatever. The *point* is, it wasn't weird. And after we rescued Darren and Marissa from wandering aimlessly through the Forest of Cheesy Smiles and Darren paid way too much money for the picture of the four of us in front of the fake ship backdrop, we all went up to our cabins, agreed to meet for breakfast at ten o'clock, and said good night.

I *was* tired, too, but as Marissa and I are getting ready for bed, I remember.

Homework.

"No!" Marissa cries when I mention it. "Just do it tomorrow."

"Tomorrow's my birthday."

"It's after midnight now, so it's already your birthday! So happy birthday. Now go to bed!"

I try to tell myself that she's right—that it's late and I'm on a *cruise* and who does homework on vacation anyway? But in the back of my mind I keep picturing Ms. Rothhammer's face when I told her that I was turning over a new leaf so I could get on the college track in high school. I thought she was going to cry from happiness, and believe me, Ms. Rothhammer is not the crying kind. I also keep thinking about how she'd helped me after school the last few weeks, and how many times she'd said she was proud of me for trying so hard and "showing such discipline."

But since Marissa's already in bed and there's no place in the room where I can work without keeping her awake, I go to bed, too. But that stupid word *discipline* won't leave me alone. Plus, it doesn't feel like my birthday yet, and the last thing I want to do on my actual birthday is chemistry problems. And if I wait until the day after, I'll be in real trouble because in the back of my mind I'm remembering Marissa saying that the two days after my birthday are "port days," when we're supposed to go on land excursions or something.

The desk clock says 12:30, but since Marissa's now *snoring* and I can't sleep, I get up and get dressed as quietly as I can, grab my backpack and sea-pass card, ease the cabin door open, and sneak out.

I know exactly where I'm going because we'd checked out the Lido Library on Deck 8 when we'd first explored the ship, and Marissa and I had passed by it a bunch of times as we'd gone up and down the stairs near our room.

There's a plaque on the door that says QUIET ZONE, and inside there's dark wood paneling and bookcases and library tables and leather armchairs the color of dried blood. There's also a long table of back-to-back computers and an alcove with a printer. So it's the perfect place to do my homework, plus it's really close to our cabin—basically, just down one flight of stairs—so I don't have to worry about getting lost.

There's only one other person in the room when I get there—a middle-aged woman with curly salt-and-pepper hair, who's putting together pieces of a big puzzle that's on one of the tables. She's only got part of the border done, and it looks like it's a really hard puzzle—the pieces seem small and are in big, yellowish mounds.

I smile when she looks over, then settle in at a table on the other side of the room with my work sheet, my notes, my pencils, paper, and calculator, and the infamous periodic table of the elements.

And then I just sit there, staring at the first problem.

I don't hate math. And I don't hate chemistry. What I hate is when the two get put together, *and* scientific words get thrown around in class before I have a really good understanding of them. It's like reading something where you keep forgetting what certain words *mean*. Or you mix up their meanings. So you spend your time sort of scrambling to keep up, looking at your definitions, going, Oh, right, then realizing that you've missed the next thing that was said and that, once again, you're lost.

Mole and *molar mass* and *mole ratio* are all words like that for me.

Anything with *mole* in it leaves me in the dark.

Which, yeah, seems pretty appropriate.

There's *atomic weight,* which I get, but also confuse with *molecular weight.* Probably because *molecular weight* has the word *mole* in it.

Anyway, Ms. Rothhammer's work sheet has us doing equations—math—with molecules—chemistry—and the first step is to calculate the molar mass of each compound in the equation.

See?

What does that *mean*?

Anyway, there I am, up to my eyeballs in math and moles, trying to fight my way out of the darkness, when all of a sudden I hear, "You're doing *homework*?"

Well, let me tell you: Concentration + Surprise = Heart Attack.

And the net reaction?

An explosion.

I bolt out of my chair, shouting, "Don't *ever* sneak up on me like that again!"

"Sorry!" Kip says, stepping back. "I wasn't sneaking."

"Were you spying on me? Were you *following* me?" And it flashes through my mind that maybe he saw me spying on his grandmother in the Forest of Cheesy Smiles.

"No! I came down to check something on the Internet!"

"To . . ." I look around. The Puzzle Lady's still there,

but other than her, it's just him and me and a bunch of books and computers.

"Sorry," he tells me, and he's backing away like I've hit him.

"Hey," I call after him, because now I feel really bad. "Sorry. I'm just stressed out by this stupid homework assignment."

"Is it chemistry?" he asks from halfway across the room. And I'm thinking, Oh, yeah—Kensingtons and chemistry. Like peanut butter and jelly.

But *then* it flashes through my mind that maybe he *hates* chemistry. Maybe he's sick to death of his granddad being Dr. Fragrance. Maybe he secretly thinks of him as being Dr. Fragrance-stein! Maybe he wants to torch the secret family formula and is embarrassed to be the nephew of the chemistry jokes guy!

So I go ahead and say it. "I hate molar conversions."

And you know what he says?

He says, "Why?"

"Because they're hard! And I don't really understand them! And I'm stuck with a three-page work sheet that I have to do on my birthday cruise!"

He takes a step forward. "It's your birthday?"

"Tomorrow is. Which I guess is already today. Never mind. The point is, I hate this."

He takes another step forward. "You want help?"

I hesitate, then shove the paper at him. "You know how to do this?"

He looks it over and starts nodding. "Sure."

"Sure?" I snatch the paper back. *"Sure?"*

He nods. "I love that stuff."

I just stare at him. And then, even though I hear a voice inside my head screaming DON'T! out of my mouth comes, "Could you help me with just one?"

"I don't have much time, but sure."

So he sits down next to me and reads the first problem out loud. "'Calculate the molarity of the solution formed when seventy-five grams of magnesium chloride is dissolved in five hundred milliliters of solution.'" He nods and grabs one of my pencils and a piece of paper. "Piece of cake."

So yeah. I'm sitting next to a know-it-all Kensington, feeling like a boulder brain. "More like stinky cheese, if you ask me."

"Huh?"

"Never mind."

"The molarity is just moles divided by liters. But you're not given moles here, so you have to calculate them first, then divide by liters."

I want to tell him that I hate moles. That moles put me in a deep, dark place, and that I would much rather be calculating birds or sunflowers or one-eyed bats, for that matter. But what comes out of my mouth is "So how do I calculate moles?"

He grabs the periodic chart. "With this." He grins. "Grandfather says this is the most elegant single sheet of knowledge ever created." Then his face kind of falls, and he goes back to the chart. "Anyway, every square in the chart has the element's atomic number, symbol, name, and atomic mass. For example"—he points to a square—"phosphorus is element fifteen, has P as its symbol, and an atomic mass of 30.97." He hands me the chart. "You try. What's the atomic mass of gold?"

Now, it's not like the chart's in alphabetic order. Plus, it turns out that gold's symbol isn't G like phosphorus' is P. And since there are over a hundred elements on the chart, I'm feeling miffed and tricked when I finally find it. "It's element seventy-nine, its symbol is Au, and it has an atomic mass of 196.97."

"Right!" he says, like I'm a star student. Then he re-reads the problem on the work sheet and says, "Do you know the formula for magnesium chloride?"

Ms. Rothhammer had given us a list of chemical formulas that were used in the problems, so I look at it and say, "$MgCl_2$."

"Right." He jots $MgCl_2$ on the paper and says, "The first step is to find the atomic mass of magnesium."

I look on the chart and find Mg easily. "It's 24.31."

"Right. Now, what's the atomic mass of chlorine?"

Cl is also easy to find. "It's 35.45."

"And how many chlorines do you have?"

"Two."

"So what is the sum of the two chlorines?"

I double 35.45 in my mind. "Is it 70.9?"

"Exactly. Now add up the magnesium and the chlorines, and what do you get?"

I scribble down the addition of 70.9 and 24.31 and say, "I get 95.21."

"Right. And that's the *molecular* weight, because we're

dealing with a molecule now." He writes down *95.21* and asks, "What are the units?"

I stare at the paper. "I have no idea."

"It's grams per mole."

I mutter, "Grams per mole," but it doesn't seem to faze him. He writes down a calculation with *75 g* in the numerator and *95.21 g/mol* in the denominator while he's saying, "It's important, because the grams in the equation are going to cancel out and leave you with"—he slashes a line through each *g*—"moles!"

Whoopee.

He ignores my frown and punches the division problem into my calculator, going, "So 75 divided by 95.21 equals . . . 0.788 moles!" He looks at me, totally excited, then writes it all down on the paper. "Now just divide moles by liters. . . ." He writes down what he's doing so I can follow it, then punches the division into the calculator. "And there's your answer!"

"That's it?"

"That's it."

I take the paper and study the steps, which is really easy to do because, just like in the non-apology note, his writing is very neat and also very unique . . . like his own special Kip font. Everything is labeled, and he has arrows helping me follow the steps, and, very slowly, something in my brain goes *click*. "Let me try the next one," I tell him. Then I calculate the molecular weight of $C_{12}H_{22}O_{11}$—otherwise known as sugar—convert it to moles, divide by liters, and circle my answer.

"Looks right," he says, then borrows my calculator, jabs in a bunch of numbers, and comes up with the same answer. "You've got it!"

And the funny thing is, I'm actually excited to try the next problem, so when he stands up, I want to yank him back and make him watch me, but he's already beelining toward the computers like he's remembered that he was in a hurry. So I wind up just saying, "Thank you!" which feels kinda lame because "thank you" doesn't even begin to cover the relief I'm feeling.

Anyway, I've just figured out the molecular weight of sodium carbonate when I hear a little snort and "I *knew* it," from over by the computers. Kip's got his back to me and is far enough away that I can't see any details, but from the screen I recognize that he's on Facebook.

Whatever. I get back to work, but then I hear him mutter, "What *idiots.*"

So now I'm curious. And before I really think things through, I get up and move closer, but all I see is a post of two girls in bikinis, holding up icy pink drinks. They're definitely older than Kip—maybe around twenty? And it takes me a minute to click into the fact that they have blond hair and blue eyes.

All of a sudden, I'm feeling really panicked. I'd jumped all over him for sneaking up on me, and now I'm spying over his shoulder?

Plus, he's a Kensington!

They have codes and rules and gag orders!

So I hold my breath and sneak back to my seat, and while Kip's fingers are flying around the keyboard, I pretend to work, but my brain's racing, remembering bits and pieces of conversation that happened in the Royal Suite.

I hear a printer activate and then Kip stands up, shoves his chair in, and heads across the room. Everything he does is fast, and he seems upset. So I call after him, "You okay?"

He whips around, then looks at his computer and realizes I can see the monitor.

"You don't seem like the blond-bimbo kind," I tell him.

He looks all around, and when he sees that the Puzzle Lady's gone and we're alone, he gets defensive, saying, "I'm not! They're my cousins."

"Ohhhh." Then I add, "The ones who are too sick to come on the cruise?"

He gives me a sharp look. "Stay out of it."

"Sure. Happy to."

And I am.

Like I want to get tangled up in the wacky web of Kensingtons?

But still, I can't seem to resist saying, "I can see why you're mad, though. Seems pretty disrespectful."

Well, stupid me, 'cause something about that pulls the gag off his mouth. "It's more than disrespectful, it's a lie!" He shakes his head. "He's a master liar!"

In the front of my mind I'm going, Stop! U-turn! Go back! But the back of my mind is calculating quick, and out of my mouth comes, "Bradley?"

"Yes! Grandfather was onto him, but Grandmother always falls for his lies." Then he says, "We're scattering Grandfather's ashes tomorrow, and he lies to cover up that his daughters are partying with their friends in Miami Beach? After everything Grandfather's done for them?"

"Maybe Bradley *doesn't* know? Maybe your cousins lied to him?"

"Oh, he knows!"

I think a minute. "His wife's supposedly sick, too, huh?"

"See? She's probably there with them!"

I study him. "Don't your cousins know you can see their posts?"

He just stands there, saying nothing.

"Ah," I say with a little nod. "Too many friends to notice an imposter?"

"Look," he says, sitting down across from me. "I helped you. Now help me by just staying out of it."

I put my hands up. "Gladly!"

"I want Grandmother to know because she should know, but there's no way anyone can find out the information came from me."

"What about your mother?"

"No one!" he says, and it comes out all fierce.

Like it's somehow a matter of life and death.

TEN

Kip took off after he went all fierce on me, and I buckled down on my work sheet. And even though I sweat bullets through every single one, I wound up finishing six problems.

Six!

Which meant I didn't have to do any on my birthday!

Well, technically, it was two in the morning *on* my birthday, but it didn't matter.

Now I could sleep!

Trouble is, as I'm going *up* the stairs to sneak back into my room, Kip's coming *down* the stairs to sneak into his. We hit the Deck 9 landing at the same time—which was awkward enough right there—but then who steps off the elevator at that exact moment?

Darren and Marko.

So of course I try to duck, and of course they see me.

And Kip.

So far, fourteen wasn't one bit luckier than thirteen.

"No!" I groan, and actually stomp my foot. "This is not what it looks like!"

Darren just stares at me, then gives Kip a look that could crush rocks.

"I gotta go . . . ," Kip stammers, and runs off, acting *totally* guilty.

So there I am, left trying to explain. "Look!" I tell Darren, yanking my chemistry work sheet out of my backpack. "I went down to the library to do homework! And Kip happened to—"

But it was already sounding so lame.

So conveniently "coincidental."

"Here," I tell him, and shove my chemistry work sheet at him. "*This* is what we were doing."

He looks it over and eyes me. "Why?"

"Because I hadn't done the problems I was supposed to do today and felt guilty! Because I kept hearing my science teacher's voice telling me she's proud of me for working so hard to bring my grade up! Because I didn't understand the assignment, and it was freaking me out, and I didn't want to be stuck doing double the problems on my birthday, and Marissa says we're doing some land excursion the next day, and I have no idea what that is or how long it's going to take! And because Marissa was snoring and I couldn't sleep!"

His look is half *uh-huh* and half *oh*. And since he's not *saying* anything, I just keep barreling along. "And since there was no place in the room to work without waking Marissa up, I went one little floor down and worked in the library. Kip came in to use a computer, which turned out to be really lucky because he actually knows how to do this stuff and tutored me. And I got *two* days' worth done, which is a huge relief, believe me."

Darren hesitates, then gives a little nod. "Ah."

Since I don't know what it means and since now I'm all keyed up, I go, "What am I, a doctor?"

Darren gives me a puzzled look, but Marko chuckles, which makes Darren look at him like, What? which makes Marko go, "You said, 'Ah'?"

Darren rolls his eyes a little and gives a kinda weak smile. And I can tell he thinks he should be doing some, you know, official parenting or something, but either he just doesn't have the heart for it or he believes me.

"It's the truth," I tell him softly.

"What, that you're a doctor?" He shakes the work sheet a little as he hands it back. "Keep this up and you will be."

I look down. "I don't want to be a doctor. I just want to turn fourteen without being in trouble."

He puts an arm around my shoulders. "Too late for that."

Marko grins at me. "Congratulations on surviving back-to-back thirteens, though. Quite a feat."

"Thanks," I grumble.

Darren studies me a minute, then lays a big smooch on my temple. "Happy birthday, kiddo." Then he pulls away and eyes me. "Now get to bed, and stay there!"

I laugh, thinking, Kiddo? And even though I'd started fourteen by getting into trouble, I do what he says and head straight to bed.

I fall asleep quick, too, feeling weirdly happy.

* * *

Even lying in a bed nine decks up, you can hear the ship's engines. It's not a roar—more a deep, steady purr that you don't really notice unless there's a big change in speed. The rest of the time it's like a calming whisper, telling your subconscious that everything's okay.

So my excuse for sleeping until ten is that engines nine decks down were sneakily lulling me to sleep.

Hypnotized by the Great Engine Lullaby!

Lucky for me, rock stars *are* notoriously late, so when Marissa threw me in the shower with, "They'll be here any minute!" I actually had nothing to worry about. It was eleven before we were all finally ready to go.

"I am *starving*," Marissa said as the rest of us hurried up the stairs after her. "I've been awake for *hours*."

For all the exploring we'd done the day before, we hadn't gone into the Schooner Buffet. It was on Deck 11, and took up the whole back end of the ship. It was in the shape of a giant U, with a wide entrance at the end of each leg. There were hot food dishes swooping clear around the middle of the U, seating along the wall of windows that went around the outside of the U, and islands with cold foods or plates and utensils or drinks in between the hot food and the seating parts.

The hot buffet was amazing. There were omelets and pancakes and waffles and bacon and . . . well, any kind of breakfast food you can think of—plus lunch foods, seeing how it was after eleven o'clock.

But the islands in between the hot buffet and the tables were my favorite. One had big bowls of fresh-cut fruit, and

I couldn't get over the way it was decorated with carved watermelons. They were crazy! Incredibly detailed—like they'd been done with a laser. There was a watermelon shark with its mouth full of melon balls, a watermelon turtle with melon balls underneath, a half watermelon where the rind was carved into a bouquet of flowers, and a whole one where the rind was a beautiful sailing ship.

Then I discovered that right next door was . . . Dessert Island! It had mousses and chocolate-dipped strawberries and pies and cakes and brownies, and it was right next to . . . Cookie Island! Which was right next to . . . Pastry Island!

"This is unbelievable!" I said, and Marko was loading up like a kid, too, going, "Dude, check this out! Dude! Check *this* out!" until finally Darren told him, "Dude! I'm checking it all out! Calm down!"

When we finally sat down, my tray was crammed with everything from key lime pie to egg-drop soup to waffles and oatmeal to a taco and pink lemonade.

"That is a strange combination of food," Darren says as we sit down at a window table.

"She gets that from Casey," Marissa says. "He's always putting weird foods together."

Which reminds me of something I'd been wanting to know since about midnight. "What's the deal with the Internet?" I ask Darren. "Is it free?"

Marissa butts in with, "Actually, it's super-expensive. Even when we weren't broke, Mom and Dad wouldn't let us use it."

I look down. "Oh."

Darren eyes her. "It's not cheap, but it's probably more that they didn't want you spending all your cruise time on the computer." He turns to me. "You're wanting to check in with Casey?"

I give a little shrug. "He's not expecting it. I told him I wouldn't be able to."

"So you'll get to surprise him." He gives me a cockeyed smile. "I set up an account yesterday, and I'm happy to share with the birthday girl."

"Really?"

"I'll show you how to use it if you promise not to spend all your time on the computer."

I laugh and nod and promise, and all of a sudden I'm feeling stupidly giddy. It's only been a day and a half, but it's my birthday! And I miss Casey!

Marissa jolts me away from thoughts of Casey by nudging me and saying, "Somebody's not happy."

I follow her gaze out to Bradley Kensington, who's standing alone near Dessert Island, holding a padded black folder and talking on his cell phone. His brow's all wrinkled, and even though I can't hear what he's saying, the vibe is definitely tense. "Busted," I say with a little laugh.

Darren and Marko whip around to look. "Who's busted?"

"Don't!" I tell them, and kick them under the table.

Marko whips back around. "Hey, you can't go, 'busted,' and have us not look!"

"That's right!" Darren says, frowning at me like I've just spit in holy water or something.

Marissa's keeping one eye on Bradley and the other on me. "Why busted?"

"That is one angry-looking man," Marko says, glancing over his shoulder.

"Stop looking!"

He does, but he keeps talking. "Obviously, his mama didn't let him play the drums as a child."

Which, yeah, seemed about right. I couldn't picture him—or any Kensington, for that matter—cutting loose on the drums.

"But why busted?" Marissa asks again.

"Uh . . . it's supposed to be in the vault?" I say, kinda low.

Marissa's eyes quit doing the splits as she focuses on only me. "How can you know something I don't?"

Darren leans in, too. "You haven't told her?" he asks, and it's maddening the way he's grinning.

Marissa punches a fist onto her hip. "Told me what?"

Marko zooms in, too, wiggling his eyebrows. "About your secret midnight rendezvous?"

"What?" Marissa asks. "With who?"

"You guys are terrible!" I tell Marko and Darren. "You're total . . . troublemakers!"

Darren seems pleased. "That we are."

"Now open the vault, matey!" Marko growls, giving me a piratey look.

So I do, telling them about Kip's little Internet adventure and how his uncle Bradley's daughters—and probably his wife—lied about being sick. And I'm just winding down when I notice someone lurking on the other side of Dessert Island.

Someone paying way too much attention to pies and cakes without actually putting anything on his tray.

"What?" Darren says, looking over his shoulder.

"Stop!" I hiss at him.

"Well, stop looking over there!" he hisses back.

"It's Kip," Marissa tells him. "Spying on his uncle."

Marko is actually *bubbling*. "Dude, don't you feel like you're back spying on the Flemings?"

"Only now we don't get to see anything!" Darren grumbles. "We just get kicked and told to quit looking."

"Who are the Flemings?" I ask.

"Neighbors," they say at the same time. And they both shake their heads in the same way as they eye each other.

Like there's no way they could even begin to explain.

"Finish your story," Marissa says, but her eyes are doing the splits between Bradley and me again.

So I finish it quick, and remind them that I'd told Kip I wouldn't tell anyone about his little computer find and that they need to close the vault about it.

"Who am I going to tell?" Marko says.

I can see the wheels turning in Darren's head, though, so I ask him, "What?"

"What what?" he asks back.

"Don't give me that. I can tell you're thinking something."

He sort of eyes me. "What I'm thinking is that kids are both stupider and smarter than we were as kids."

Marko's eyebrows go flying. "Stupider than us? Than *us*?"

"Well, it is *we*," Darren says.

"Okay, Mr. Grammar. *We* hid from the principal on the roof of the school and then couldn't get down, remember that?"

"Hey, that was *your* idea."

"Whose idea was it to sneak into the Flemings' basement? And why?"

Darren mutters something that none of us can understand.

"Say it!" Marko demands.

He sighs. "Because there was gold down there."

"Gold. In the Flemings' basement. They didn't even own a car, and you thought there was gold."

Darren gives a little shrug. "Or maybe maps to gold?"

Marko turns to us. "But instead we found gnats! Thousands of mean, biting gnats."

Darren shudders. "They were no-see-ums. Invisible stealth biters."

"The bites lasted weeks!"

"And *itched* . . ."

"And you told everyone we'd been attacked by biting ghosts."

"Biting ghosts!" Marissa and I cry.

Darren frowns. "I was eight, okay?"

"And then there was the time we were playing dodge, and we crashed our dirt bikes *into each other* fifteen miles from anywhere, remember that?"

"You can stop right there," Darren tells him through his teeth.

Marko backs down. "Just sayin'. We had our fair share of stupid."

Now, really, I want to say, Don't stop! Because I'm having a really good time picturing the two of them as kids, getting into scrapes and trouble.

It makes me feel like . . . well, like we have something in common.

But then Marissa gets out of her seat and says, "Bradley's leaving. Dessert time. You take the far end, I'll come in from this side."

The weird thing is, I know exactly what she means, but the real question is, Why?

So I ask.

"Why?"

"Kip heard everything!"

And for probably the first time in our friendship, I'm the one to go, "Who cares?"

But she gives me one of her stern looks and a scoopy little wave, so what can do? I roll my eyes and follow her.

"Watch out for gnats!" Marko warns.

"And biting ghosts," Darren adds.

Which makes me laugh. I mean, how cool is that, to be able to make fun of your own dorky selves?

Anyway, Marissa circles Dessert Island from the left and I swoop in from the right, and Kip doesn't stand a chance.

"Whoa!" he says, jumping back a little.

"Did you get all that?" I ask him.

His eyes dart back and forth as he death grips an empty tray. "Get all what?"

"Uncle Bradley's intense conversation."

"You've been spying on me?"

"Uh, I think *you* were the one spying?"

Marissa nods. "We were just observing."

"And what we observed," I tell him, "is that you were spying."

He blinks. First at me, then at Marissa. Then all of a sudden I notice that his eyes are getting all glassy, and he's all, like, choked up. Or maybe choked off. Or, you know, *trapped*. And in that moment I feel really sorry for him. I mean, who spends their cruise spying on some angry uncle? Why isn't he hanging out with his cousin or his mom or some random teens in the arcade, or rock climbing or mini-golfing? Or at least eating some dessert!

Obviously, being part of a fragrance empire isn't as easy as it seems.

So I grab a dish of chocolate mousse, stick in a huge strawberry, put it on his empty tray, and make my confession. "I told Marissa about last night."

I'm expecting him to freak out, but he just shakes his head fast and says, "This isn't about that." He looks down. "This is actually really bad."

Marissa and I both stare at him like, Well?

"Grandmother's missing."

Now, excuse me, but the first thing I do is laugh. I mean, come on. It's a big boat. And when you're rolling in dough and your nephew's the cruise director, you could be anywhere!

"This is serious!" he says, all serious-like.

"Sorry," I tell him, "but she's got to be someplace, right? The casino? Having breakfast with the captain? Drinking champagne in the Cloud 9 Bar?"

Kip shakes his head. "They haven't found her, and I don't think they will."

"Why not?"

"Because I don't think she's on the ship."

"But we haven't docked and—" I blink at him as what he said sinks in. "You think she *jumped*?"

He shakes his head super-fast. "Grandmother would never jump. And Grandfather's urn is still in the suite."

"So?"

"So if she did jump, she would have taken him with her!" He looks all around, then drops his voice. "I think she was pushed."

ELEVEN

"Pushed?" Marissa gasps. "As in overboard? As in *murdered?*"

Kip's death grip on the tray sure isn't getting any looser, and he's shaking so much that the giant strawberry I'd jammed into his mousse is sorta falling over, and the shiny strawberry seeds suddenly seem like tiny windows on a big red ship to me. A big red ship that's tilting over in a sea of foamy chocolate.

I shake off the thought and grab him by the arm, 'cause obviously he's having a meltdown. "Come with us."

But when he sees we're headed over to Darren and Marko, he pulls back. "I've got to go."

"You've got to sit," I tell him, and kinda shove him into a chair.

His tray thumps and bumps and the Strawberry Titanic keels completely over.

"So we meet again," Darren says with an eyebrow cocked.

"That's one sad-looking dessert," Marko tells him, eyeing the Strawberry Titanic.

I look Kip square in the eye and just come out with it: "They know, too."

"About . . . ?" He searches my face, but fear's written all over his because he knows exactly what I'm talking about. "But you said—"

"That was before you ditched me in the hallway at two in the morning."

"But . . . why did you tell them? Why didn't you just make something up?"

Darren focuses on him. "What was that?"

Marko shakes his head and does a little tisk. "Kipster, that was a bad move."

Kip tries to get up, but I pull him back down. "Look, I wasn't going to *lie,* but you also don't have to worry—it's not like you did anything wrong. And it's not like we're going to be talking to anyone in your family about it."

"You don't understand!" he cries, jumping up.

I yank him down again. "What I *do* understand is that you're sneaking around this ship all by yourself, spying on people, and freaking out about your grandmother."

"The alien queen?" Marko asks.

Marissa and I cry, "Marko!" and Darren does his best to run interference by asking, "What happened with your grandmother?"

He's asking sincerely, so I look at Kip like, Well? and finally Kip says, "She's missing."

Marko's and Darren's eyebrows go flying, and they say, "Missing?" Then they look at each other quick, the eyebrows come down, and they turn back to Kip and go, "Did you check the casino?"

106

"She's not in the casino!"

"How about somewhere in here?" Marko asks. "It's a big buffet."

Darren nods. "Or the bars? The bars are always open."

Now it's my turn to run interference. I give Darren and Marko a cool-it signal, then tell Kip, "Look, you're obviously upset about your grandmother, and you obviously need someone to talk to."

"Well, *you're* a bad choice!"

So yeah. He's also obviously ticked off.

"Actually, she's a great choice," Marissa tells him.

He snorts. "Right."

"She is. And I don't know what I'd do if I didn't have Sammy to talk to."

"Likewise with Marko here," Darren tells him.

"Dude!" Marko gushes, and blows him a kiss.

Well, after *that* has a few seconds to clear, I tell Kip, "The point is, if you think someone shoved your grandmother overboard—"

"Whoa! Wait!" Marko says. "What's this?"

"Hold on," I tell him, then turn back to Kip. "Who *can* you talk to?"

He just looks down and shakes his head.

"Your mom?"

He shakes it some more.

"JT?"

His head snaps up. "No way!"

"So . . . ?"

There's a long silence, and finally he says, "Grandfather was the only one."

I just blink at him. "Uh . . . not much conversation happening there."

"I know," he says, and really, it looks like his eyes are about to bust loose with tears.

"Dude," Marko says. "You want to come play my drums?"

Marissa and I turn on him. "Marko!"

"I'm serious! It's great therapy."

Darren slaps Marko on the back. "It would probably help if we left."

"Dude, it's just getting interesting!"

Darren stands and drags Marko out of his seat, then gives Kip a little smirk. "It's not like I talked to my mother when I was your age, and I sure didn't talk to other people's parents. Mostly I talked to Marko here, even though he's always given questionable advice."

"Dude! I give great advice! This boy needs to bash on something, can't you see that?"

Darren just pulls him along, telling us, "So maybe we'll go catch some rays while you talk things through." And since none of us are begging him to stay, he adds, "How about I meet you in that Lido Library at three o'clock? We'll get you online."

"That'd be great!" I tell him.

The minute they're gone, I scoot around so I'm facing Kip better and look him square in the eye. "The person I love most in the world is my grandmother."

"Hey!" Marissa cries.

"Sorry!" I turn back to Kip. "But it's true. There'd be this huge hole in my heart that nobody could patch up if she died. So I get what you're saying about your grandfather."

Which, big help, makes him actually cry. I hand him a napkin, but he wipes his face with his hands instead. And when he's mostly dried up, I ask, "Your grandfather was your mother's father, right? And Kate's your mother's mother?"

He nods.

"So your mom's got to be upset about all this, too. She would understand how you feel, wouldn't she?"

Only instead of nodding, he shakes his head. "She resents them. Maybe even hates them."

My eyes squint down. "She *hates* them? Why?"

"Because of me."

"You?"

"Grandfather brought me here from Kenya. He thought my mother needed a child."

"Wait. Whoa. *What?*"

Kip nods. "That was pretty much my mother's reaction."

"Can you actually remember her reaction?" Marissa asks. "How old were you?"

"Eight."

"But . . ." I shake my head. "What was he doing in Kenya? And why you?"

"He was buying a shea tree plantation."

"A what?"

"You know—the stuff they make shea butter out of? For creams and stuff?"

"So . . . ?"

"And I was an orphan and a . . ."

He just drifts off, so I say, "And a what?"

He looks away. "A thief. You know."

"No! I don't know!"

"You do what you have to do to eat, okay? There was never enough at the orphanage." He shrugs. "But he caught me, and instead of punishing me, he hired me to help him. He taught me things, too. The second time he came, I was so happy to see him. I didn't want him to leave."

"So he brought you back with him?" Marissa asks, and when he nods, we both just stare until Marissa finally says, "So it was your grandfather's idea and your grandmother went along with it?"

"That's the way it always was. I never saw her disagree with him." He shakes his head a little. "And I spent a lot of time with them. Grandfather seemed to really like having me around. And Grandmother has always been very kind to me."

"But not your mother?" I ask as gently as I can.

"She hasn't been *un*kind," he says with another little shrug. "She just never wanted a child. She travels a lot and is really into her fashion business."

Marissa shakes her head. "So why didn't she just tell him no?"

"None of them ever told him no."

Now, he doesn't actually have a sneer on his face, but I can sure hear one in his voice. So my brain races around and finally out of my mouth comes, "Because he was so . . . powerful?"

He eyes me. "Because he was so rich."

110

My brain races around some more. "So he could, what, *bribe* her into taking you?"

He frowns. "Right before he and Grandmother took that last trip where he had his heart attack, I overheard him begging my mom to become a real mother to me—to stop doing it just for the money." He shakes his head. "Everything started making sense."

"Wow," I say after a minute. "That's awful."

"Still better than my life before," he mutters. "By miles."

"Okay, but back to your grandmother," Marissa says. "Why would anyone want to push her overboard?"

"Things were always tense between my uncles and my mother, but since Grandfather died, it's been really bad—especially since Grandmother was so mysterious about the will."

Marissa scoops out a bite of chocolate foam. "We overheard that she wants to sell the company and build a hospital in Africa last night at dinner."

"You did?"

She nods. "It didn't seem to go over too well. And why get everyone on a cruise to tell them what's in the will?"

Kip takes a deep breath. "Grandfather wanted his ashes to be scattered at sea, and Grandmother used the will as a bribe to get everyone together. She said a week at sea would tell her things she needed to know."

"Like whether Bradley should run the company?"

His eyes pop. "How do you know about *that*?"

So I tell him how JT's parents had come storming down the hall all angry about what Bradley had said, and at first Kip's kinda stunned, and then he shakes his head fast and says, "There's no way Grandfather said Bradley should run the company. It's just another one of his lies!" Then he kind of scowls and says, "It's true about Uncle Lucas and Aunt LuAnn, though. I don't think either of them has ever had a job."

"But still," Marissa says. "None of this means anyone pushed Kate overboard!"

Kip looks at me, then at Marissa, then back at me. And I can tell he's weighing something in his head, so I say, "We're obviously trying to help, right? So just tell us."

He gives a little nod and keeps his voice low as he says, "Last night when I finally got up the nerve to slip that printout of my cousins under Grandmother's door, I could hear voices. There were people in there, yelling."

I lean in a little and drop my voice, too. "Could you tell who?"

"No. But for their voices to make it through that cabin door? They had to be pretty loud."

"Could you tell if the voices were male or female?"

"Both. But I didn't stick around! Or leave the paper. I was afraid of getting caught, so I came running down, and that's when I bumped into you." He looks down. "Which is why I was so freaked out. I'm sorry I just ran off."

I study him a minute and ask, "Was your mother in your cabin when you got back to your room?"

"No. She snuck back in at two-thirty."

"So she could have been one of the people fighting in the Royal Suite, which means if your grandmother really is missing, she might have had something to do with it."

He covers his eyes with a hand. "I was so grateful to her. I tried so hard to please her! But then I found out about Grandfather paying her, and now this?" He gives me a pleading look, then says, "But she is a night owl. She works on her designs on her laptop clear through the night sometimes. So maybe that's what she was doing."

"You didn't ask her?"

He shakes his head. "She wouldn't have told me anyway."

Now, I've been trying to avoid telling him something else, because when you line up all the "overhearing" I've done, well, it sounds like I'm the world's worst snoop. But it just doesn't seem fair *not* to tell him, so I finally fess up about Kate and Ginger in the Cheesy Say-Cheese Aisle and about, uh, *accidentally* overhearing Kate say she was going to call a midnight meeting to discuss the rest of the will.

At first Kip does look at me like I'm the snoop monster. But then he focuses on what's important. "So they were *all* in there?"

I give a little shrug. "Your grandmother seems like someone who can get people to show up at midnight meetings."

Kip thinks a minute, then goes, "Wow. Whatever else is in the will must be really bad."

"Is the hospital actually written in it?" Marissa asks.

Kip shrugs. "I don't know."

"What else is there besides the company?" she asks. "Stocks? Bonds? Cash? Real estate? Valuable art?"

"I don't know! It's not like I sat around talking about

it! Grandfather and I talked about things like astronomy and chemistry and physics . . . not money!"

"Okay," Marissa says, scraping out the mousse dish, "so let's assume that the company is the main thing, and that selling it to build a hospital is *not* actually in writing. What happens if your grandmother dies before that gets carried out?"

Kip looks a little lost. "It depends on what's in Grandmother's will?"

"And if what's in her will is that the kids inherit everything, then getting rid of your grandmother would mean your mother and uncles would go from getting whatever's left over after the hospital is built to getting *everything*."

Kip stares at her a minute, then looks over both shoulders. "They can't know we suspect them," he whispers. Then he looks right at us and says, "And they can't know *you* know."

"Us?" I try to laugh it off, but the truth is, I do have the creeps.

The big-time, don't-ignore-me creeps.

And I can't help looking around, too, and feeling worried that we're being watched. Because as big as the ship is, I'm realizing we're trapped.

Trapped on the high seas, with psycho-rich killers who are not afraid of tossing their problems overboard.

TWELVE

I'm feeling totally paranoid as I'm checking around every-where, but then I realize something.

It's only about noon.

What if Kate was just . . . shopping?

So I take a deep breath and say, "Okay. Back up. *Why* do you think Kate is missing?"

"Aunt Ginger called everyone together and told us she was!"

"Well, how does *she* know?"

"She said Grandmother's bed was not slept in, and that when she got up to use the bathroom at six o'clock, she had to close the balcony door, because it had been left open."

"Wait, so your great-aunt is staying in the Royal Suite, too?"

Kip nods.

"Well . . . she must've been there, then! And she wouldn't let someone throw your grandmother overboard!"

"I don't *know* that she was there! After she told us Grandmother was missing, my mother made me leave. I said I wanted to help, but she made me leave, and I haven't seen her since."

I think about that a minute, then ask, "What did you hear Bradley say when you were over by Dessert Island?"

"Dessert Island?"

"You know . . ." I wave over to where he'd been standing. "Over there!"

He covers his face, and at first I think that, after all this, he's still worried about telling us, but it turns out he's just trying to remember. "He kept saying, 'Find out. Find out and get back to me.' He said it over and over."

"Who do you think he was talking to?"

"A lawyer. I'm pretty sure it was a lawyer."

"Why?"

"Because he told him, 'I'll litigate it all the way to hell, if that's what it takes!' "

"Wow." I think about it a minute, then ask, "What *do* they do if someone goes missing on a cruise? Ginger's reported it, right? If they think she's overboard, wouldn't they turn the ship around and look for her floating in the water?"

"You don't just turn a cruise ship around," Marissa says. "It's like turning an island around."

"Then what do they do if someone falls overboard?"

Marissa gives a little shrug. "Put out a life raft? Throw out a buoy? Call the Coast Guard?"

"Have they done that?" I ask Kip. "Have they done anything?"

"I don't know!"

We're all quiet a minute, and then Marissa gets us back on track with, "What about Noah? Could he help figure out where your grandmother is?"

"Noah," he says, and it comes out all breathy. Then he stands up, saying, "Noah's a great idea. Let's go!"

We hurry to keep up with him as he hightails it out of the Schooner Buffet and down the stairs. Trouble is, he stops after one flight and heads for the hallway.

Right for the Royal Suite.

"Wait!" I cry, grabbing his arm.

"We're not going in *there*," he whispers, then takes off down the hallway to the front of the ship.

"Then where?" I ask when we're past the alien hive.

"Noah's room is up by the bridge."

Marissa zips ahead of me to catch up with him. "Is it by the captain's quarters?"

I try to walk next to her but there are trays of dirty dishes and cleaning carts in the way, so it's not easy. "How do you know where the captain's quarters are? And what's the bridge?" I was picturing something arching over water.

"You know—the control center?" Marissa throws over her shoulder. "It's full of computer screens and monitoring systems and stuff. My parents were platinum club members and we got a tour once."

We're passing by the forward sets of stairs now, plowing straight ahead, and Kip says, "Uncle Noah told me his room was second from the end on the port side."

"That's the left side, right?" I ask, and he goes, "Right, the left," and actually grins over his shoulder at me.

It turns out that the door to the room second from the end on the port side was open. So Kip sticks his head inside and calls, "Uncle Noah?"

But there's a cleaning cart out in the hallway, and

instead of Noah, a woman with black hair pulled back into a bun comes to the door. "Mr. Marlowe is not here," she says, flashing top teeth that are outlined in silver. She pulls a paper from her smock's pocket, unfolds it, and shows it to Kip. It's today's Cruzer Calendar, and she points to the events column and says, "Mr. Marlowe is at bingo now."

I glance at the list of activities scheduled for the day and ask, "He has to be at *all* those things?" Because there are events listed from seven in the morning until eleven at night.

"Oh, yes," she says. "Mr. Marlowe is a hardworking man."

We tell her thanks, then do a U-turn and zip down the stairs to Deck 3, where bingo is already in full swing inside the Poseidon Theater.

Now, compared to how sunny and bright it had been at the Schooner Buffet, the theater seems really dim. There's a big digital board with lit-up numbers and letters in front of the closed stage curtains, and the room is speckled with players—not packed, but with the size of the auditorium, there are actually a lot of people, maybe two hundred? But they're all spread out and . . . quiet.

And mostly old.

There is someone on the stage announcing squares, but it's not Noah, and after we've scanned the room for a minute, I ask Kip, "Do you see him?"

He shakes his head, and Marissa pipes up with, "Usually the cruise director opens and closes shows and activities. He doesn't stick around for the whole thing."

"Maybe he's backstage?" I look at Marissa. "Do you know what's back there?"

She shrugs. "Never been."

Well, that was a first. And for once I was wishing she *did* know all about it already, but since she didn't, I started thinking that there had to be a door off to the side of the stage, and that going through it would be like sneaking through an employees-only door at the Santa Martina Mall—you go in, look around, and either find what you're looking for or get kicked out.

So I start cutting through an empty aisle of seats, heading over to where I figure the door must be.

Right away, Kip gets nervous. "Where are we going?"

I whisper, "Backstage, I hope," and keep on moving.

"Why don't we just wait for bingo to finish?"

Behind me, I can hear Marissa whisper, "Because that would be too easy."

I glance at them over my shoulder. "Do you really want to watch old people play bingo for an hour?"

Well, the answer's obviously *no*, because they follow me.

And I'm right about there being a door.

Actually, there are two.

Trouble is, both of them are latched and have key-code pads.

"Look at you," Marissa whispers as I scout out the area. "Your eyes are all bright, your cheeks are all flushed, that crazy brain of yours is off to the races trying to figure out how to get back there." She leans in toward me and says,

"Of all the things you might get for your birthday, nothing's going to compete with this, is it?"

"What are you talking about?"

She just snickers. "You know what I'm talking about."

"So we wait?" Kip asks, not really tuning in to what Marissa's teasing me about.

Marissa snickers again, but this time she doesn't actually *say* anything.

And she's right.

I'm terrible at waiting.

So I do the only thing I can think to do when I'm blocked by a locked door.

I knock.

"What? No!" Kip whispers.

"Why not?" I ask him, and knock again.

"Because it's *loud*," he hisses.

Which it is.

But I've already done it twice, so after a few quiet seconds, I figure what the heck and try again.

The door does not open, but a guy with a walkie-talkie comes running toward us from the back of the auditorium. His blue shirt has patches and lots of brass buttons, so I know he's some cruise official, but it's not like we've done anything wrong, so I'm not worried.

Kip, though, is sweating bullets. "Look what you've done!" he whispers.

Now, Marissa's usually the one getting all nervous, but I guess Kip acting that way makes her switch to cool and collected, because when the Walkie-Talkie Official asks,

"May I help you?" Marissa jumps right in with, "We need to find Noah. It's sort of an emergency."

The WTO asks, "Noah Marlowe?"

Kip nods and says, "That's right," and then Marissa pipes up with, "He's his uncle. Family emergency."

Walkie-Talkie studies Kip, and I'm thinking he's thinking that Kip and Noah sure don't *look* related and that we're probably just a bunch of annoying kids causing trouble, when out of his mouth comes, "Are you Kip?"

Kip nods.

Walkie-Talkie looks around. And I can tell he's thinking rapid fire, but I can't tell what about. I know what *I'm* thinking, though. And when I look at Marissa and Kip, I can tell that they're thinking the same thing I am.

How did he know Kip's name?

Then all of a sudden the rapid-fire thinking seems to have hit its mark. "Come with me," the WTO says, and in a flash, he's keyed in the access code and is leading us backstage.

THIRTEEN

Walkie-Talkie takes us down a corridor that starts out narrow and dim but then turns and opens up to a bright hallway with racks of clothes and wigs and props along one wall, and open doorways to dressing rooms along the other.

"Where are we going?" Marissa asks.

"Right back here," Walkie-Talkie tells her. And he keeps hurrying along until a voice behind us calls, "Kip?"

We come skidding to a halt, and when we whip around, there's Noah, leaning out of one of the dressing rooms.

Walkie-Talkie hurries back. "I was told you were in the entertainment office, sir."

"Thank you, Jacques," Noah tells him as he wraps Kip in a bear hug. Then over his shoulder, he calls, "Mom! He's safe. He's right here."

"Shall I call off the alert?" Jacques asks.

Noah nods. "Right away. I'll let my family know."

"Is there anything else, sir?" Jacques asks him, and when Noah tells him no, he leaves, going back the way we'd come.

So Noah says, "I'll be right back," and suddenly Ginger's there, gasping, "Oh, Kip! We've been so worried!"

Kip blinks hard and fast. Like he's having trouble making sense of any of this. "About me?"

"Of course about you! Where have you been all morning?" Then she looks at Marissa and me and says, "But I see the answer's right here in front of us. Tell me your names again?"

"I'm Sammy," I tell her, "and this is Marissa."

"Have you found your sister?" Marissa asks. "Kip's really upset."

"We have not," Ginger says, and she's doing one of those brave-face adult things. "But we really don't want you to worry! Leave that to us, okay?"

Just then Noah returns, and Kip asks him, "Does the captain know Grandmother's missing? Is the Coast Guard looking for her? Why didn't we turn around? What's being *done?*"

Noah and Ginger exchange concerned looks, and then Noah takes a deep breath and says, "You know I love your grandmother, right? So please believe that I'm doing everything I can."

"But if she was shoved overboard—"

"Shoved?" Ginger gasps. "Sweetheart, who would have shoved her?"

"Any of them!" Kip cries.

"Any of . . . who?"

"Any of the Kensingtons!"

Ginger blinks at him. "Why on earth would you think that?"

Kip backs down. And I'm thinking, *Tell her,* only he doesn't. Which seems insane. I mean, how will they ever get to the bottom of things if they won't talk to each other? So I decide to say it for him. "Because of that big fight last night."

Kip shoots me a look, but he seems more nervous than mad. So I'm thinking, Okay. Sticking my nose in was a good thing for once.

Until Ginger zeroes in on me.

"A big fight?" she asks.

She made it a question but I can tell that a) she definitely knows about a big fight, and b) I'm definitely *not* supposed to know about a big fight.

Now, the way she's looking at me is pretty unnerving. But Kip is either feeling braver because of what I said or he doesn't know where else to turn, because instead of backing down again, he pulls his computer printout out of his back pocket and hands it over. "I came up last night to slip this under the door. I thought Grandmother should know."

Ginger takes the paper, and an eyebrow goes creeping up as she figures out what it's about. Noah studies it over her shoulder and frowns as he says, "Well. This shouldn't be a big surprise. Bradley's always been a master at pulling the wool over her eyes."

"Exactly!" Kip cries. "But Grandmother never *believes* it, and this time I finally had proof. But when I heard the fighting . . ." He gives a little shrug.

"You didn't want to get caught?" Ginger asks.

Kip looks down, and I can tell he's feeling really uncomfortable, so I pop in with, "So it was Bradley and Lucas and Teresa fighting? Anyone else?"

She studies me a minute, and I can tell she's dying to say, "What business is it of yours?" but instead she gives a little nod and says, "The three of them. And when they left, Kate was extremely upset."

"Did you talk about the fight after you were alone?"

She raises an eyebrow at me, then turns to Noah, who cuts in with, "Let's leave the questioning to the authorities, shall we?" Then he looks at Kip and says, "You trust me, don't you, Kip? That's why you came looking for me . . . that's why you let me see that paper . . . that's why you're asking me for help . . . right?"

Kip nods.

"Then please know that I'm doing everything I can. I'm hoping that she's just somewhere cooling off. It's a big ship. Almost four thousand passengers, over a thousand crew members . . . lots of places she could be." He forces a smile. "I'm so relieved we don't have to worry about you, too."

"But I don't understand why you were worried about *me*."

"Your mother told us that *you'd* disappeared, too."

Kip blinks at him. "I've been in the wide open all day!"

"Where?" Ginger asks.

"At the Schooner Buffet!" He looks at Marissa and me. "We were all just sitting there in plain sight!"

"Well," Ginger says. "Your mother was very agitated."

"But why? She kicked me out of the suite this morning, remember? She couldn't care less!"

Ginger and Noah look at each other *again*, but before they can say anything to try to smooth that over, Kip blurts out, "I know Grandfather was paying her. I overheard them talking about it."

Ginger studies him a minute, then says, "I think you should come stay in the Royal Suite with me. There's *plenty* of room."

"But . . ." Kip stares at her. "Why do you want me to stay with you? And what would I tell my mother?"

Ginger frowns. "Tell her what you overheard. That's all the explanation she deserves."

"I think staying in the Royal Suite is a very good idea," Noah says. "At least until things settle down."

Something about that didn't make sense to me. And I couldn't help thinking that *I* sure wouldn't want to be staying in the alien hive—the place where fights happen and people disappear. So why were they trying to talk him into it? If Teresa was really worried about Kip like they said, then . . . it just didn't fit together. And all of a sudden, I start to picture Noah as the big snake from *The Jungle Book*, hypnotizing Kip as he hisses, "Trust in me. . . ."

It's feeling very creepy.

I guess Kip thinks so, too—well, at least that it's strange—because he shakes his head and says, "I . . . I can't."

Ginger nods, and she keeps on nodding. Like she's rappelling down to some deep, dark cranny in her mind. Then all at once she pulls herself back out, cups Kip's cheeks in her hands, and says, "If you change your mind, you know where I am. Day or night. Just come over."

Noah checks his watch and gasps. "Come on, kids. I've got to wrap up bingo and get poolside for limbo!" He starts down the hallway, calling, "Meet you later, Mom. Shut down the lights, won't you?" over his shoulder as Kip, Marissa, and I hurry along behind him. And when we're almost to the security door, Noah tosses a grin at Kip and says, "What happens when you breathe out two heliums?"

"You laugh," Kip says without even a hint of a smile. "He He."

"Aw, Kip—you've heard them all, haven't you?" Then he opens the door and tells him, "I'm not making light of the situation. Really. I'm just trying to make you smile and think optimistically. Worrying won't help, so go try to enjoy yourself!"

He bounds up to the stage, and while the three of us file out of the Poseidon Theater, I try to tell myself that none of this is my problem, but I can't help feeling sorry for Kip. No wonder he sneaks notes under doors. No wonder he eavesdrops on relatives. No wonder he acts suspicious and frustrated and upset. *All* his relatives seem to be hiding something. *All* of them seem to be cloak-and-daggering around.

In a very sophisticated, oh-we're-Kensingtons way, of course, but still.

Now, I don't want to *say* any of this, so as we're leaving the theater I ask, "So, uh . . . did you get anything out of that?"

"Yeah," he says with a scowl. "They think I can't handle the truth."

But before I can ask him what truth he's talking about, we run smack-dab into JT.

Which is weird.

127

I mean, out of four thousand passengers and another thousand crew members, we bump into a Kensington?

Plus, he's out of breath.

"Hi, guys! What's up?" he says, acting way too friendly.

I just glare at him, and so does Marissa.

"What's up," Kip says as he pushes past him, "is that Grandmother is missing." He stops and turns to square off with him. "Unless you've tracked us down to report some good news?"

"Tracked you down?" JT says with a fake little laugh. "You make it sound so . . . sinister!"

Kip crosses his arms. "Is there news on Grandmother or not?"

"News?" His face goes sour. "Like that she drinks too much? Like that someone saw her flirting with the bartender at the Sky-High Bar last night? Like that she's probably sleeping off a hangover on some lounge chair?" He gives Kip a little squint and adds, "What's your deal? Why do you care so much anyway? It's not like she's your real grandmother."

And just like that, JT's on the floor, screaming in pain, with blood streaming out of his nose.

FOURTEEN

Kip didn't hang around after he punched JT in the nose. And I think he expected us to follow him, but Marissa and I were in such shock that we just stood there with our jaws dangling.

What finally made me snap to was the blood. A little of that stuff goes a long way, and there was more than just a little coming out of JT's nose. So I tracked down a bathroom, and snagged some toilet paper and a bunch of paper towels. I made some of the paper towels wet, then hurried back to the big open area outside the Poseidon Theater where it had all gone down, but bingo people were filing out of the theater right across the spot where I'd left JT.

"Over here!" Marissa calls, and now I see that she's got JT sitting on a bench by a wall. So I jet over and hand JT my selection of blood blotters.

He's got his nose pinched to stop the blood, so he sounds all stuffy when he says, "Thanks." He jams some of the toilet paper up his nose, then wipes around with the wet paper towels to clean up.

Marissa and I just stand there watching, and after a

minute I'm itching to leave. I don't like what JT said to Kip, and I don't like *him*. But what's keeping me there is that I also don't like that Kip punched him in the nose, which is actually kinda confusing to me.

See, *I've* punched someone in the nose before.

Someone who turned out to be my future boyfriend's sister.

Blood went spurting then, too, but the difference was, she'd jabbed me with a pin. She'd been physical, so me being physical back seemed justified. Not that the school agreed—they'd suspended me for "brawling."

But here, JT hadn't touched Kip. Still . . . something about what he'd said had obviously really hurt Kip, so what was the difference?

Anyway, I'm trying to sort through all this when a voice behind me goes, "What happened here?"

I whip around and there's Noah, looking really concerned.

"Kip happened here," JT grumbles.

"He *hit* you?"

"A total ninja attack."

"Wait a minute," I say, and then tell Noah the whole story.

"You actually *said* that?" Noah asks him.

"Oh, come on!" JT cries. "It's stupid that everyone pretends that he's really one of us!"

"JT . . . ," Noah warns.

"I'm serious! He doesn't *look* like us, he doesn't *act* like us, he doesn't *sound* like us . . . the whole thing's a joke! And you know what? The next time you or my parents tell me to chum around with him or keep an eye on him, I'm going to say forget it!"

Noah's face flushes a little, but he manages to keep his cool. "Legally, he's part of the family, so if I were you, I'd find a way to accept him."

JT stands up and snaps, "Who are you to tell me what to do?" And he may not *say* it, but we all hear what he's thinking loud and clear: *You're not a Kensington, either! You're just a dorky cruise director! And by the way, your jokes are totally lame!*

Then he storms off, leaving all his bloody blotters behind.

Noah mutters, "Arrogant little . . . ," as he picks up JT's garbage. Then he looks at us and says, "Sammy and Marissa," like he's double-checking that he's got our names right. When we nod, he says, "I'm worried about Kip. It's not like him to hit someone. He must be very upset, and I'm just wondering if you could try to get his mind off of all the family drama. There's rock climbing, golf, swimming, Ping-Pong, ice-skating, basketball, board games . . . or the Serpent's Lair is a cool hangout just for teens. And the Arena Arcade is always popular with kids your age. . . ." His voice trails off, and he shakes his head. "I can't manage all this while doing my job."

Marissa gives him a kind of pinched look. "Uh . . . we just met him yesterday? And this is Sammy's first cruise? And it's her *birthday* today? So . . ."

He gives a little wave. "I get it, I get it. And I'm sorry for asking." He turns a half-watt smile on me and says, "Obviously, enjoy your birthday."

And I guess I'm feeling bad about not jumping at the chance to babysit Kip, because I have this urge to *explain,* and out of my mouth comes, "I was thirteen twice, so today's actually kind of a big deal for me."

He cocks his head a little. "You were thirteen twice?"

I shake my head. "Long, complicated story."

"Well, it sounds like you may have more in common with Kip than you know."

Now, he says this as he starts for the stairs, and it makes me all curious. So even though Marissa tries to hold me back, I chase after him, going, "What do you mean?"

"The orphanage claimed he was eight, but I've always suspected he was older. Maybe ten? But he was undernourished and such a scared little guy. . . ."

He's going up the stairs two at a time and *fast,* so I'm having trouble keeping up. "How long ago was that?"

"It's been seven years." He bounds up another half flight, *boing-boing-boing,* then says, "It's too bad that good fortune is mostly wasted on those who have it."

I can't keep up, so I just stop and *look* up as he switchbacks onto the half flight above us. "But . . . ," I call, "Kip seems to really appreciate what his grandparents have done for him."

He looks down at me with a wry smile. "I wasn't referring to Kip." Then he disappears to the next level.

Marissa stops next to me. "So Kip's either fifteen or sixteen or *seventeen*?"

"He's not seventeen."

"But how weird not to know!"

"Tell me about it," I grumble.

"No, Sammy. That is way worse than thinking you're one year older than you actually are. Plus you were never undernourished or in an orphanage."

I try on a wry smile of my own. "Maybe my good fortune was wasted on me."

She laughs. "Maybe!" Then she says, "But that doesn't mean I want to waste any more of your birthday with any ungrateful or hotheaded Kensingtons." She grabs my arm and drags me to the next landing. "Deck 5. Promenade. Let's shop."

I groan, "Nooooo," but it turns out we actually have fun. Marissa drags me into a hat shop where we try on everything from cute little caps to huge feathered monstrosities. "They wear these in England," Marissa whispers as she balances a ridiculous green one on my head. Then she steps back and giggles. "Your head, at least, is palace ready."

So I turn and look at myself in the mirror, and after I shriek, the lady behind the counter escorts us out.

That kind of sets the tone for the ten-dollar jewelry store, where you can buy old-lady beads and crazy fake diamond rings and bangles galore . . . and nothing's over ten dollars.

We wind up getting escorted out of there, too.

So we try to be a little more civilized when we go into the perfume store, and keep it on the down low, even when we get into a spray war with the sample bottles.

But then Marissa notices something. "Look at these!" she whispers. "It's the Kensington line!"

The bottles are in a hexagonal shape, and the stoppers are, too. They all have chains around the necks, which hold tags with the names of the perfumes, and the tags are in the shape of two connected hexagons, with lines etched parallel to the edges of every other side.

Like how Ms. Rothhammer diagrams molecules.

I pick up a bottle that has a tag that says REACTION. "I never really thought about perfume being chemistry related until Kip said something about it." Then I laugh and say, "Oh, this is really clever!"

"What?"

"There's a *chain* attached to the tag?"

"So?"

I grin at her. "Chain reaction?"

"Oh!" She laughs, then takes the bottle from me and studies it. "The question is"—and then she gets a totally bratty look on her face—"how does it smell?"

So yeah, I get sprayed, and yeah, that does start a chain reaction, which, yeah, gets us escorted out.

The only store we didn't get kicked out of was the Logo Shop, because one short tour through it and we left without any, you know, *encouragement*. Everything had the ship's logo on it, and let's just say, if you're not gray, stay away!

We finally wound up at Le Petit Café, where little sandwiches and desserts are served round the clock and the tables are set up so you can watch people walking by, which is always entertaining.

And yes, we were entertained!

"Have you noticed," Marissa asked as we watched people walk by, "that there are different categories of people on the ship?"

"What do you mean?"

"Like those guys," she said, nodding out at a family wearing Hawaiian shirts, shorts, and sandals. "Those are family-vacation cruisers." Then she gave a sly nod at a small group of women walking by. Lots of makeup, fancy fingernails, silver jewelry, and rotisserie tans. And they were all squeezed into clothes about two sizes too small and about ten years too young for them. "Cougars," she whispers. "On the prowl."

We watch them strut by, and then I point out the obvious. "The biggest category is old people, but what's weird is they're nothing like the ones in the Senior Highrise."

"Right," she laughs. "These are hipster seniors!"

"But a lot of them seem to be on the prowl, too," I whisper, "which is kinda creepy."

"Like her?" Marissa says as a woman wearing a black velour sweat suit and a long string of fake pearls comes out of the Logo Shop. She is walking with a cane, but she's obviously trying to look young, because her hair's way too black for her age, and she's wearing sunglasses.

"Why do people wear sunglasses inside the ship?"

"So you can't tell they're watching you!"

"Are you serious?"

"Or they want to look stylish? Or they didn't have time to do their makeup?" We both watch the velour lady a minute, and as she gets closer, Marissa whispers, "No wedding ring. And see how she's scoping people out? She's definitely on the prowl."

I study her as she goes by. "I don't think she's gonna get any takers with that mole on her lip."

"Yeah, scary, right?"

I sigh and shake my head. "I never want to be her, okay? Never let me turn into *that*."

She gives me a funny look. "What kind of crazy thought is that for you to be having on your birthday?"

And that's when I see that it's past three o'clock. "I'm late!" I cry, jumping up like the White Rabbit.

"Oh, right!" Marissa says, and we scurry up to Deck 8, where Darren is already in the library, sitting in front of a computer. He's wearing a backward ball cap and nerd glasses, so he looks really different, but I recognize him anyway.

Now, even though it's a "quiet zone," we sort of gust in 'cause we're late and, you know, out of breath. So yeah, we're a little loud, and yeah, there are other people there—including that same woman working on that same puzzle—but it sure doesn't seem like we deserve the extreme look and finger-to-the-lip *shh* that Darren gives us.

Besides, it's very old lady–like and not at all rock 'n' roll.

But then he does a little point between computers, and I see that there are two people huddled around the monitor that's backed up to his. I can't see their faces, but the tops of their heads are both blond.

Kensingtons.

I give Darren the oooooh look, letting him know I get it, and he does some hand signals—first a hand push telling us to take it easy, then a little come-here wave.

So Marissa and I hold our breaths and ease forward, then crouch in next to him.

Darren puts his finger to his lips again, then taps his ear with a little grin. So I give him a got-it nod and grin back, and then we strain to hear the whispering that's going on at the other computer.

It's a man's voice, and I've heard it enough times to recognize that it's Lucas', and I can tell that he's reading something off the computer. "'After seven years from the date of the last known contact with the individual, persons who have just cause can file a petition in state court to have the missing individual declared legally dead.'"

"Seven years?" a woman's voice chokes out. "Seven *years?*"

So okay. It's definitely JT's parents huddling at the computer, and it's pretty clear that they're talking about Kate.

Lucas continues reading, "'If the individual disappeared under unusual circumstances—for example after a threat was made upon their life—then the process becomes even more complicated, especially when it relates to insurance benefits and other financial matters.'"

"Oh my God," LuAnn gasps.

There's a moment of silence, and then Lucas says, "This is not good."

They're quiet for at least a minute, and then LuAnn says, "Maybe if there was a note?"

"A note?"

"You know . . . a *note*," she hisses.

Again there's a short silence, and then JT's dad says, "Let's go."

I give Marissa an uh-oh! look, 'cause if they glance over

the computer bank and see us, they'll know we've been listening, no matter how much we pretend to be looking at our monitor.

Darren must have been thinking the same thing, because he rolls his chair back just a little, and does a move-it-now double point. And, boy, do we! By the time the Whispering Blonds are standing up, we're crammed under the table, with Darren's chair running block.

Luckily, there are no other people seated in our row. So when Lucas and LuAnn are gone and Darren rolls back, I get out and whisper, "Did they recognize you?"

He shakes his head. "I kept my back turned and my head down."

"Wow," Marissa gasps. "That was incredible."

Darren whispers, "I saw them sitting there, and you could just tell—they were wound tight and ready to pop. So I thought I'd slip in and give a little listen."

"Wait, whoa," Marissa says, staring at him. "You planted yourself here so you could snoop?"

"You thought I landed here by accident?" An eyebrow arches above the nerd glasses. "And I prefer to call it information gathering. For you two, of course." He grins at me. "And I did good, huh? Those two sound like they're up to their golden eyebrows in this disappearance thing."

Marissa's jaw drops, and she looks from me to Darren and back to me. "All this time, I thought snooping was something you did for survival. But no. It's genetic!"

I laugh, but something about what she'd said was more than just funny.

Better than just funny.

It made me feel . . . happy.

Which also made me stand there all tongue-tied and awkward until Darren says, "All right—let's get you online."

So he shows me how to access his account, and in no time, I've sent Casey a quick "Hey, are you there?" message. Casey doesn't message back, though, so I write another, longer note that's half news and half mush, and log out.

"That's it?" Darren asks, 'cause I was pretty quick.

"He wasn't online, so I'll try again later, if that's okay."

"Sure." He turns to Marissa. "Want to touch base with your parents?"

"Nah," she says. "They're not expecting it, and what am I going to say? Sammy's dragged me into a murder mystery?"

"Shh!" Darren and I say at the same time, because she hadn't exactly whispered it.

She stares at the two of us a minute. "Unbelievable."

Darren and I give each other a little one-shouldered shrug, then he asks me, "You hungry?"

"Starved!"

"But we just ate!" Marissa says.

"It's the stairs," Darren tells her.

"Definitely the stairs," I agree.

"And eavesdropping."

I nod. "It always makes me hungry."

"Unbelievable," Marissa grumbles.

So off we go, first to Deck 9 to wake Marko up from a nap, then up to a fifties diner on Deck 12. It cost extra to eat there but Darren joked that we were hiding out from Kensingtons, and Marko seemed jazzed to be someplace where burgers were delivered by girls in poodle skirts. And since Marko was way behind on *everything* and Darren was clueless about our little adventure backstage at the Poseidon Theater, we caught them up on the Kensingtons.

"So you think the dame's really dead?" Marko finally asks.

I bust up. "What's with this dame stuff all the time?"

"*Dame* seems very appropriate," he says back. "Conjures up visions of cigars and daggers and trench coats, don't you think?"

Darren nods. "And a dank, cluttered office."

Marko acts like he's pulling a cigar away from his lips and growls, "She walked into my office with a bottle of booze and an attitude so bad, she coulda killed with it."

Darren fakes like he's got a cigar, too, and hunkers down a little. "And maybe she had. From the blood on her hand, I knew whoever'd crossed her was sleepin' in a pool of sticky red sorrow."

Marko nods. "So I told her to sit and said, 'Honey, what brings you to the corner of Fifth and Scotch?'"

"'Desperation,' she snarled. 'Now get me a glass.'"

Darren and Marko give each other fist bumps and little-boy grins, so I go, "Wait, that's it? I was just getting into it!"

"Hey!" Marko cries. "You know that game lounge near the casino? Do you think they have Clue? Because right now I am jonesing for an old-school game of Clue."

"Are you serious?" Marissa asks.

"I've never played," I tell him.

"No!" they all three cry, and let me tell you, their eyes are totally bugging out.

"It's the classic whodunit game," Marko says, and Darren goes, "You know"—he drops his voice and looks around—"it was Professor Plum in the library with a candlestick!"

"I challenge that!" Marko cries. "I say it was JT in the hall with a lead pipe!"

"No, no!" Darren cries. "It was Ginger! In the dining room! With a revolver!"

Marko scowls at him. "You already made a prediction."

"What *are* you guys talking about?" I ask.

"That does it," Marko says, standing up. "I'm finding Clue and we're gonna play. It's the least we can do to further your daughter's regrettably limited experiences."

"I agree," Darren says, standing up, too. "It's the least we can do."

So we wind up going down to Deck 4 to the game lounge, where Marko manages to unearth a board game that has CLUE in big letters on the box.

"Unbelievable," Marissa says. "That's the word of the day. *Unbelievable.*"

And it kind of was. There was no cake, there were no

presents, and I was playing a *board* game on a *cruise* ship. It had all the makings of the Lamest Birthday Ever.

But somehow . . .

Unbelievably . . .

It felt like the best.

FIFTEEN

The game lounge isn't a room—it's more of an open area with four-person tables and a big cabinet of board games. It's next to the walkway that leads into the casino, so although there were people playing chess and cards, there were others just hanging out, watching people walk by, or reading books.

It wasn't crowded, so we found a table off to the side of the game lounge, and the others taught me how to play Clue, which uses a game board with cards and playing pieces and dice—and lots of note taking—to figure out who committed a murder, and where and with what. It takes a while, but when you think you've figured out who killed "Mr. Boddy," you make your accusation by announcing the suspect, place, and weapon, saying something like, "It was Miss Scarlet! In the kitchen! With the lead pipe!" If you're right, you win. If you're wrong, well, you don't.

After the second game, I'd gotten the hang of it, but then Marko decides we need to "relevantize" the game to "increase the intrigue."

"What's he doing?" I ask Darren when Marko disappears into the casino. "And what does *relevantize* mean?"

"To make relevant?" He laughs. "It's Marko. We just have to wait and see."

When Marko hustles back into the game lounge a few minutes later, he's got a pack of playing cards, a magic marker, and a wicked grin on his face. "Time to make us some real suspects!" he whispers, and starts fishing the jacks, queens, and kings from the deck. "Expose their double dealings and criminal pursuits!"

"What are you talking about?" Marissa asks.

He turns his wicked grin on her and whispers, "Kensingtons!"

Marissa rolls her eyes, but she's the first one to jump in to help name our new suspect cards. "The queen of diamonds should be Kate," she says.

Marko nods and writes *KATE—the Diamond Dame* on the card and puts her over to the side, facedown.

After all, she's the victim.

"And the queen of hearts should be Ginger!" Marissa says.

So Marko writes *GINGER—Suspicious Sister* on that card, then asks, "Next?"

"The jack of diamonds should be JT!"

"Right on," Marko says, and writes *JT—Bratty Grandson* on that card.

And pretty soon everyone but Kip has their own card.

Well, except JT's parents—they get put together as *LUCAS & LUANN—Sneaky Spouses,* because Marko thought we should stick to six suspects, like in the original Clue, and with *BRADLEY—Sulking Son, TERESA—*

Money-Grubbin' Mama, and *NOAH—Cruisin' Cousin* already labeled, we had only one card left.

Then Marko shuffles our custom suspect cards and passes them out randomly, and we play our own version of Clue—Kensington Clue!

We do a good job of keeping our voices down at first, but after a couple of games, we get kinda rowdy. Especially since Marko keeps winning. Plus I think it sorta slipped our minds that we were playing a murder mystery game using the names of people who . . . well . . . who might actually have committed a murder.

Not that I *believed* that yet.

Anyway, I'm sure not thinking about actual murder when I jump out of my seat and announce, "It was Noah! In the library! With the rope!"

Now, at first I think Marissa's just in shock that I've figured it out, because her eyes are big and her mouth is kinda gaping. But then Marko starts gathering our notepapers together super-fast, and the next thing I know, there's a voice behind me, going, "Did I hear my name?"

I whip around, and sure enough, there's Noah.

I try to cover up by going, "Oh, hey! Any news?" But there are still papers with Kensington names all around the table, and it doesn't take long for him to pick one up.

"No," he says, studying the paper. "But I'll have you know that at no time was I in the library with a rope." He places the paper down slowly and says, "Glad to see you enjoying your birthday, Sammy," then gives a little nod and leaves.

"Whoa!" Marko says when he's gone. "Busted!"

"How embarrassing," Marissa whispers.

Darren shrugs. "I thought he took it quite well."

Marko nods. "Played it close to the vest, that's for sure."

And that was exactly it about the Kensingtons. They all seemed to play it close to the vest. It wasn't *just* that they weren't going to show you their cards—they were also going to try to make you believe they were holding high cards instead of low.

Or low instead of high.

Or whatever.

Except for Kip. He'd kind of abandoned the whole Kensington code of honor. He'd even punched his cousin in the nose.

In public!

So maybe JT was right. Maybe being adopted and steeped in Kensington ways couldn't actually *make* you one.

Blood was obviously thicker than ink.

Except . . .

Except Kip sure seemed to love his grandfather. And grandmother. Which was more than I could say about any of the blood Kensingtons. From what I'd seen, they were more interested in talking to lawyers and scouring the Internet for legal clues than they were in looking for clues about where Kate might be.

Anyway, I couldn't help thinking about it a little, but I tried not to think about it a lot.

It was my birthday!

I'd escaped thirteen!

"So what now?" Darren asks. Then he checks his watch and goes, "Wow. How did it get to be eleven?"

My eyes pop. "It's *eleven*?"

Marko nods. "Time flies when you're solving crime."

"Okay," Marissa says, looking at him. "That was just corny."

"Get used to harvesting," Darren tells her, "because there's always an abundance of corn when you're hanging with Marko."

"Hey!" Marko says, and gives a little pout. Then he eyes the board. "It looks like Sherlock Holmes could have walked the halls of this mansion, don't you think? Can't you just see him and Watson going through the secret passageways with Gladstone sniffing the way?"

"I thought the dog's name was Toby," Darren says.

One of Marko's eyebrows stretches up, the other one angles down. "I believe, my dear Darren, that Sherlock co-opted any available bloodhound. The name was irrelevant."

"Irrelevant? If the dog helped solve the crime, how can its name be irrelevant?"

But Marissa's not a bit interested in Sherlock Holmes' dog. She's moved on, checking out her Cruzer Calendar, going, "Karaoke's starting right now in the Aqua Lounge on Deck 5."

Darren and Marko both make like they're choking.

Or barfing.

Or choking on barf?

Whatever, it's definitely rock 'n' roll.

"It's fun, you goons," Marissa says. "Not all of us get to be onstage in real life, you know."

Darren eyes the Cruzer. "What else is there?"

"Oh!" she cries. "Ice sculpture and a chocolate fountain are happening right now on the promenade level, aft!"

That's basically right above us, so we go up the swoopy stairs to Deck 5, where hordes of people are already waiting in the chocolate fountain line.

"Uh, I don't need chocolate that bad," I tell them.

"Me, neither," Marko says. "But the ice sculpture's cool."

It's in the shape of a big sea serpent, glistening away on a long table near the chocolate fountain mob, and it *is* cool, but after watching ice glisten and chocolate flow for a few minutes, I finally just say, "What I'd really like to do is message Casey and then maybe raid the buffet again. Is that okay?"

Darren says, "Let's do it!" and before you know it, we're up on Deck 8, whooshing into the Lido Library.

The place is deserted except for one person.

The Puzzle Lady.

This time she gives me a little smile and says, "You just missed your friend."

"My friend?"

"The African American boy? He was just here."

Now, something about her makes me feel . . . uneasy. I mean, obviously she's a snoop. But also, what sort of person pays a bunch of money for a cruise to sit by herself in a library all day, doing a puzzle?

You can do that for free at home!

She's being friendly, though, and I feel kind of bad for thinking right away that she's a crazy, nosy puzzle lady, so I smile back and say, "Thanks," and get on a computer across the room from her.

Luckily, Casey's still awake and at his computer, so I have an awesome time messaging back and forth with him. And I guess I was typing away a lot longer than I knew, because after what seems like only five minutes, Darren taps me on the shoulder and says, "The birthday pumpkin appears in ten minutes."

"Really?" I check the time, and sure enough, it's almost midnight.

So I send Casey a bunch of hugs and kisses, and sign off. And when I stand up, I see that the Puzzle Lady is gone and sitting in her place is Marko.

With a rope.

"Where'd you get that?" I ask, but he just gives me a wicked grin and says, "Marissa claims to know where the cruise director sleeps. I thought we'd have a little fun."

I bust up, and really, I think it's a brilliant idea—a funny way to maybe smooth things over. So I scrawl a note that says, *You left this in the library!* and before you know it, we're up on Deck 10, acting stupidly suspicious as we tiptoe down the hallway and plant the rope in front of Noah's door.

Then we knock and race out of there, giggling like a pack of kids as we escape up a flight of stairs to the Schooner Buffet.

"That was awesome!" I pant as we plop into seats at a window table, because something about it seemed really, you know, *clandestine* to me. Even though it would be totally obvious that we were the ones who put it there.

Anyway, we wind up getting a midnight snack, and then we go back to Dessert Island for big wedges of cheesecake. Marko tries to light a toothpick on fire for a candle, and even though it doesn't work very well, he jabs the smoking stick in my cheesecake, and they all sing "Happy Birthday."

Which, let me tell you, sounded great in Troublemaker harmony.

"Big day tomorrow," Darren says after we've practically licked our plates. "Off the ship and onto foreign soil."

"Cabo San Lucas, Mexico," Marko says, like he's announcing a fighter getting into the ring.

"So . . . what do we do?" I ask, 'cause really, I haven't given thought to any of it.

Instead of answering, Darren and Marko both look at Marissa like, Well?

"Oh!" Marissa clears her throat. "Well, we get up early, eat, disembark, walk or catch a tour bus or do an excursion—"

"An excursion?" I ask.

"You know—like ATVing through the backcountry or zip lining or swimming with dolphins. We just have to be back on board by five o'clock or whatever time they tell us we're set to sail."

The rest of us kind of shrug like, Sounds good.

She hesitates, then says, "You have to sign up for excursions ahead of time, though. And they're expensive."

Darren's looking like he's not sure what to do, so I tell him, "I'm fine with just walking around. I've never been on 'foreign soil' before, so I don't need to tear it up with an ATV."

Marko gives Darren an accusing look. "Dude, what happened to your planning skills? I totally wanted to swim with dolphins."

"The water's right there," Darren says, pointing out the window.

I look at the two of them, and it hits me that Darren and Marko have made it through their entire lives together. They're friends who *get* each other and can joke and act stupid and not worry about being judged. And, I don't know, something about that sort of chokes me up. I don't want Marissa to move to Ohio. I want her to stay and be my friend so we can grow up and be the girl version of Darren and Marko.

Finally, I take a deep breath and tell them, "This has been a really great birthday."

Darren scratches the side of his jaw. "My present was the cruise, but I'm feeling like I should have bought you something tangible."

"Yeah, where's my pony?" I demand.

He laughs, and then Marko says, "Dude, you could at least have gotten her a dolphin, come on."

"My present's still at the store," Marissa tells me, "'cause you wouldn't buy anything today!"

"And my present is my *presence*," Marko says with a little head bow. "Unparalleled by anything you'll find on this ship."

"Hello," Marissa says. "Where's the corn husker?" And Darren slaps five on her.

But I still want to make my point. So I tell them, "What I'm trying to say is that this has been the best birthday, and there hasn't been a single bow or any wrapping paper." I give a little shrug. "Thank you."

After that, we head back to our rooms, where Darren gives me a one-armed hug good night, and Marko smothers me with both arms and says, "You're an awesome kid."

"And you're a beast!" I laugh, 'cause I'm suffocating.

"The Beast from Corn Alley," Darren announces, and then they shove each other and disappear inside their cabin.

"They remind me of Billy and Casey," Marissa whispers as she opens our door.

"They do, huh?" I laugh.

And I'm still laughing as we walk into our cabin.

And then I see what's on my bed.

SIXTEEN

Marissa and I stand stock-still, staring at the rope on my bed, until finally Marissa whispers, "That is very creepy."

Which it is. Not only because it means that Noah had been in our room, but also because the rope is now tied into a noose.

"So he can let himself in and out of anybody's room?" I whisper back.

"He's the cruise director," Marissa whispers. "I'm sure he has access to everything. And I don't think the stewards work this late." Then she adds, "Maybe there's a note? We left *him* one."

So we inch over to my bed like it has a coiled rattler on it and check for a note.

Nothing.

"Maybe he thinks this is funny?" I say.

Marissa nods. "Like we thought playing Kensington Clue was funny?"

But even looking at it from that angle, the noose on my bed does not seem funny.

It seems creepy.

Like a threat.

"Do you think Kate's turned up?" I ask.

Marissa shakes her head. "Kip would have told us, don't you think?"

I shrug, 'cause the last time we saw Kip, he was running off after punching JT's lights out. Who knew if he'd bother to tell us. Or if Noah would. Especially not after he'd caught us playing Kensington Clue.

Marissa takes a deep breath. "I'm starting to think that maybe Kip's right."

"About?"

"About his grandmother and foul play."

"Foul play?"

She looks at me. "That's what they call it, right?"

I grab the rope and head for the door. "Yeah. I guess. I just haven't ever heard anybody actually *say* it. It seems so, you know, Agatha Christie."

Marissa chases after me, saying, "Wait! Where are you going?"

Where I'm going is next door to tell Darren, but there's a little hitch in my brain stopping me from saying so. "I'm gonna tell my dad" is not something I've ever said or even *thought,* and it flashes through my mind that a) it's childish, and b) it's . . . well, it's weird to even be having the whole tell-my-dad thing cross my mind.

So instead, I just beat on his door.

"Oh, good," Marissa gasps. "I thought you were going to storm the castle again."

I knew she meant beat down Noah's door, because

I've got a kinda bad reputation with her for doing stuff like that. "The last person I want to see right now is Noah Marlowe."

The door flies open, and there's Marko, holding a toothbrush. "What's up?"

I dangle the noose, and his eyebrows go for a big stretch as he moves aside to let us in. "Dude!" he calls, tapping on the bathroom door. "Be decent when you come out."

"What?"

"Your offspring is here!" he calls, louder. "She brought a noose."

We hear another *"What?"* but then the bathroom door flies open, and there's Darren, also holding a toothbrush. "Everything okay?" he asks, then sees the noose.

"It was on my bed," I tell him.

He takes it from me. "Not cool."

"So, bro," Marko says, "what's our course of action?"

"Kick his ass?" Darren says, and he's looking really ticked off.

I try to bring it down a notch. "Look, he obviously didn't like our joke. And we obviously don't like his."

"I don't care who you are or what your passkey allows you to do, you don't just let yourself into the room of two young girls! And after midnight?"

"It was Noah! After midnight! With a key!" Marko cries, and when we all scowl at him, he looks kinda sheepish and goes, "Sorry."

I nod. "Or maybe someone else saw us put the rope in front of Noah's door."

"You think someone's been spying on us?" Marissa gasps.

Darren kinda shakes his head. "Who would be spying on us?"

"Kensingtons!" Marissa and I cry together. Then Marissa adds, "And since Kip knows what room Sammy and I are in, probably all of them do!"

"Like they would care?" Darren asks, and Marko goes, "Why would Kip tell anybody? Isn't he mad at the rest of them?"

But then something hits me. "What if JT's parents *did* see us at the library?"

Marissa's eyes get all big and she jumps in with, "They could've bribed someone to let them into our room!"

"Girls! Girls!" Darren says. "You are really letting your imaginations run wild."

I give him a scowl, because how many times have I heard *that* in my life? And now from him?

But then something *else* hits me. "Wait a minute," I say, with a finger in the air, and what's weird is, they all *do* wait a minute. And stare at me. Which is kinda distracting. Especially since my wait-a-minute thought is actually kinda mind-boggling.

"Well?" Marissa finally asks.

I take a deep breath. "According to the way we're registered, I'm supposed to be in *this* room with Darren, and Marko is supposed to be in *that* room with Marissa."

"Oh. Right," they kind of mumble.

And then we all stand there, thinking.

"So maybe he knows I'm the instigator," Marko says. "Maybe it wasn't meant for the girls at all."

As we mentally chew on that, I look around Darren and Marko's cabin, and there's stuff scattered everywhere, including an acoustic guitar propped up in the corner by a bed. But stuff everywhere does not explain ten hats on the desk. They're not all ball caps, either. There are a couple of cowboy hats, a Panama straw hat, and a *fishing* hat.

There are also, like, fifteen pairs of *glasses* that range from cop-style sunglasses, to ones with narrow rectangle lenses, to cheap plastic hipster glasses, to the nerd specs Darren had been wearing in the library.

And I'm sorry, but I've just got to know.

"What's all that about?" I ask, pointing at the desk.

Darren sort of raises an eyebrow at the hats, and when he doesn't say anything, Marko goes, "Things can get a little crazy when people start recognizing us. Once it starts to build, it sort of tidal waves. And it's starting to build."

"So those are *disguises*?" I ask, thinking that a ball cap and sunglasses have got to be the lamest disguise ever.

Darren can tell what I'm thinking, though, and says, "A ball cap and sunglasses is the ultimate disguise. It doesn't fool *you* because you know us. But it works remarkably well on people who only know us in a different context."

"Like from posters, which are now up outside the theater," Marko says.

"To hide, you just wear what half the population of men wear. It's how you blend in and disappear in a crowd."

"We've gotten pretty good at laying low," Marko says.

"And switching it up. Like poolside today? Total peace and quiet." He grins at Darren. "The goatees were genius."

I blink at them. "You wore goatees to the *pool*?"

Darren shrugs. "My face was a little annoyed, but the rest of me was very happy."

"Right, huh?" Marko says with a happy little sigh.

Darren looks at the clock. "Okay. It's almost two in the morning. What are we doing about the situation? Do you want me to beat on Noah's door?"

"Or maybe some other part of him?" Marko asks.

"No!" I tell them, 'cause something about your *dad* storming the castle seems so . . . childish.

"Okay," Darren says. "Then do you girls want to stay in here with us? Would that make you feel safer?"

Marissa and I pull faces. "No!"

"No?" Darren says, and he looks kinda hurt. "Marko could sleep in your room, and you two can share one of the beds in here?"

"Uh, that's okay," I tell him, thinking how a) I was totally starting to feel like a little kid afraid of the boogeyman, and b) I did not want to share a tiny bed with someone who snored. Being in the same room was bad enough.

"Or we could just switch rooms?" Marko says.

"We're fine," I tell them, and drag Marissa toward the door. "It was probably Noah, and he probably thought he was being funny."

"He does tell bad chemistry jokes," Marissa says.

"Plus I hadn't thought about the room-switch thing before, so I'm sure he didn't think he was threatening a couple of helpless girls."

Marissa snorts. "Helpless. Right."

"So forget about it," I say over my shoulder. "We're fine."

"I'd argue with you," Darren tells me as we go out the door, "but I agree with you, so I wouldn't know where to begin with that."

Marko calls, "Just dial our room number from your cabin phone if you get scared," and Darren pokes his head out the door and adds, "And jam a chair under the doorknob."

"Got it!" I call back. "We'll be fine."

I do actually jam a chair against the door, but only because I said I would.

Not because I'm scared.

And I do dial their room.

Just to try it out.

Then I brush my teeth and wash my face and collapse into bed. And the last thing I remember before drifting off is Marissa's sleepy voice coming through the dark, murmuring, "Your dad is awesome."

My brain says to tell her, "His name's Darren," but I'm so tired it just comes out, "Mmm."

Sunshine started creeping in through the curtains way too early, but nine decks down, the Great Engine Lullaby kept me in Snoozeville.

Until the engines stopped lullabying and started sputtering. And cranking. And *va-va-vroom*ing.

We didn't seem to be going faster, but something was definitely happening and I did *not* like the way it felt.

I guess Marissa knew I was starting to freak out, because she groans, "We're pulling into dock," then wraps a pillow over her head.

"Pulling into dock?" I kick off the covers and go out to the balcony and see that lots of other people are also on their balconies, watching as our giant floating city moves slowly toward land.

It's already warm out, and humid. At the end of a long, rocky pier, there's a lighthouse, and the town itself looks nestled sort of haphazardly up rocky hillsides around a bay. The buildings are mostly boxy, with flat roofs and lots of square windows, and the water is really blue and busy with motorboats and small sailboats.

I just stand there, taking it all in. It's not like I've ever really traveled anywhere, but something about this does seem foreign.

And exciting!

But when Marissa finally stumbles onto the balcony, she takes one look and says, "Yup. Mexico," then stumbles back inside.

I check Darren and Marko's balcony, but it's empty. The balcony where I'd seen Kate's white pants the first afternoon is empty, too.

After a little while I go back inside, where I find Marissa back in bed. "You want a lemonade?" I ask, 'cause all of a sudden I'm dying for the pink lemonade they have at the buffet.

"You offering to deliver it?" she moans.

"Sure."

She rolls toward me and unburies her head. "How can

you be so awake?" And before I can answer, she buries her head again and says, "Extra ice, okay?"

So I get dressed quick and head up two decks, and the first thing I notice when I get off the stairs is that there are a *lot* of people waiting for elevators to show up. So many that there's no way they'll all fit in one trip. Some of them are carrying bananas and bagels or pastries, and some have whole trays of food.

The *next* thing I notice is that one of the people waiting at the elevators with a tray is Ginger.

Well, there's no way I want her to see me. I mean, I'm sure by now Noah's told her how insensitive and crass we are, playing Kensington Clue and leaving ropes outside doors. And even though part of me wants to go up and ask, Hey, did your sister ever show up? the smarter part of me ditches it into the Schooner Buffet.

The place is packed with people. Lots of them have backpacks and cameras and are eating like they're in a hurry. And while I'm looking the breakfast foods over, thinking I'll take a tray down to Marissa and we'll eat in the room, Captain Harald comes on over the PA and starts making announcements about disembarking and remembering your sea-pass card and getting back to the ship by five because we'll set sail at five-thirty, and anyone not onboard has a long walk home.

After that, people start eating faster and moving faster and grabbing bananas and pastries and leaving. Which makes me feel like I'm missing out on something big, or at least running really late.

So I pile a bunch of stuff—including bananas and

bagels—on a tray, get two glasses of lemonade and two more of milk, then head down two flights of stairs with my getaway tray.

Marissa can't believe her eyes. "Wow!" she gasps when she sees the tray. "This is awesome!"

We wind up having breakfast on the balcony. And even though the balcony is tiny and boxed in on three sides, it's warm and balmy, and we can see the hills of Mexico, and eating breakfast out there feels really *decadent* to me.

Like something I would never have pictured for myself.

Plus, Marissa smiles at me and says, "This is so great. I've never done this before," and something about that makes me feel extra happy.

And then there's a ringing sound.

At first I think it's just some random ringing sound.

And then it dawns on me that it's a phone.

Our phone.

So I rush inside, sure that it's Darren giving us a wake-up call, only when I pick it up and say, "Hello?" the voice on the other end goes, "Don't hang up."

"Why would I hang up?"

"It's Kip."

"I know that."

"You could tell? From three words?"

"Technically four. Two words and a contraction."

"Well, don't hang up."

"Does it look like I'm hanging up?"

"I don't know. I can't see you."

I sigh. "Kip, why are you calling?"

"Can I come over?"

"To our *room?*"

"Shh! Yes!"

"Why am I shushing? And no, that's not a good idea."

"Please?"

"No. I promised I wouldn't—"

"Coded notes were put under our doors," he whispers. "Everyone's freaking out."

My ear perks up. "Wait, what? Notes in code?"

"Yes! And for some reason everyone's acting mad at *me.*"

"Well, you did punch your cousin in the nose."

"Can I *please* come over?"

"How about I meet you by the stairs?"

"No! I can't risk any of them seeing."

"Seeing what?"

"I can't explain it now!" he whispers, and it comes out all frantic.

"Look, I—"

"I'll be right there."

"Wait!"

But he's already hung up the phone.

SEVENTEEN

"Great," I grumble, then I dial Darren's room and hear a gravelly, "Hello?"

Obviously, I'm waking up the rocker boys, so I get right to the punch line. "It's Sammy. We'll have a visitor here in about seven seconds. A boy."

That wakes him up. "A boy?" And now I can tell that it's Darren on the other end.

"Kip. I tried to tell him not to come because I agreed to the no-boys rule, but he's on his way over anyway."

"So am I," he says, and hangs up the phone.

Sure enough, seven seconds later, Kip's there, knocking on the door. And sure enough, by the time I've answered it, Darren and Marko are stumbling out of their room into the hallway.

"Oh, good!" Kip says when he sees them.

Darren and Marko look at each other like, Oh good? but Kip's already inside, at the desk, scribbling like mad on a piece of notepad paper.

"What are you doing?" I ask him, but all I get is a frantic little head shake. So I look over his shoulder and watch him write:

90 – 49 – 19 / 4 – 39 – 8 – 60 / 42 – 10 – 39
19 – 53 – 60 – 10 – 16 – 16 / 53 – 16 / 99 – 34 – 7 – 22 – 13
9 – 53 – 60 / 17 – 18 – 53 – 9 – 53 – 20 – 22 – 8 – 7
49 / 20 – 83 – 7 / LIONN

When he's done, he stands up straight and lets out a huge sigh of relief. "There. That's it."

Now, I know Kip said it was a coded message, but to me it looks like some complicated order-of-operations problem that Mr. Tiller might have assigned us in math.

Well, except for the *LIONN* part.

But still. I didn't understand how he could have held anything that long and complicated in his head. I would have had trouble with just one line of it. So I stare at him and say, "That's impossible. No one can do that."

"What is it?" Darren asks him.

"A coded message!" Kip gasps. "Copies of it were under Uncle Lucas' and Uncle Bradley's doors, with their names and *TICK TOCK* typed on the front."

"Whoa," Marko says, clicking into what just happened. "You mean to tell us you *memorized* it?"

Kip looks down and gives a little nod.

"Sammy's right," Marko says. "That's impossible."

And then we all stare at his bowed head until it's totally awkward, and he finally volunteers, "Grandfather taught me. He called it Picture and Pattern." He shrugs. "I've worked at it for years, but this is bigger than anything I've ever done before."

We stare at him some more. "Do the others know you can do that?" I ask.

"Uncle Bradley might." He eyes me. "Either that or he's just naturally paranoid about his passwords."

We all raise eyebrows and sort of mentally look around for things we should be hiding from view, but nobody says anything until Darren finally asks, "So what's this about?" He sits on the edge of Marissa's bed and says, "And start at the beginning, would you? No skippin' around."

"Yeah," Marko says, plopping down next to him. "Our sleep-addled brains can't take you skippin' around."

So Marissa and I sit on the edge of my bed, and Kip starts pacing a little, going, "It was a weird night. I couldn't sleep. The phone rang at one-thirty, and after my mother answered it, she said, 'I'll be right there,' and was gone until three-thirty."

"Do you know who called?" I ask.

"The only person she really talks to is Lucas, but I can't be sure."

"What about Ginger and Noah?"

"Oh." He sort of frowns and says, "She's fine with them, too."

Darren shakes his head and says, "We're skipping around." He looks at Kip. "You couldn't sleep, the phone rang, your mom disappeared for two hours, and then what?"

"In the morning, there was a note shoved under our door."

"Who found it, and at what time?" Darren asks.

"I did. Around seven."

Darren focuses on him. "From what you said before, I'm guessing the note was folded, with your mom's name and *TICK TOCK* typed on the outside of it?" And after Kip nods, Darren says, "But you opened it anyway."

"She was sleeping! And it wasn't in an envelope or anything!"

"So why not just copy it? Why memorize it?" Marko asks.

Kip looks away. "You don't understand Kensingtons." And then when we all just stare at him, he says, "Because if she'd caught me, she would have taken it away! And now she can't!" We're quiet a minute, and finally I ask, "So what did your mother do when you showed her the note?"

"She freaked out and got mad at me for looking at it. She called me a sneaky punk kid."

"Your *mother* did?" we cry. And then Marissa asks, "Because you looked at some weird coded note?"

He gives a little shrug. "Like I said, she never wanted me."

I eye him. "Or maybe she thinks you planted it."

"Why would I do that?"

"Did you?"

"No!"

"Well, you've been known to slip anonymous messages under doors, you know."

"That's not fair."

"Sure it is. There was the one you wanted to put under the Royal Suite door the night of the big fight, there was the non-apology you left slipped under our door—"

"Non-apology?!"

Marko interrupts with, "If you ask me, this is a classic case of skippy-doodlin' around," and Darren nods and goes, "You're definitely skippy-doodlin' around. There are big holes in this story, and Marko's right—our sleep-addled brains can't handle it."

Marko gives him a happy bro grin, then makes a little rewind motion with his hand and goes, "You couldn't sleep, the phone rang at one-thirty, your mom disappeared for two hours, then returned and went to bed. Around seven in the morning you found a note shoved under your door, she freaked out and called you a sneaky punk kid, and *then* what? How and when was there a convergence of Kensingtons?"

I blink at him. "A convergence of Kensingtons?"

Marko nods. "You know—how'd they all decide to get together?"

Marissa eyes me and kinda mutters, "So much for being sleep-addled."

"No kidding," I mutter back.

"Hey," Marko says. "I like things sequential. No rushing, no skipping beats, no jumping to the bridge before you finish the chorus."

Darren adds, "And absolutely no breaking into the chorus before you finish the verse."

"You can *start* with the chorus, though," Marko says, looking at him. "Like we do in 'Echo Man'?"

I blink at him. "You're accusing *us* of skippy-doodlin' around?"

"Right, right," he says, then turns back to Kip. "So tell us about the convergence of Kensingtons."

Kip kind of nods and then goes, "My mother called

Lucas, Lucas called Ginger, Ginger called Noah, Noah called Bradley, and they all met in the Royal Suite. It was at around eight."

"Did you go?"

He shakes his head. "My mother wouldn't let me."

I zero in on him. "So you stayed in your cabin?"

He toes the floor. "Not exactly."

"You listened through the suite door?"

He nods. "But I couldn't hear anything!"

"Back to the notes," Darren says. "What *are* they?"

Kip gives a kind of wild shrug. "I don't know! Threats? A sick joke?"

"Hmm," I say, eyeing Marissa. "We happen to know that at least one of those people likes sick jokes. . . ."

"Right," Marissa says. "The noose."

"The noose?" Kip asks.

So we tell him about the noose, only—dopey us—that means we have to back up and explain about the rope and playing Kensington Clue.

Kip looks horrified. "You were playing Kensington Clue? And Grandmother was Mr. Boddy?"

"She was actually Kate, the Diamond Dame," Marko tells him.

Darren nods and says, "And the culprit turned out to be Noah, in the library, with a rope."

"Only that last time, though," Marko adds. "The time before, it was Lucas, in the—"

"Stop!" I cry, then tell Kip, "Sorry! But . . . none of us really thought she was dead. Just, you know, *misplaced*."

"Misplaced," Kip says, like it's the stupidest thing anyone's said all day.

Which it actually might be.

"Skippy-doodlin' around again," Marko warns, which definitely *sounds* stupider than saying someone's misplaced, but I still feel bad, so I tell Kip sorry again, and Marissa adds, "And we don't *know* she's dead, right?"

Darren picks up the paper with the code on it. "This would seem to indicate she's not."

Marko shrugs. "Or maybe it indicates that time is running out for one of the three heirs. Or maybe all of them!"

Marissa and I look at him like, WHOA! and Kip nods and says, "That's what Bradley, Lucas, and my mother think."

"What about Ginger?" Marissa asks. "What does she think?"

"Noah said she tried to talk everyone into working together, but it started another yelling match."

"Whoa. Wait," I say, putting up a hand. "How do you know any of this? When did you see Noah?"

"Skippy-doodlin' around," Marko mutters with a little tisk.

Kip frowns. "Noah sorta caught me spying."

I eye him. "Sorta caught you?"

"He came storming out of the suite."

"Because . . . ?"

Kip shrugs. "He said Bradley called him a dim-witted sycophant."

"What's a sycophant?" Marissa whispers, and when

I shrug, Marko goes, "A toady," and Darren adds, "A kiss-up."

"Ouch," we both say, and Kip frowns and says, "Exactly."

"But what's the deal with the codes?" Marko asks. "Maybe they're from the Diamond Dame?"

Kip shakes his head. "It's not her style. Not at all. She's basically allergic to numbers."

"So maybe they *are* a threat. Or a scare tactic?" Darren says. "But who has something to gain from this?"

Kip just shakes his head some more, and then Marko says, "*Tick Tock* does sound pretty ominous."

Kip looks right at me. "Can I borrow your calculator? I'm hoping I can decipher the code." Then his forehead goes all wrinkly and he says, "Because what if it *is* a threat? Or a ransom note? And what if there's a time limit? I don't think the others are going to do anything but fight and if—"

"Dude!" Marko says, putting up a hand. "A ransom note wouldn't be in code! It would say, *Fork over a billion bucks at the big clock at midnight!*"

Kip looks around at us. "So . . . you think it's a threat?"

"Who would threaten them?" I ask. "I mean, who are their enemies?"

"I don't know!" Kip cries. "Each other!"

That zaps us quiet for a minute. Then I try, "So maybe one of them did the codes, and gave himself one, too, just to cover it up?" And Marissa throws in, "Or what if it's just a distraction? What if someone's trying to get them to quit thinking about Kate by making them worry about themselves?"

Kip gives me a pleading look. "Can I *please* just borrow your calculator?"

So I dig it out of my backpack and hand it over. "I need it back tonight, okay?"

"Sure."

"I'd try to help, but we're going into Mexico today."

He shakes his head. "I need to think and I do that better by myself anyway." He gives me a halfhearted smile. "But thanks."

Then we all just kind of watch as he takes my calculator and his code and hightails it out of the room.

EIGHTEEN

As much as I tried to tell myself to stay out of it, the whole time Darren and Marko were downing coffee and eating breakfast, I kept thinking about Kip.

Worrying about Kip.

And it kept creeping back into my mind that if it was Grams who'd gone missing, I'd be going crazy trying to find her.

Plus, maybe my mother never called me a sneaky punk kid, but I *do* know what it's like to think that your mother never wanted you.

So when everyone's finally ready to go, *I'm* the one who winds up lagging behind.

"Hey!" Darren calls over his shoulder. "Something wrong?"

We're barreling down the stairs, and I feel really stupid saying it, but I blurt out, "I'm worried about Kip."

"Oh," Darren says, stopping.

"We are *not* not going ashore because of Kensingtons," Marissa says, and, boy, does she look serious.

"I know," I tell her. "I just feel really bad."

We all stand on the stairs for a minute until Darren finally says, "So what do you want to do about it?"

I give a stupid little shrug, and then Marko pipes up with, "I say we take the Kipster with us."

"No!" Marissa cries. "The two of them will spend the whole time with that stupid code and a calculator and not want to do anything!"

"Hey," I tell her, "I've never been to Mexico. You think I'm going to spend the whole time with a *calculator*?"

"Yes!"

I roll my eyes and then we stand around some more until Darren asks again, "So what do you want to do?"

And that's when my gut takes over. "I want to invite him to come with us."

"Nooooo!" Marissa wails. "Besides, can you even take someone else's kid into a foreign country?"

"Let's find out." Darren says.

I give him a grateful smile. "He's probably in the library. Or his room, if his mom's not there. Or in the Royal Suite."

"He could be anywhere," Marissa moans.

"All those places are close by," Darren tells her. "Let's just check."

We're almost down to Deck 8, so we start by looking in the library, and the first person I see is the Puzzle Lady.

"You've got to be kidding," I mutter, 'cause while the rest of the ship is off exploring Mexico, here she is in a windowless room, putting together a boring brown puzzle.

"Hi, there," she says with a little smile, then nods

toward the other side of the room and whispers, "Back there."

So yeah, I get hit with that same weird combination of feeling bad and feeling creeped out, and I wind up doing what I did before—smiling and telling her thanks.

Marissa hangs back while Darren, Marko, and I pass by the computer tables and find Kip hidden away in the very back of an alcove, punching numbers into my calculator. "Hey," I tell him, and even though we hadn't exactly snuck up, he looks at us like we've got butcher knives ready to slash and jab.

"Dude!" Marko laughs. "We're not here to hurt you."

Darren takes over, saying, "We'd like you to come ashore with us."

Kip just sits there, blinking.

"I know you're obsessed with this," I tell him, nodding at the code paper, "and believe it or not, I get that. But we're, you know . . ."

My voice just trails off, so Darren finishes for me, "She's worried about you. Doesn't want to leave you here alone."

"I'm fine," he says. "But thanks."

"You're *not* fine," I tell him, but I recognize the look on his face. It's been on my own face enough for me to realize that there'll be no talking Kip out of this. He's going to spend the day holed up with my calculator and his code, and nothing I can say will change his mind.

Darren and Marko give it another shot, but they finally throw their hands up, too.

Now, as we're leaving, I'm kinda shocked to see Marissa

chatting with the Puzzle Lady. Darren and Marko head for the door while I zip over to Marissa and go, "Ready?"

She says, "Sure!" but then I notice that the whole top third of the puzzle is put together and that it's a picture of a man straddling a big branch of a gnarly old tree. The artwork looks very detailed and classic—like it might be a puzzle of some famous old drawing or something. And even though I know it's not a good idea to start chatting with a crazy puzzle lady, I can't help asking, "What's the puzzle of?"

The Puzzle Lady laughs, "Very good question! So far, it's of a man in a tree, but I have no idea why he's up there. He seems to be looking at something, don't you think?"

I look closer, then nod and ask, "Isn't there a box with the picture on it?"

She smiles. "No box, no printout, nothing. Which I think is why I can't seem to leave it alone. I want to find out!" Then she puts out her hand and says, "I'm Sue Taylor, by the way."

So Marissa shakes her hand and says, "I'm Marissa," and I give her a little wave and say, "I'm Sammy."

"Very nice to meet you." Then she smiles and says, "Have fun in Mexico."

Which for some reason creeps me out all over again.

To get off the ship, Marko and I switched our sea-pass cards, then went through the checkpoint turnstile on Deck 4 and onto a smaller boat, which motored us to a dock in a big marina. Now, since the cruise ship was air-conditioned and really cool, and since we were running late and tangled up with the whole Kip situation, I guess we'd all kind of forgotten that Mexico would be humid and hot. By the time we'd walked the length of the dock, we were totally wilted.

"Shorts woulda been thinking," Marko says, because all of us are wearing jeans.

"I *knew* that, too," Marissa grumbles. "I feel so stupid!"

There's a big sign on a nearby building that says MARINA MERCADO over a doorway, and Darren leads us inside, where it *is* cooler, but not a whole lot. The place is like a giant maze of small, packed booths, where the booth dividers are about eight feet tall and covered on all sides with stuff like leather purses and hats and bright clothes and wrestling masks and Elvis paintings and wooden puppets and zarapes and wool blankets. And inside the little booths there's silver jewelry and wood carvings and brightly painted pottery and knickknacks galore.

We zig and zag around the booths for a while, checking stuff out, and although a lot of the booths have electric fans blowing air around, after a while all I can think about is how hot and claustrophobic I am.

"See anything?" Darren asks me, and at first I don't get the question.

And then I do.

"As in anything I would want to *buy*?"

He nods.

Now, maybe it's because for the longest time I had zero money and still don't know how to spend it, or maybe it's because of the heat and being boxed in by Elvis paintings

177

and zarapes and wool blankets, but I just shake my head and go, "No."

"No?" Darren asks, then looks over at Marko to see if he heard my complicated answer, too. Marko just shrugs, so Darren looks back at me and says, "You didn't see *anything* you'd want? A souvenir?"

"Maybe a blanket?" Marko says with a mischievous grin.

I grin back at him. "I definitely could use one of those right now." Then I look back at Darren and say, "I also don't need a wobbly-headed turtle or a glass chessboard or a glow-in-the-dark painting of Elvis."

"Jewelry?" he asks, like he can't believe what he's hearing.

"I've got plenty," I tell him, then show him my Casey jewelry: the lucky horseshoe charm on my shoelace and the skeleton key necklace that I keep tucked inside my T-shirt.

And I've just put away my necklace when from my right I hear, "Hh-hh-hmm!" and there's Marissa, holding out the skirts of two little halter dresses that are hanging from a booth wall. The dresses are both white, one with red and yellow flowers, the other with blue and yellow flowers.

Now, okay. Normally, I would have given her the are-you-*nuts*? look, but I'm about to faint from heatstroke and just looking at those dresses is cooling me off.

"The girl's a genius," Marko says. "I'm going to find us some shorts." And before I can say *anything*, Darren's hauled out his wallet and is paying for the dresses.

The Mercado doesn't have a dressing room, but after

Marko shows up with two pairs of swim trunks and Darren buys a knapsack, which has drawstrings that double as shoulder straps, we go back outside, where we find a public bathroom and take turns changing. And since the three of them are all wearing some kind of low-cut sneakers, they look okay, but I look like a complete dork in my little dress and scribbled-on high-tops, even with the ankle flaps flipped down.

But feeling twenty degrees cooler is worth being Little Miss Dorky!

After we've all stuffed our jeans inside Darren's knapsack, he slings it on his back and says, "Okay, gang, *now* I think we're ready to tackle Mexico!"

Which turns out to mean walk and shop.

Which, really, I'd had enough of inside the Mercado.

I do my best to be, you know, interested and impressed, but the only thing that really interests or impresses me is air-conditioning, which seems to be on in just the expensive shops. So I wind up spending a lot of time looking at stuff that I would never in a million years buy, just so I can soak up some coolness.

On our way out of each shop, Darren asks me, "Anything?" but each time I just shake my head, step outside, wilt, and start looking for the next shop with air-conditioning.

Marko finally catches on when I step inside a shop full of glass vases and platters, and he grins at me and whispers, "Takin' shelter from the swelter?"

I feel totally busted, so I just make a quick tour through before leaving.

"Anything?" Darren asks, and he sounds kind of desperate. Like he can't believe I'm passing up all this cool stuff.

"Nah," I tell him. "I'm not into dangerous art."

"Dangerous art?"

"You know—stuff that might break if you happen to look at it wrong?"

"So why'd we . . . ?" And then, *ding-dong,* he gets it. And after he's studied me a minute he goes, "Okay, so what *do* you want to do?"

"Swimming with dolphins woulda been good," Marko says.

I can tell he's only joking, but Darren snaps, "Shut up, man. I checked. They were sold out."

"Hey," I tell them. "I don't want to swim with dolphins!" But then it hits me what I *do* want to do. "But can we maybe get down to the water and just stick our feet in? That sounds really great to me."

At this point we'd been shopping for hours, so we were a ways from the marina, but we headed in the direction we thought the ocean was, and somehow we found a little patch of sand right by the water. It wasn't an official beach, and at first I wondered if we were even allowed to be there, but nobody yelled at us to scram, so we took off our shoes and socks and went wading.

The water was warm, but it was definitely cooler than we were, and it felt amazing! Trouble is, we hadn't been in it very long when a man comes beelining toward us.

"Uh-oh," I say, nodding out at him. And we're all sure we're busted for . . . well, for wading in foreign waters without a permit or whatever. But instead he calls, "Tacos? *Pollo asado, pollo colorado, carnitas* . . ." Then he tries, "Coca-Cola?"

Darren and Marko are out of the water in a flash, ordering stuff, and faster than you can say, "Boy, I didn't realize I was so hungry, but now that I know there are tacos coming, I'm *starving,* and really, the thought of an ice-cold soda is making my mouth water buckets, because an ice-cold soda is going to have double the thirst-quenching power of anything else I can think of," the guy is back, carrying a box lid full of food and glass bottles of Coke.

We spread out our jeans, and as we get all set up on our little beach for a picnic, I notice Darren moving my shoes around more than he needs to. I can tell he's trying not to be nosy, but while we're eating, he finally breaks down and says, "Okay, 'Cute Feet' and 'Cool Your Heels,' I get. But where is Sassypants Station?"

"Sassypants Station is a grave site in the Santa Martina Cemetery," I tell him. And before he can say anything about *that,* I add, "And you may *think* you know what 'Cool Your Heels' is about, but I promise you, you are clueless."

"And that's how you want to stay, believe me," Marissa tells him.

Darren's looking a little worried, so I add, "It has to do with the way a condor cools itself off. And that's all I'm gonna say."

"Yeah," Marissa adds. "We're eating." She eyes him. "And even if we weren't? You wouldn't want to know."

"What *are* you people talking about?" Marko asks.

Darren grabs one of my shoes and tosses it at him. "We're decoding the shoes." Then he grins at me and says, "I like how he put 'Left Foot' on both of them."

I nod. "Sums up my dancing perfectly."

Marko starts reading from my high-top. "'Umbrella Girl,' 'Miss Notorious,' 'Triple-T,' 'Drool Monster' . . . Wait—'Drool Monster'?!"

I shake my head. "Don't ask. It's not pretty."

He goes back to reading the shoe. "'Cute When Baffled,' 'Shiver Me Timbers!' 'Fruity Chicken Salad Sammich,' 'Startle = Pain' . . ."

And then Darren picks up my other shoe and reads from *it*. "'Ice Blocking,' 'Kickin' Crime,' 'Zombies to the Rescue,' 'Storm the Castle!' 'Race Ya!' . . ."

Marko laughs. "Good thing you don't have size elevens like your dad, or we'd know way too much about you!" Then he tosses me my shoe and goes, "Dude, that is the coolest thing ever. I'm talking *ev-er*." He looks at Darren. "Man, why wasn't I cool like that when I was a teenager?"

"I don't know," Darren tells him. "I wish you had been."

"Hey!"

"Man, I'm kidding. *I* was the dork, remember?"

"Good of you to admit that."

Darren hands me my other shoe and says, "How long have you known him?"

I take my shoe back. "Casey? About a year and a half. Why?"

"Just wondering how long it takes to get to the place where little phrases can be code for whole stories." He shrugs and looks away. "It feels like I've missed out on a lot."

I think about that a minute, then tell him, "If I were to scribble on your shoes, I could already say stuff like, 'Let the Adventure Begin!' and 'Don't Fall!' and 'Anything?'"

Marissa chimes in with, "Hey, you could put 'Port' on one shoe and 'Starboard' on the other! And 'Fore' and 'Aft' on both!"

"But which would be which?" I laugh. "And would those be one-way shoes?"

Marissa's bouncing up and down, totally getting into it. "How about 'No Breakin' into the Chorus Before You Finish the Verse'!"

"Or 'Stop Skippy-Doodlin' Around!'" I cry, and *I'm* bouncing now, too. "And don't forget 'Hoity-Toity' and 'No Five-Fork Dining!'"

"Or the best one of all," Marissa cries, and when she looks at me, I know exactly what she's thinking, so we both shout, "'Kensington Clue'!"

Marko raises his Coke bottle. "And I would definitely add 'Tacos on the Beach.'"

I smile at Darren and say, "See? We're already filling up your shoes."

He smiles back at me, but even through his sunglasses, I can't help noticing.

I've made a rock star cry.

NINETEEN

My souvenirs from Cabo San Lucas were the sundress, a sunburn, and my Coke bottle.

When Darren saw that I was keeping my bottle, he kept his, and then Marko and Marissa decided not to throw theirs out, either. We got caught in a downpour on the way back to the shuttle boat, which was weird and warm and funny. And over as fast as it started.

On the boat ride back to the ship, I started blowing on my Coke bottle like a flute, and pretty soon the four of us were doing it, making sounds that Marko called the foghorn song. It wasn't actually a song. It was more just noise and a lot of laughing. I think we drove the other people on board a little nuts, but whatever.

Now, I didn't think much about Kip when we were in Mexico, but the minute we were back on the ship, I started to. Marissa could tell, 'cause as we're shuffling up the stairs, I could feel her watching me, and finally she says, "There's no way he's still there."

"Wanna bet?"

"No. I want a shower!"

I did, too, but I still wanted to peek inside the library. "You don't have to come," I tell her.

But we all wind up going, and sure enough, Kip's right where we'd left him, only now the whole table where he's working is covered with papers.

"Any luck?" I ask, which totally makes him jump.

"Dude," Marko says, shaking his head. "Have you been out of that seat at all today?"

Kip blinks at us, then says, "What time is it?"

"Dinnertime," Darren says.

"Shower time," Marissa grumbles.

"Time for you to give that a rest," Marko says.

"Tell you what," Darren says to him. "The four of us are going to take showers, then we're going to come back here and drag you to dinner."

Kip's head bobbles like a dashboard doll, where the head moves because someone's jolted the car, not because it wants to.

"Does anyone even know you're here?" I ask him.

"Noah." His voice comes out groggy. Like it's still waking up. So he clears his throat and adds, "He was here . . . a while ago."

"Well, we'll be back as soon as we take showers," Darren tells him as he scoops an arm around my shoulders and pulls me away. And since I'm still wet from the downpour and cold from the ship's cranked-up air-conditioning and looking mega-dorky in a halter dress and high-tops, I don't put up a fight.

"Dude," Marko says as we're going up the stairs. "That poor kid."

Which about summed it up. And since Marissa could tell I felt awful about leaving Kip alone in the library, she let me shower first so I could get back down there while she took hers.

The foghorns blasted as I was getting dressed, so I knew I'd be missing the sail out of port, but I hurried back down to the library anyway.

"Hey," I said, sliding into a chair next to Kip. "Catch me up."

First he looks around to make sure no one can overhear. There are quite a few other people in the library, but they're mostly on the computers, and no one's near us. And the Puzzle Lady's gone, so really, there's nothing to worry about.

Not that there would be anyway, but obviously Kensingtons are paranoid, so whatever.

Then he starts raking in all the papers that are spread across the table, going, "I started with a simple substitution cipher."

"Like where 1 is *A* and 2 is *B*?"

"Right."

"How high do the numbers on the note go?"

"To 99."

"But there are only twenty-six letters."

"If you loop the alphabet, it could go on forever."

I let out a really intelligent "Oh."

"Anyway, that got me nowhere. So I started shifting the origin of the numbers."

"So 1 is *B* and 2 is *C* . . . like that?"

"Right. It's called a Caesar cipher, and I did it for twenty-six one-letter shifts." He watches me, waiting for what that means to sink in. And when my eyes have stretched wide enough, he gives a little shrug and says, "I still wound up with gibberish."

"Wow."

"So I went online and found out about something called an Atbash cipher, which is a Caesar cipher in *reverse*."

"Oh, so *A* is 26 and *B* is 25?"

"Right. And I did *that* for twenty-six shifts and wound up with . . . ?"

"Gibberish?"

He nods. "Then I found out about this thing called a Vigenère cipher." He fishes through printouts from the computer and shows me a page that looks like a cross between a word search puzzle and a letter graph, where there's a set of alphabet letters across the top and another set going down the left column.

"So what do you do with this?" I ask.

"A Vigenère cipher uses a key word. So I thought maybe that's what the word on my note was."

"You mean the *LION* with the extra *N*?"

"Exactly."

I study the big letter grid for a minute, then say, "But . . . this gives you back letters, not numbers."

He frowns. "Yeah. But after you Vigenère cipher it, you can Caesar cipher the resulting letters and—"

"Whoa! Stop. That is *way* too complicated. And it seems like the possibilities are endless! I mean, if the first one didn't work, you'd have to try the shift thingy through the whole alphabet, right? And if *that* didn't work, you'd have to try the whole reverse shift thingy!"

He holds his head and groans, "Exactly! It may also be a polyalphabetic cipher. Plus the notes were written as subtraction problems, so what does *that* mean? Or are they incremental dividers and *not* minus signs?" He shakes his head and says, "There's also deranged alphabet ciphers."

"Deranged?"

"Yeah. Like, rearranged? Where you take the letters of a word and move them to the front of the alphabet, then continue with the alphabet with that word's letters missing." He gives a defeated little shrug. "So I tried *LIONN* and *KENSINGTON* and *KATE* and *KATHERINE* with about a hundred numeric position shifts and wound up with nothing but gibberish."

I paw through the pages on the desk and shake my head. "Unbelievable what you've gone through to figure this out."

"It's driving me crazy!" he cries, and actually yanks at his hair with both fists, just like you'd see in some cartoon.

I sort the papers into computer printouts, the code sheet, and piles of scribbled-on pages. Then I tell him, "Okay, let's back up."

He takes a deep breath and closes his eyes for a moment, then nods.

And out of my big mouth comes, "It can't be as hard as you're making it."

"Not as—" He grabs for the papers. "What do *you* know?"

I slap down the pages and look him right in the eye. "Why would someone put coded notes under doors if they're too hard to decipher? I'm sure they mean *something,* but whoever's done this can't scare you or extort money from you—or whatever the idea behind them is—if you can't figure them out!"

He keeps on gripping those pages, staring at me.

I keep them slapped down, staring back.

Finally, he lets go and says, "Then what? And I *did* start simple." He rolls his eyes. "It doesn't get any simpler than a straight substitution." He slaps the pages with the back of his hand. "And if *LIONN*'s not a key word, why's it there?"

"What if it translates to a number? You know, like the numbers in the code would translate to letters?"

He blinks at me a minute, then real quick goes through each number's place in the alphabet and comes up with 12, 9, 15, 14, 14, which he then writes down as one big number, and then as a big number with commas: *129,151,414.*

I sigh and shake my head. "That doesn't tell us anything, does it? And it's one digit shy of a phone number." Then I go back to the paper with the coded message and say, "So the smallest number is 4, and the biggest number is . . . 99." I study it another minute, then ask, "Did you check for a pattern? Or any repeats?"

"Like, frequency?"

"Yeah. What is the most common letter of the alphabet?"

"*E,* I think."

"Can you Google it?"

He jumps up, and while he's heading over to a

computer, I ask, "Can I try to work something out? Look for patterns?"

"Sure," he says with a little wave.

So I take a blank sheet of paper and start tallying up numbers that repeat, and by the time Kip's back, I've got the stats. "So 53 is in here five times. And 7, 16, and 60 all happen three times, and everything else is once or twice." I look up at him. "What's the most common letter?"

"*E* is number one, *T* is number two, and *A* is number three." And after he's studied the code paper a minute, he says, "There are also two occurrences of a 53, 60 combination."

I nod. "And two 9, 53 combos."

He looks at me. "So 53's our *E*?"

"But . . . we have to figure out what 53 is if you cycle the alphabet, don't we? Like, 53 would be the first letter, right? Twenty-six plus twenty-six plus one?"

He sort of stares at me, then a little smile flashes onto his face. "Right."

So real quick I make a chart that goes from 1 to 26, then cycle around until I get to 99. Then I take the tally of numbers I'd already done and find out that *A*, *H*, and *P* have the most tallies.

Which makes me feel like I've gotten a whole lot of nowhere.

So finally I say, "Seems like a total dead end."

He shakes his head. "To me, too."

"Okay," I say with a sigh. "Let's get back to simple."

But before we can get back to simple, Darren and Marko walk in. They're wearing ball caps and old-school

Wayfarer glasses, and I can tell Kip actually doesn't recognize them until he sees Marissa trailing behind.

"I told you," Marissa says when they get close. "She's already totally sucked in."

Darren ignores the comment and smiles at us. "Ready for dinner?"

I grab Kip's arm and kind of turn him to face me. "Don't *even* tell us you're not hungry."

He laughs. "I'm *starving*." Then his face falls, and he says, "No. I know what starving is, and I'm not that." Then he laughs again and says, "But I *am* really hungry!"

It's so weird to see him transform from Deranged Decoder into Hungry Teen that I laugh, too, and say, "Well, let's go!"

I start to fold up my paper, thinking I'll work on it more later, but while Kip hands over my calculator, saying, "Thanks for the loan. Maybe I can borrow it again?" I notice Marissa nudging Darren, and before I can put the paper in my pocket, Darren takes it and the calculator and slips them into his sports coat. "Not tonight," he tells Kip. "There's a comedy show and we're dragging you to it."

What's funny is, Kip doesn't argue. He just tucks away his papers and follows us to the Schooner Buffet, and during dinner and the comedy show, he even laughs out loud a few times.

Maybe that's because dinner with Darren and Marko turned out to be a comedy show all by itself, once Marko whipped out a deck of cards and he and Darren pretended to be dogs playing poker. All the growling and yipping and chomping and snarling . . . It was bizarre, especially with

191

the Wayfarer glasses, and really funny, especially since they seemed to know exactly what the other one was snarling about.

So yeah, the night was like a double feature of laughs. And even though I really wanted to ask Kip some basic questions—like how come nobody but Noah seemed to ever check on him, and what he was going to do about the situation with his mother—there was never a good time.

Especially since Marko seemed to want to keep Kip's mind miles away from Kensington madness, so anytime there was a lull—like sitting around waiting for Darren to get out of the bathroom, or waiting for the comedian to hit the stage in the Poseidon Theater—Marko gave him drum lessons. There were no drums, but that didn't stop Marko. First he got his right hand going, *tap-tap-tap-tap-tap-tap-tap-tap,* then he added his right foot, telling Kip, "That's your bass drum, *boom, boom, boom, boom!* Now here comes the snare!" And his left hand started slapping his left thigh. Everything Marko did, Kip copied.

Marko recruited Marissa and me, too, but we were just sort of extras in the Great Drum Escape—it was Kip he was really paying attention to. And while it didn't take long for Marissa and me to be like, Okay, enough of that, Kip kept at it everywhere we went.

Which got annoying!

Even Darren thought so, 'cause when we were raiding Dessert Island after the comedy show, he finally said, "Can we maybe just eat?"

Kip stopped slappin' and tappin' and said, "Sorry!" but

Marko went, "Are you kidding? I wish I had some sticks on me, man. This young dude would be rockin' right now!"

So I don't know—maybe Marko had been right all along. Maybe Kip needed some drum therapy to get his mind off his family and help him through this cruise. All I know is Kip seemed to be a completely different person when we wound our way back down to Deck 9. He even stopped outside our cabins to give Marko a spastic, out-of-nowhere hug.

At least that's what I think it was. It happened so fast, and then he was jetting down the hallway toward his cabin, going, "See you tomorrow!" and waving like a lunatic.

"Yeah, dude!" Marko called after him. "We'll get you some sticks tomorrow. And maybe you can help us with sound check on Thursday!"

"Awesome!" Kip called back.

And it would have been, only sometime during the night, Kip Kensington disappeared.

TWENTY

That night my brain must've been wrestling with the Kensington code, because I had a weird nightmare where numbers were chasing letters. At first it was like a big swirl of digits and letters, but then the numbers got legs and arms and *knives,* and became an angry mob, hunting down letters. They had voices, too, and I could hear them yelling, "Get 'em! Get 'em!" but I don't remember any faces.

The *letters,* though, definitely had faces. And no knives. Or legs. My face was in an *S,* Marissa's was in an *M,* Kip's was in a *K,* and Darren's and Marko's faces were on the top arms of an *X.* None of us could move. We were just petrified Letter People being attacked by the Number Mob.

What was weird—well, *weirder*—was that the knives didn't hurt. Those numbers hacked away at us, but we were like sponges or something and just sealed back up.

And then an *N* appeared with Noah's face, and for some reason he had a voice and hollered, "Why was six afraid of seven?" into the Number Mob.

All the numbers stopped and waited.

"Because seven eight nine!" Noah the *N* shouted.

Now, even though the numbers didn't have faces, it

was clear they were all going, Huh? So Noah the *N* hollered, "Get it? Seven *ate* nine?" and all at once the Number Mob turned on the number seven.

Luckily, the phone rang and woke me up from my stupid number wars dream. The curtains were closed tight, so I thought it was deep, dark nighttime, but when I stumbled over to the desk to answer the phone, the clock said it was almost ten in the morning. And I could sort of hear Captain Harald's voice announcing something over the hallway speakers about us being in Puerto Vallarta.

I fumbled with the phone before finally getting it up to my ear. "Hello?"

"Rise and shine, sleepyhead! I've booked us on a sailing and snorkeling expedition. Leaves in an hour."

"In an hour?"

"What are you, a rock star? I can't believe you're still in bed."

"Very funny," I grumble, because he's obviously having a good time paying me back for yesterday's wake-up call.

Darren laughs. "Wear your swimsuit, flip-flops, shorts, and a T-shirt. And bring a towel. We'll grab breakfast on our way out."

"What's going on?" Marissa asks after I hang up.

I stumble over to the balcony and about blind us both when I open the curtain. "Darren booked us on some sail and snorkel expedition." I open the balcony door, and sure enough, it's already roasty-toasty outside. "It leaves in an hour."

"In an hour?" she says, flinging off the covers.

So we hustle to get ready, and before you know it, the four of us are heading up the stairs to the Schooner Buffet.

After one flight, Marissa eyes my feet. "You're serious?"

At first I think she can't believe I'm wearing something besides high-tops, but then I notice that everyone else has their flip-flops under control.

Mine are wild.

And loud!

FLIP-FLAP, FLIP-FLAP!

And I can't seem to shut them up.

"How do you *do* that?" I ask her, 'cause her feet are just . . . quiet.

She gives my feet a little squint. "How do *you* do *that*?"

So yeah, there'd be no sneaking around in these things, but I figured, Who cares? But as we're cruising the buffet, I spot Lucas and LuAnn over at Fruity Island, and all of a sudden I *start* caring.

The first thing I do is look around for JT, because the last thing I want to do is deal with JT. I don't see him anywhere, but Lucas and LuAnn are obviously uptight. I can't hear what they're saying, but from the way they're putting stuff on their trays and talking to each other in manic little bursts, I know they're not discussing the fine carving details of the watermelon shark.

So I turn to Darren and whisper, "Can I borrow your hat and glasses?" and before he can ask me why, I've snagged them.

"Hey!" he says, like I've stripped him down to tighty whities.

"Shhh!" I say back as I shove my hair inside the cap and

put on the shades. "Get me something to eat, okay?" Then I abandon my tray and head over to Fruity Island.

Trouble is, my feet are flippin' and flappin' so loud that Lucas actually turns and looks as I walk up. Luckily, he doesn't seem to recognize me, but they still move away, and the only thing I manage to overhear before they leave is LuAnn saying, "How can they trap us on here? We're not under arrest!" and Lucas going, "And that's how we want it to stay! We have to stay cool and be cooperative and just play this thing out." He takes a deep breath. "At least Noah's agreed to do what he can to keep it quiet."

I do try to follow them over to Pastry Island, but my feet are being so loud that Lucas looks *again*, so I just head back to Darren and the others at the main buffet, where my spot's been taken by three very tan women with tight shorts, silver jewelry, and dainty, manicured feet.

Cougars.

And they are definitely prowling around Darren.

"No," he's telling them, "I'm here with my daughter." He puts a hand on my shoulder as I wedge back into the buffet line. "Family time."

"Oh!" they say, and give me the kind of smile that says, Aren't you cute, and I'd like to kill you, all at the same time. Then they tell Darren, "Can't wait for the concert!" and leave, carried off by their ridiculously quiet feet.

The instant they're gone, Darren snatches his hat and glasses back from me, saying, "Let's eat and get out of here."

Which is what we do.

And even though Marko says something about wishing

"the Kipster" was going with us, Marissa cuts that idea off quick by pointing out that Darren had bought only four excursion passes, so unless one of *us* wants to stay home . . .

Which none of us does. And besides, we're barely going to make sail time for the excursion as it is.

No time to track down the Kipster!

Luckily, we can walk right off the ship and onto the dock, so we don't have to wait for a smaller boat to shuttle us over. And almost right away we spot a man with a sign that says Los Arcos Sail & Snorkel. He leads us and a handful of other people off the dock and over to, well, I guess it's a truck. Or maybe a converted van? The back where we climb in has low sides with posts holding up a bright green canopy, and there are bench seats that go around the perimeter. There's a big open window between the cab, where the driver is, and the back, where the rest of us are. And once we get going, Mexican music blares from speakers wired through the window.

Everyone on board seems to be in a great mood, holding on to one of the canopy posts or the side of the truck as we jostle through town and then blast along dusty roads into the countryside. The driver keeps shouting, *"Ándale,"* as we zoom around cars and people and livestock, so Marko starts shouting it with him, and pretty soon all the adults are going, *"¡Ándale! ¡Ándale!"*

After about half an hour we park at a dock where a sailboat is waiting, and guides give us some instructions before we all pile into the boat.

Now, at first I'm kinda nervous. I mean, this is a *boat*.

Not tiny, but not big, either. It tips a little side to side as people walk around. There are masts and sails and ropes, which seem solid and secure, but the whole thing feels somehow . . . dicey. Like once we get out to the real ocean, a whale might come along and flip us right over.

Plus, it's crowded. Besides the five crew guys and eight passengers, there are three big coolers and a bunch of snorkel gear and not enough places to sit. I wind up on a wooden bench near the front of the boat, with Marissa on my right and Darren on my left. It's actually a good spot, but poor Marko gets stuck sitting on an ice chest.

Anyway, after some more instructions and a little over-view of where we'll be going and what kind of wildlife we might be lucky enough to see, they put up the sails and off we go.

I'm still nervous as we sail away from the dock, but after we've been going for a while, I start to relax. Everything is so beautiful. The water, the birds overhead, the coast-line, the mountains . . . And I love the *sounds*. The gush of water against the boat, the seagulls crying, the *wind* . . . Something about the wind—in the sails, against flags at the top of the mast, and especially across my face and in my hair—it makes me feel like I'm soaring over the water.

Like I'm *flying*.

After a while one of the crew points and shouts, *"Delfines,"* and when we look, we see dolphins arching in and out of the water not far from us.

I cry, "Holy smokes!" and it comes out all squealy, because I'd never seen anything like it before. And then the dolphins swim *toward* us instead of swimming away, and pretty soon the boat is sailing along in the middle of a group of them.

I look over at Darren with a big ol' smile and tell him, "This is *awesome*," and he smiles back and nods like, No kidding!

After that, I was definitely over my fear of being on the sailboat. I think the dolphins made me feel like we were welcome. Even after they took off, I just quit worrying about us being kicked out of the water by angry whale tails or whatever.

Then we arrived at our snorkeling place, which was called Los Arcos, where there were huge rock formations jutting out of the water, one in the shape of an arch. And after some basic snorkeling instructions, we put on our flippers and masks and jumped overboard!

It was really warm on the boat, so jumping into the ocean was a shock, but after just a couple of minutes, the chill was gone and the water felt great. And when Darren was sure we had the hang of breathing through the snorkel tube, we kicked off toward the arch rock, because that's where all the fishies were supposedly hanging out.

And, boy, were they! Whole schools of yellow-and-black ones and green-and-blue ones. Plus we saw a sea turtle and an *octopus*.

It was awesome and I could have stayed out there all day, but after we'd been through the arch a few times, we heard the time's-up! whistle blow and had to swim back to the boat.

The return trip didn't feel much like the sail out to the rocks. For one thing, we seemed to be moving a lot faster—like we were in a rush to get back. But also, the crew turned on music, which kind of killed the whole symphony of nature thing. Marko didn't seem to mind, though, 'cause he slapped and bapped the side of the ice chest he was sitting on to the rhythm of the music. "Dude!" he called over to Darren. "I got me a cooler *cajón*!"

Darren laughed, "You have a way cooler *cajón* at the studio!"

Marko had to give up his ice chest when they served food, but he didn't seem to mind that, either, seeing how the food that got served was delicious fruit and shrimp and fresh-baked rolls.

On our sail out to Los Arcos, one of the crew had been snapping pictures, and apparently there was a setup somewhere on board where they could print them, because after the food was put away and we were all air-dried, they brought out a three-ring binder with plastic-sheeted pictures in them. I didn't even want to look, because come on—you want to sell me a little snapshot for twenty bucks?

But when it was Marissa's turn with the binder, she gasped and said, "Oh, Sammy!" and shoved it in my lap.

Now, okay, the truth is, I hate pictures.

Maybe because I take *terrible* pictures, but whatever—I hate them.

But looking at the one in my lap, I knew right away—I had to have this picture.

Twenty bucks?

Shoot, I would pay a hundred!

"Sammy, that is *way* better than anything you would get at formal night," Marissa whispers.

Well, pinchy shoes and a dress are not going to produce anything *anyone* would want, but really, this picture is more than just not tortured.

It's like a small miracle.

For one thing, I'm smiling.

Really smiling.

For another, it's a picture of . . . well, of me and my dad.

There are no pictures of me and my dad.

Zero.

Well, okay. There's the cheesy say-cheese picture of the four of us, but none of just him and me.

And there sure are none with him grinning at me while the ocean's glistening and *dolphins* are arching out of the water in the background.

Marissa takes over, shoving the binder into Darren's lap. "You have to buy this picture!"

He takes one look at it, then calls out to a crew guy, "Señor," and just like that, the picture's mine.

"Promise you'll scan it for me?"

I nod and look away, wishing hard for some sunglasses to hide my stinging eyes.

TWENTY-ONE

It was nearly five o'clock by the time we got back to the marina, and I could tell Darren was kinda keyed up as we went through the turnstiles and boarded the cruise ship.

I guess Marko could, too, because he says, "Dude, they're here. Relax."

"Who are we talking about?" I ask.

"Drew and Cardillo," Marko tells us. "Bass and keys. We won't be causin' much trouble tomorrow without them."

"Oh, we could still cause some major trouble," Darren says. But then he frowns and adds, "But we'd be in violation of our contract."

"Why haven't they been on the cruise the whole time?" Marissa asks.

"What's actually unusual is that we *have* been on the ship the whole time," Darren tells us. "The way entertainment on cruise ships works is acts go from ship to ship, switching at ports. Or on sea days, they helicopter talent in and out."

My eyes bug out. "They *helicopter* people around?"

Darren nods. "There's a landing pad on the bow of the ship."

"That's a little over-the-top, isn't it?"

"They've got a system down. And it makes for cabin efficiency. They don't want you taking up a room for five nights when you only entertain for one or two."

I think about that a minute. "So the comedian we saw last night . . . ?"

"Is probably doing the same show on a different ship tonight."

Marko throws in, "Sleeping on the same pillow some other entertainer used last night."

As we enter the arctic zone of cruise ship air-conditioning, Darren adds, "We also would have been down on Deck 3 if I hadn't upgraded. Drew and Cardillo decided last minute that they couldn't be gone the whole week. They had other commitments."

"Yeah," Marko mutters, kind of rolling his eyes. "Soccer."

Darren eyes him. "Hey, it's important to *be* there." Then he looks at me and says, "Which I'm afraid I won't be much of tomorrow. We've got setup, sound check, and two shows."

"And he's a total mother hen," Marko says.

"Hey!"

"Well, you are." Marko puts his hands up. "Not that there's anything wrong with that! Especially since we've got no techs."

"We've got techs, just not *our* techs."

"Variety show techs?" Marko says, pulling a face. "Comedian techs?"

"We'll be fine," Darren tells him. "It'll all be fine." But it's like he's trying to convince himself.

We're at the Deck 4 stairs now, but instead of going up with us, Darren stops and says, "I do want to go check on Drew and Cardillo, and touch base with Archie before we leave port."

"So is he hairy?" I ask, remembering how they'd called him the Wolfman earlier.

Marko kinda grins. "No hair, no sharp teeth . . . a big disappointment."

I laugh, and then Darren gets us back on track. "How about we meet at our staterooms at seven and then go to dinner?"

Marko makes a quiet little *brwak-brwak-brwak* sound, which gets him backhanded by Darren. "Dude! I'm kidding," Marko laughs. "And you know what? I'll come with you."

So they go down the stairs while we go up. And no, I haven't gotten any better at the walking-in-flip-flops thing. They're loud and I'm kinda slow, and on the Deck 6 landing, Marissa actually stops and says, "Take them off, would you? Just go barefoot."

So I do, and it feels . . . great! I can totally zoom!

I zip up, up, up the stairs until Marissa finally calls, "Hey!" 'cause her quiet little feet cannot keep up.

I wait on the Deck 8 landing, and for the first time since we'd left the ship, Kip Kensington takes over my mind.

"No," Marissa says when she meets up with me, because I'm seriously eyeing the library door.

"He's probably not there," I tell her. "It'll just take a minute."

She grumbles, "He probably *is* there, and it *never* takes just a minute," but she follows me inside anyway.

And it *would* have taken just a minute, because Kip's *not* there, but the Puzzle Lady spots us. "He hasn't been here all day," she says from across the room.

Which means she *has*.

Now, really, I would have waved and said thanks, but Marissa notices how far she's gotten on the puzzle and goes over, saying, "Wow, that's"—and then she sees the image that's shaping up—"one weird puzzle."

"Isn't it?" the Puzzle Lady says. "What on earth is a skull doing in a tree?"

Which anyone would agree is a great question. I mean, it's just perched there. On a branch. By itself.

It's definitely a human skull, but it's way bigger than the head of the man straddling the branch of the tree. And it's smiling. Even though there's a spike coming out of the side of the head.

And I don't know if it's a perspective thing—you know, where the man in the tree is farther back than the skull in the tree—or if the artist didn't know what they were doing. Or maybe was on drugs. Or whatever. All I know is that this puzzle is more than hard.

It's *creepy*.

"Obviously, I can't stop now," the Puzzle Lady tells us. "Got to figure out the rest of it." Then she looks at me and says, "I'm guessing you and your friend decoded your own puzzle?"

So yeah. Can you say *eavesdropper*? But I just shake my head and try to be polite. "He might've. I don't know. We've been gone all day."

"Ah," she says, going back to the puzzle.

Now, I don't know how one little *ah* can make a person feel so guilty, but that one little *ah* sure did. It seemed to be all wrapped in a giant bow of disappointment. Like, Ah . . . you're one of *those*. Abandons her friends. Puts pleasure before problems. Lives in a haze of take-it-or-leave-it ignorance.

Which ticked me off!

So I wag my flip-flops at her a little and say, "That's not fair! I barely even know him! Am I supposed to spend my whole cruise trying to help him figure out his crazy family's problems?"

"My," she says as she puts a piece into place. And without even looking up, she says, "Aren't those supposed to be on your feet instead of wagging in people's faces?"

Well, that does it. I tell Marissa, "Come on," and walk my bare feet right out of there.

"Wow," Marissa says as we're heading toward the stairs. "What was that all about?" But the weird thing is, she says it like she doesn't understand *my* reaction.

"Didn't you get that?" I snap. "The way she said, 'Ah'?"

"The way she said, 'Ah'? You bit her head off because she said, 'Ah'?"

"It was the *way* she said it." I start stomping up the steps. "And I didn't bite her head off!"

"Like you're not biting mine off right now?" she mutters.

Then I put my sea-pass card in the door lock and nothing happens.

"What?" I cry, and try again.

Still nothing.

And I can feel myself getting all *flushed*.

Mad.

I can't even open a stupid door when I have the *key*?

Finally, Marissa asks, "Did you forget to switch back with Marko?"

Which for some reason makes me feel even stupider, and I actually stomp my foot when I go, "Maaaaaan!"

So Marissa lets us in and tells me, "There's no reason for you to be feeling guilty about not helping Kip today."

I follow her inside. "Who says I feel guilty?"

"Please," she snorts.

"Besides, he must've decoded it or he'd have been in the library today, right? So what's there to feel guilty about?"

"Hmm. Then maybe you feel like you missed out?" She gives a little shrug. "You're the one who always figures things out. Maybe you're jealous?"

"What?!"

She laughs at the face I'm pulling. "Oh, just go take a shower."

"I can't believe this!"

She eases my picture and flip-flops from me. "Shower. Go. I promise you, you'll feel better."

The truth is, I did feel like a crusty crab from all the seawater and sun.

But I wasn't jealous!

Good grief.

And it turns out I *did* feel a lot better after the shower.

But I wasn't jealous!

Good grief.

I *was* kinda curious, though.

Had Kip broken the code?

And if so, what did the note say?

Was it from a kidnapper?

A blackmailer?

A *murderer*?

Or maybe Kate had been found?

So while Marissa's taking her turn in the shower, I sit and think. And there comes a point where I just can't stand it—I really want to know! So since there's no way Marissa's going to want to run around and track down Kip, I finally decide to just call his room.

I know he's probably not there, but it feels like an easy place to start. So I pick up the phone and punch in 9584. And after four rings, I'm about to hang up when suddenly there's someone on the other end saying, "Yes?"

It's a soft voice.

Female.

"Uh, Ms. Kensington?" I ask, not really knowing what to call her.

"Yes?"

"It's Sammy. Kip's friend?"

"Why . . . hello." She sounds calm with maybe just a hint of being surprised. "What can I do for you?"

"Uh . . . I was hoping Kip might be there?"

"Here?" She hesitates, then says, "I thought he might have been spending the day with you."

"With *me*?"

"Like he was when we didn't know where he was before?"

"Uh, we've been gone all day? We went to shore."

"Oh, well, *that* would have been nice," she says, which reminds me of what I'd overheard JT's parents saying over by Fruity Island.

About being trapped on board.

"So . . . you haven't seen him all day?" I ask.

She heaves a little sigh. "You probably know he's miffed at me?" My brain races around for what to say to *that*, but she saves me from having to answer by saying, "It's okay. I'm sure you have issues with your parents, too. The teen years are tough, and he's certainly a teen. Moody, impulsive, not always rational . . ." She laughs, "Not that I'm trying to insult *you*, but I'm sure you've noticed these tendencies in him, hmm?"

There's a lot I could say or maybe *should* say, but the person on the phone is not really matching up with the person Kip's talked about. And a lot of what she's said about Kip is true—he's definitely been short-tempered and hotheaded in front of us, and we're basically strangers. What's he like in front of people he actually *knows*?

Anyway, I'm kind of thrown by all this, so instead of

answering her, what comes out of my mouth is, "I'm just wondering if someone broke the code?"

"The . . . code?"

A little chill tickles through my ear to my spine. And my brain's going, Uh-oh, because there's definitely been a shift in her voice. So I tell her, "Never mind. Not important," but before I can get off the phone, she asks, "He told you about that? When?"

Now, the way she says *when* is pretty intense. Like she really wants to know.

Like it *matters*.

So I try to sound all casual as I tell her, "Yesterday he said he didn't want to go rock climbing or anything else until someone had 'cracked the code,' whatever that meant. I figured it was a brainteaser, but . . . it was more than that?"

She hesitates, then says, "Things are always a bigger ordeal in this family than they should be." The intense edge in her voice is gone now, and before I can even try to get a real answer, she adds, "I'm sorry he's not here. Have you tried the teen lounges? Or the pool? Or maybe the pastry shop? That boy loves pastries."

I can tell she's getting ready to hang up, so I just blurt out, "When's the last time you saw him?"

"Like I said, he's playing the teen card. My advice would be to check the Royal Suite. He may have moved in there."

"Moved in?"

I can practically see her shrug. "Some of his things are gone."

I want to cry, Are you serious? But you don't know where he went? but I hold back and ask, "Has Kate turned up?"

There's a short silence before she says, "No."

"And you're not worried about Kip?"

"Like I said, some of his things are gone."

"Like what 'things'?" I demand.

"Look, I overreacted once already on this trip. I'm not going to do *that* again." Then she says, "I suggest you check the Royal Suite. I'm sure that's where he's staying. Ginger just *loves* to interfere."

And without another word, she hangs up.

TWENTY-TWO

Marissa did *not* want to go up to the Royal Suite. "Why can't you just leave it alone?" she moaned as I dragged her up the stairs. "Or why not just call there like you called Kip's room?"

She already knew the answer to her first question, but I did answer the second one. "Because I don't know the number. All it says on the door is ROYAL SUITE, remember?"

"No," she snaps. "I don't remember. I don't spend my life noting every little detail of every little door I see!"

So yeah, she's miffed, but as we reach the Deck 10 landing, an idea suddenly storms my mind. "Hey! You know how sometimes phone numbers are given as words—like 1-800-GET-RICH?"

She's obviously somewhere else in *her* head, too, 'cause she goes, "Get rich—what?"

"Or GET-THIN or GET-FISH or whatever!"

"Get Fish? Who would have a number that was Get Fish?"

"A fishing company!" I shake my head. "Never mind! The point is, what number would *Royal Suite* translate to on the keypad of a telephone?"

"What?"

"Forget it. It's stupid. It would be way too long to be a cabin number . . . unless maybe you used just *Royal* . . . which"—I tick off the letters on my hand—"would still be one number too long."

"Sammy, I'm sorry, but could you stop thinking out loud?"

Which I do for all of three seconds.

But then another thought hits me, and it's so big that it stops me in my tracks, and I just *know* that Marissa will want to hear it. "What if the decoder to the Kensington notes is the keypad of a telephone?"

Marissa squints at me. "The keypad of a phone."

"It could be, don't you think?" I whisper, and even though we'd already decided *LIONN* didn't decode to a phone number via the alphabet, something about using the keypad as a decoder has me all excited.

"Sammy!" she whispers back, but instead of sounding excited, her voice comes out all fierce. "You said yourself he's probably figured it out. Can't you just let it go?"

"But what if he hasn't? And what if it's as simple as decoding from a phone? What if—"

"Sammy!"

Well, I can't believe she isn't even a *little* bit excited and I'm about to tell her so, only right then the door just to the left of the Royal Suite opens and Bradley Kensington steps out.

My first thought is *Hide*. But we're standing *right there* with nothing to hide behind, so instead we just freeze.

Bradley's wearing the same kind of clothes we'd seen him in at the Schooner Buffet two days ago—they could even be the *same* clothes—but the shirt's all rumpled and half untucked, the tie's gone, and the black folder is now bursting with papers, sticking out like too much lettuce on a tuna fish sandwich.

His jowls are kinda red, too.

So is his nose.

He closes the door, then tries the handle to make sure it's locked, and pushes on the door to make sure it's latched.

Then he sees us and freezes, too.

So there we are, like silly ice sculptures on the Deck 10 landing.

I make myself thaw out and go, "Hi, Mr. Kensington. Any word on your mom?"

His eyes sharpen down on me as he goes from frozen to dripping at the temples. "You know about that?"

"Uh . . . yeah?"

"Oh, right, right," he says, wiping a hanky over his brow, "from the kids." His voice is a little slurred, and I can tell he's trying to act cool, but he's rumpled and sweaty and, it hits me, drunk. "It's not looking good," he says. "But we've been told to keep it quiet so as not to worry other cruisers. Which is why I asked. Now if you'll excuse me . . ."

But I kind of follow him over to the glass elevators and ask, "We're actually looking for Kip. Have you maybe seen him?"

He punches the down button. "I have maybe *not* seen

him," he snaps—well, as much as you can snap when your words are sort of tumbling over each other. Then he jabs the elevator button a bunch and turns an angry eye on me. "And if I never see that conniving little weasel ever again, it'll be a *good* thing." And when an elevator opens, Bradley gets in without even looking at us.

I race around so I can watch it go down, and Marissa follows me, going, "Well, that was . . . interesting."

The elevator stops just one deck down, and even though there are other people on board and I can't be sure, I have a hunch Bradley's getting off.

"Come on!" I tell Marissa, and run for the stairs.

"Wait! What? Why?"

I laugh, "Who? Where? When?" Then I say, "It was Bradley! In the elevator! With a folder!"

"You're driving me crazy, you know that, right?" Marissa calls as she flies down the stairs after me.

But when we get to the Deck 9 landing, I peek down our hallway and whisper, "Crazy, maybe, but I'm right."

"About *what*?"

I nod down the hallway. "There he goes."

"So *what*?"

"So just watch!"

Sure enough, Bradley stops about midship and knocks on a door. Then he goes next door and knocks on another. And a minute later, Lucas steps out of the second room, and both men go into the first.

Teresa's room.

At least, I figure, it must be.

"Wow," I gasp after the doors are closed.

" 'Wow'?" Marissa asks. "Why 'wow'?"

"Three of them, mortal enemies, all in one room?" I look at her. "This is big!"

She just rolls her eyes. "Who says they're mortal enemies? They're siblings. They fight. So what?" Then she does a smarty-pants hike of an eyebrow and says, "Kip's mom and JT's parents were in line together when we boarded the ship. They booked rooms right next to each other. That doesn't seem like mortal enemies to me."

"I'm pretty sure Kate's the one who arranged everything. And since then one of their sons has punched the other's son in the nose!"

Marissa's eyebrows stay in smarty-pants position. "Seems like Teresa would be pretty apologetic about that. Especially since, according to Kip, she doesn't act very motherly toward him."

"Well, what about Bradley? They were barely talking when we saw them in the Royal Suite, and now he's meeting with them, carrying a big ol' sandwich of papers?"

She squints at me. "A big ol' sandwich of papers?"

"Folder! Portfolio! Whatever! The point is, the three of them are meeting, and not in some public place." I grab her by the arm. "Come on."

"Come on where?" she cries as I drag her along.

"Up to the Royal Suite."

"Why?"

"To see if Kip's there!"

So up we go, back up to Deck 10, and this time we

don't make like ice sculptures on the landing. We go straight to the Royal Suite door and ring the bell.

Now, I know the place is big and that it would take a little while to walk from, say, the living room to the door. So I'm willing to be patient, but Marissa is not. After five seconds she says, "No one home, let's go."

I yank her back. "Give it a minute." Then I wait, like, two more seconds and ring the bell again, this time twice.

After a few more seconds, Marissa frowns and says, "Obviously, nobody's here."

"What if they're on the balcony and can't hear?" I ask.

"They? Who're they?" Marissa asks while I jab the bell, like, twenty times.

"Kip or Ginger!"

She rolls her eyes. "Can we please go? We already missed the sail, but there's still yogurt cones and sunshine calling our names!"

But just then the door pulls open, and we find ourselves face to face with Ginger.

She doesn't smile when she sees us, that's for sure. And all of a sudden I remember about Kensington Clue, and I'm pretty sure the frown's not just because her sister's still missing—it's because I'm on her blacklist.

So instead of asking her if Kip has moved into the suite, I tell her, "We have news."

She stares at me. "News?"

I nod. And I try to look very serious and a little mysterious, because now I want *in* so I can check for Kip myself.

"Well?" she asks.

So I look over both shoulders, then whisper, "Probably not a good idea to discuss it in a hallway?"

She stares at me some more, then calls, "Company!" over her shoulder and lets us inside.

Now, she's not exactly *young*, but she's walking so slowly that I can't help but think that she's trying to block us from getting down the hallway too quickly. And my mind is racing around, wondering why she would have to warn Kip that we were there, but then it hits me that they're probably working on decoding the notes and she doesn't want me to see them . . . which means they *haven't* figured out what they say yet, which means that Kate is probably still missing, which means . . .

Only it's not Kip we see when we turn the corner.

It's Noah.

Noah and I both go, "Oh!" and do a little bob backward, but then almost right away, I hit him with, "Nice noose."

"Noose?" Ginger says, and looks back and forth, back and forth between us.

"You didn't think that was funny?" Noah asks me.

"You put it in my room! On my bed!"

"A noose?" Ginger asks. "In her room?" She blinks at him. "On her bed?"

Noah looks away. "Yeah, I thought later that it might not have been the best idea."

"Noah!"

"Sorry, Mom," he says, like a sheepish little boy.

"But why on earth would you do such a thing?"

All of a sudden, I feel kind of defensive of Noah. I mean, maybe grown men shouldn't be putting nooses in girls' cabins, but watching him be scolded by his mother?

It's embarrassing.

And besides, we'd started it, right?

So I cut in and say, "It's a long story. And we, uh, we gave him the rope to begin with, so . . ."

She does the whole back-and-forth thing again, and it's obvious she wants to know what in the world this rope thing's about, so Noah finally says, "I'll explain later, okay, Mom?"

"Yes, you will," she tells him, then turns a stern eye on me. "Now, what news do you have?"

I move a little deeper into the Royal Suite, saying, "First, have you seen Kip today?"

"Kip?" Ginger says, and when I look back at her, she's just standing there, staring at me.

"Yeah, you know . . . ," I say as I edge toward the living room, ". . . your grandnephew?"

"Of course I know who Kip is!" She hurries after me, asking, "Why do you think he's here?"

Now, the way she says it makes me think she's hiding something. Either that or she doesn't want me snooping around her sister's fancy suite. So I do a quick scan around while I tell her, "I didn't say that I did. I just asked if you'd seen him today."

Noah steps in, saying, "It's okay, Mom. They heard you offer to have Kip stay here, remember? I'm sure that's why they're looking for him here." Then he looks at us and says, "Can we offer you something to drink?"

Just like that, Ginger seems to switch gears. "Yes," she says. "Sorry for my lack of hospitality. There's been so much . . . turmoil. But my sister would be mortified by my behavior." She moves to the wet bar, saying, "What would you like to drink?" and it comes out kinda choked up.

"How about a round of pink lemonades?" Noah says. "And why don't we talk on the balcony? It's beautiful out there!"

Now, the first thing that flashes through my mind is, How does he know we like the pink lemonade? And the *next* thing that flashes through my mind is, There's no way I'm going out on that balcony! I mean, didn't Kip say that the balcony door had been open the morning after Kate went missing? So just the thought of going out there is giving me the creeps.

Only then my mind flashes back to Darren peeking through the deck dividers and telling me, "Don't fall!" as I looked down a skyscraper of decks at the ocean below. And *that's* when I connect the dots.

Or, I guess, the balconies.

All of a sudden, my heart is like a racehorse galloping away. I try to reign it in, try to tell myself, *Eeeeeasy, Sammy, whoa!* But I can't help wondering if Bradley might have come back into the Royal Suite after the big fight by sneaking from his balcony to Kate's, and then coming in through the balcony door.

What goes jolting through my mind is, *Wow. Yes. Murder.* So instead of telling Noah, Uh, no way I'm going out there, I say, "Sounds nice," and head for the balcony so I can check it out.

"You think he wants us out here because they're hiding something inside?" Marissa whispers as she follows me.

I blink at her. "Wow."

She blinks back. "So what *are* you thinking?"

What I'm thinking is that I'm stupid, and that I should have listened to my gut about not going out onto the balcony. And I go to do a U-turn, only there's Noah, standing in the doorway.

Noah, the guy with the key to any room.

Noah, the guy with the noose.

"So," he says, corralling us like a couple of sheep, "what news do you have?"

I blink at him like, Oh, right, and then Ginger's there with two glasses of lemonade. "Here you go, girls," she says, as Noah lets her by and plants himself back in the doorway.

It feels like we're trapped, and that any minute Noah's going to charge and shove me overboard. I tell myself to calm down. I mean, it's broad daylight! There are two of us! We would scream! People would see!

Besides, why would they kill us? We haven't *done* anything.

But my mind's also scrambling around, trying to figure out what we *might* have done. Or seen. Or heard.

Maybe we knew something we weren't supposed to know and didn't even know we knew it!

Maybe . . .

"Your news?" Ginger says, all sweetly.

I gulp down some lemonade. "Right. Well, a little while ago we ran into Bradley coming out of his suite.

His clothes were all rumpled, he was sweaty and blotchy-faced and his speech was slurred." I look right at her. "He seemed drunk."

Ginger gasps. "Are you sure?"

I look at Marissa, who nods and says, "Definitely drunk."

"Oh, this is bad," Noah mutters.

I turn to Noah. "We asked him about Kip, and he called him a conniving weasel, so I'm wondering . . . did you tell him about the printout? The one of the supposedly sick cousins?"

"No!"

"So why did he say that?"

Noah shakes his head like he doesn't know, but what I'm picking up from him is that he *does* know but doesn't want to say. And the way he's still standing in the doorway is really starting to freak me out.

So I take a couple of casual steps toward Bradley's balcony, thinking that moving away from Noah might lure him onto the balcony, so I can ditch it around him and get *off* the balcony. And after I've scooted away a bit, I tell Noah, "We followed him."

"You followed *Bradley*?" Noah's eyes get big, but he doesn't budge. "That was not a wise thing to do."

I take another step away from him and pretend to look out at the water. "You know where he went?"

Finally, he comes onto the balcony. "Where?"

"To Teresa's room. He and Lucas and Teresa are all in there right now, having a meeting."

"Are you *sure*?" Ginger asks.

"Positive."

At this point I'm all out of news. And Noah may be on the balcony, but there's no way I'm going to be able to grab Marissa and duck around him. So I go over to the panel that divides the Royal Suite balcony from Bradley's balcony and point to the big gap at the bottom of it. "Do you think he could have fit under here?"

"Who?" Noah says, coming toward me.

"Bradley. I'm thinking maybe he squeezed under and came in the balcony door after the big fight."

Ginger is coming over now, too, going, "After the big fight?" and my heart is slamming around as I move aside and give Marissa a wide-eyed look.

Like, GET READY!

And the instant Ginger is far enough away from the door, I charge across the balcony, grab Marissa by the wrist, yank her through the balcony door, slam it shut, and lock it!

"What are you doing?" Marissa cries, and there's Noah on the other side of the glass, all wild-eyed and manic-looking.

"Check the suite!" I cry to Marissa.

"For what?"

"For any sign of Kip! Or Kate! You go that way! I'll go back here!" She's just standing there, so I yell, "GO!"

So while she checks the bedrooms, I race through the rest of the suite, looking inside closets and under couches and in the bathroom and the kitchen and the trash baskets for any signs of Kip or blood or ropes or, you know, foul play. And I'm scouring the living room when Marissa *screams* like she's just found a corpse.

Only when I race over to her, I see that she hasn't found a body.

Somebody's found her.

TWENTY-THREE

It was Noah.

With Marissa.

In the hallway.

He had her by the arm and his face was all flushed and his eyes were zapping scary blue sparks.

"Let go of her!" I shout, and pick up the first thing I see that I can use to bean him with.

The urn.

Only the urn is really awkward. Heavy, with nowhere to really grab.

"Put that down!" he shouts, and blue sparks are flying!

"Let her go!" I shout back. Then I hear the *bam, bam, bam* of Ginger beating on the balcony door, and it clicks that the door is still locked and that Noah's just proved my theory.

A grown man *can* fit under the divider.

Noah must have done that, gone in through Bradley's balcony—which had to have been unlocked—gone out Bradley's front door, and then come into the Royal Suite with his master key.

"Put that down *now*," Noah shouts.

"Let go of her *now*," I shout back.

Bam, bam, bam! Ginger beats on the door.

And it looks like Noah's thinking about hauling Marissa over to the balcony door to let his mother in, which would make it two people against us instead of just one. So I shout, "Hey!" then hurl the urn into the air, sort of toward him but over to the side a ways. And since it's out of his reach and not the kind of thing you can catch one-handed, he lets go of Marissa to dive for it, and I leap over the coffee table and grab Marissa. I must've kind of misjudged where to hurl the urn, though, because as we're escaping the Royal Suite, we can hear it crash to the floor.

"Are you crazy?!" Marissa screams as I haul her out the door. "Why'd we *do* that?"

"I was trying to figure out what might have happened to Kip! Or Kate! I was trying to keep us from getting killed!" Then I mutter, "But it all got kinda confused and messy."

She yanks her arm free and storms toward the stairs. "I've been on a lot of cruises, and I have never wound up locking people out on their own balcony while I cased their suite. Never!"

I chase after her. "Sorry."

"Sorry? *Sorry*? Sammy! It was the *cruise director*. And his *mother*. In the *Royal Suite*. You don't think we're getting kicked off the ship? Maybe *arrested*?"

"Better than getting shoved overboard," I grumble.

She stops and glares at me. "Sammy, I am so mad at you right now. A cruise is supposed to be *fun*. A cruise is supposed to be *relaxing*. But somehow you've turned it into locking people out on balconies and hurling a dead man's ashes through the air!"

"Sorry."

She shakes her head and starts running up the stairs two at a time. "I need a yogurt."

So I follow her up to Deck 11 and outside to the frozen yogurt dispensers, begging her to forgive me, but she's basically not talking to me. So I finally give up and focus on behaving myself as we park on two loungers near the swimming pools. I don't make excuses or talk about Kensingtons. I don't mention Noah proving that Bradley could have squeezed under the balcony divider and murdered his mother. I just sit there, trying to act relaxed and like I'm loving soaking in the sunshine as I lap up my yogurt like a best friend should.

I'm still totally freaked out about what happened in the Royal Suite, but I'm trying.

I'm really trying.

It's *Marissa* who suddenly goes into bloodhound mode when we hear loud laughter come from the whirlpool area. She perks up and sits forward, and her nose points straight ahead as she zeroes in on one of the whirlpools.

"Let me guess," I say from my kick-back position. "JT."

"JT and about eight girls!" she says, all disgusted-like.

I slurp up some dripping yogurt. "Be glad you're not one of them."

I can tell she's still all fired up about what I'd put her through, because she says, "Exactly!" in a real don't-mess-with-me way.

But a couple of minutes later she's still in pointer position, and doesn't even seem to notice that her yogurt's dripping down her hand.

I lap up some more yogurt. "Obviously, *he's* not too worried about his grandmother or cousin. . . ."

"Obviously!"

Lick, lick. "Out there having the time of his life."

"What a jerk!"

Lick, lick. "Uh, Marissa?"

She stays in pointer position. "What?"

"You're dripping?"

She finally snaps out of it and sees that her hand is covered in melted yogurt. "Oh!" she cries, jumping up like she can somehow escape it. "Oh!"

All she has is one tiny napkin, so I run to get a bunch more while she slurps like crazy. Only the napkins don't exactly cut it. "I'm a sticky mess!" she moans. "I need to wash up. Let's go."

But even leaving, she can't help watching JT and his little, you know, *murmuration* of mermaids. "Who does he think he is?" she mutters.

And the truth is, I'm really relieved she's shifted her anger away from what had happened in the Royal Suite and onto JT. So instead of saying nothing, or something like, Yeah, really, out of my mouth pops, "Uh, future heir to the Kensington throne?"

Now, I knew it didn't really work that way, but something about it did ring true. JT had his grandfather's actual name, was a guy, and was a blood relative. Even if he wasn't the first or only grandkid, it still seemed like he had more perks built in than two granddaughters or an adopted African boy.

A real chip off the ol' block.

"It's disgusting," Marissa grumbles, eyeing the whirlpool. "They look like they should be feeding him grapes."

I laugh, picturing a fat old Roman guy with grapes.

"And you're right," she huffs. "What kind of person frolics in a whirlpool while his family's in crisis?"

I laugh again. "Frolics?"

"It's a good word," she growls. "Even if he's just sitting there."

"Waiting for someone to feed him grapes."

"Exactly."

When we get to our room, Marissa lets us in and the first thing we see is a folded note on the floor. I snatch it off the ground and unfold what turns out to be a full sheet of unlined paper with three computer-printed words on it:

I'm OK—Kip.

"See?" Marissa says, slapping it with the back of her hand. "You did all that stupid stuff in the Royal Suite for nothing!"

But something about the note seems . . . off. "Except I don't think this is from him."

She turns back to the note. "Why not?"

"Because he wouldn't waste time printing something he could write in three seconds, the other note he left us was handwritten, and his writing would be really hard to forge."

"But . . . who else would leave a note like that?"

"Someone who wants us to think Kip's okay when he's not."

"Who would do that?"

I sit down on my bed. "Someone who knows we're looking for him."

"Like Noah?" Marissa asks. "Or Ginger?"

"Or Bradley." I eye her. "Or even Teresa."

She thinks a minute, then says, "Or maybe someone told Kip we were worried about him and it *is* actually from him?" Her face screws to one side and she adds, "And how many of them know which room is ours?"

I look at her, and all of a sudden there's a huge lump in my throat. She isn't acting all miffed at me. She isn't telling me to shut up about Kensingtons. She's trying to help me *think*.

"I'm really, really sorry about before," I choke out.

She plops down next to me. "Can we please just stay away from Kensingtons and try to have some *fun* before we get thrown off the ship?"

My eyes get all big.

"Not that kind of thrown off, stupid! I mean *escorted* off. Like we were in the hat shop? And the perfume shop? And the ten-dollar store?"

"Hey, *you* started the spritz war, remember? And *you* put those stupid hats on my head."

She does a little tisk and shakes her head. "You and I have a long, checkered past."

"Yeah," I tell her, and heave a sigh. "We sure do."

* * *

While Marissa was in the bathroom washing up, I remembered the brainstorm I'd had about decoding the *other* Kensington note by using the number pad of a phone.

Which got me up and looking at the phone.

Which got me drawing the keypad on the *I'm OK* note and jotting down which letters went where.

"What are you doing now?" Marissa asks when her hands are all de-stickified. And then she sees what I've drawn. "Oh, right."

"Did you know that one and zero don't have any letters?"

"Is that a problem?"

"I'm remembering ones and zeroes on the coded note."

"But . . . do you remember any of the actual numbers?"

"Kip and I were looking for patterns and I remember the combinations that had 53 in them." So I write them down: *9–53–60, 19–53–60,* and *53–9–53.*

"Don't forget *LIONN*," Marissa says over my shoulder.

So I write that down, too, and then start trying to decode it, putting *WXYZ* under the first 9, *JKL* under the first 5, *DEF* under 3, and *MNO* under 6.

"You think the zeroes are maybe *O*s?" Marissa asks. "And the ones are maybe *I*s or *L*s?"

I look back at her. "Wow. Could be."

Then we both stare at the paper, trying to fish words out of the little pool of letters under 9–53–60.

"There's nothing here," Marissa finally says. "What about the *LIONN*?"

So I go back to the keypad decoder and write down *54666* under the letters.

Marissa shrugs. "You've got a 6-6-6. Sign of the devil, right? Maybe somebody born in fifty-four is the devil behind all of this?"

I heave a sigh. "Just tell me it's a dead end."

"It's a dead end."

"Thanks."

Just then the phone rings, which about shoots me through the roof. Marissa snatches it up and says, "Hello? . . . No, this is Marissa. . . ." and then I sit there, watching as her eyes get bigger and bigger, and she gasps, "Really?"

"What?" I whisper, because I'm sure there's been some big breakthrough with the Kensingtons.

But she stands there with her eyes about ready to pop, going, "Really? Wow! Okay! I'll tell her!" She puts the phone down and gasps, "Unbelievable!"

"What?"

"Change of plans! That was your dad. We have a private seating *with the captain*!"

"A private seating for what?"

"For dinner!" she squeals. "It's not just at the captain's table, either. It's actually a private dinner *with the captain*!"

"What's the difference?"

"The captain's table is a big, long table in the middle of one of the dining rooms. He hardly ever actually *eats* there, but even being invited to sit at the table—whether he shows up or not—gives you bragging rights."

"Bragging rights? Who would you brag to?"

"Other cruisers! Only platinum cruisers or VIPs get to

sit at the captain's table. But we're actually eating *with* the captain and not at the captain's table!"

"Why have a captain's table if he's not going to eat at it?"

"Oh, Sammy," she sighs as she heads for the closet.

"No, I'm serious. Why are other people invited to eat at the captain's table where there's no captain and *we're* invited to eat at some *other* table that *isn't* the captain's table *with* the captain?"

"Because the captain," she says, all breathy, "is a fan of your dad's!"

"You're not serious."

"I am!" She gives a little giggle. "Apparently the Troublemakers are huge in Norway." Then she adds, "It was a personal invitation and your dad didn't think he could say no, even though it's at eight and you have to dress up."

"Dress up? Why?"

She frowns at me. "You can't dine with the captain looking like *that*."

"Dine?" I pull a face at her. "You make it sound like he's the king."

"It's like that, Sammy. It's just like that!"

I squint at her. "But why? So he drives the boat. So what? I don't dress up for the bus driver. Or the taxi driver. Or—"

"This isn't a bus! Or a cab! And it's not a *boat*. This is a floating island! It's its own little sovereign entity on the high seas. And he's in charge of it, okay?"

"'Its own little sovereign entity'?"

She flings a dress at me. "Just get dressed, would you?

And be glad he's inviting us to dinner instead of kicking us off the ship!" She shakes her head and actually giggles. "Wow. What a roller coaster today has been!"

Well, obviously she's over the moon about having dinner with the captain, but while I'm getting dressed, my brain wanders back to the *I'm OK* note and how all the coded notes slipped under the Kensingtons' doors had also been typed and printed on plain white paper.

Marissa's packing a little purse, so I ask her if she has an extra one, which of course she does. And she's happy to lend it to me, but when she sees me fold up the *I'm OK* note and slip it inside it with a pen, she goes, "No!"

I give her a back-off look, and she just mutters, "Whatever," and leaves me alone.

Anyway, at 7:45 there's a knock on the door, and when Marissa answers it, she calls, "Troublemaker time!" at me over her shoulder, because the whole band's out in the hallway.

Darren's hair's still wet from a shower and he's wearing the snazziest suit coat I've ever seen. It's a smoky gray with a darker gray pattern and really dark red—almost black— buttons. And I can't help saying, "Wow. I *love* that coat."

"Yeah?" he asks, and gives me a happy-guy grin.

"You look nice, too," I tell Marko, 'cause he's doing a big ol' pout. "And I love what you've done with your hair."

"Thanks," he says, running his hand over his shiny scalp. "Took hours."

"You remember Drew and Cardillo?" Darren asks, and I nod, because I *had* kinda met them once before.

In Las Vegas.

When I found out who my dad was.

Let's just say it was good to start over.

So I shake their hands and tell them, "And this is Marissa."

Well, Marissa practically *dies* as she shakes their hands, 'cause yeah, they're younger than Darren and Marko and have definitely got that whole rock star thing going on.

As we head for the stairs, Darren tells me, "Sorry about the dress requirement, but you do look great." He gives me a quick one-armed hug. "Have a fun couple of hours without us?"

I laugh. "*Fun* doesn't even begin to describe it."

"Oh?"

Marissa snorts. "Can you say Kensingtons?"

"I can!" Marko says as we start down the steps. "I saw one!"

I turn around to look at him. "You did?"

"Yup. I stopped in at the library on our way up to see if maybe the Kipster was there."

I blink at him. "Really? Why?"

"I thought we'd have some fun with these." He pulls a pair of drumsticks out of his back pocket as we keep going down the stairs.

"You're bringing those to dinner?" Marissa asks with a definite squint.

Darren laughs and I notice Drew and Cardillo roll their eyes. And in a flash I understand that we've been really lucky the last few days to have Marko's equipment locked away somewhere down in the hull.

"So you saw him?" I ask.

"Nope. The Kensington I saw was"—he does a little drumroll along the handrail—"the Kipster's mother."

"Teresa?" My eyebrows go shooting up. "When?"

"About an hour ago."

"And . . . ?"

"Well, I didn't *talk* to her." He grins. "Most moms don't want their sons influenced by the likes of me or my drumsticks." Then he kinda shrugs and adds, "Besides, she was talking to that puzzle woman."

"She *was*?"

He eyes me as we turn another bend. "That's a big deal?"

"No . . ."

But it did feel like . . . *something*.

"Anyway," I tell Marko as we start down the next flight, "Kip hasn't been seen by anybody all day and we've been kinda worried about him." I open my purse and show him the *I'm OK* note. "We did get *this* shoved under our door, but we're not sure he wrote it."

"Hmm," he says, after reading it. "Well, maybe he'll come out of the woodwork tonight."

"What's this part?" Darren asks, taking the paper and pointing to my writing. "Why 6-6-6?"

"Told you!" Marissa cries.

So I fill him in on my not-so-brilliant decoding idea, which he kind of nods along with, then says, "So this is what you've been doing for the past two hours?"

"This?" I laugh. "No! That took about thirty seconds."

Now, I don't want him to think I'm some decoding

dork, but I also don't want to tell him how I locked the cruise director and his mother outside on a balcony, rummaged through the Royal Suite, and tossed Dr. John Tyler Kensington through the air.

So I try to straddle those extremes by saying, "We spied on Kensingtons and, uh, tried to get some answers about Kip and, uh, watched JT flirt with a murmuration of mermaids in the hot tub. . . ."

"A murmuration of mermaids!" Marko says. "Dude, all we did was talk to the hairless Wolfman and get wrangled into a hoity-toity dinner with the captain." He eyes me over his shoulder as we get to the Deck 4 landing. "I'm totally ditchin' your dad for the two of you from now on."

"You have no idea what you're saying," Marissa tells him. "Being around her is nothing but trouble, trouble, trouble."

Marko laughs as we follow Darren into the dining room. "Just the way I like it."

TWENTY-FOUR

It was just the six of us and Captain Harald. We were seated in a way-back corner of the fancy dining room, which was one deck down from the one we'd eaten in our first night, and the first thing I thought when I saw the captain was, Oh, *no*—another blond?

His eyes were brown, though. And he didn't look or act anything like a Kensington. Plus he had that Norwegian accent, which *was* very cool.

Once we're settled in, the captain gushes to the band, "I saw you in Oslo! At the Spektrum Arena!"

Drew looks at Marko and says, "Wasn't that the place where you got lost on some lunatic quest to find a troll and almost didn't make the gig?"

"Right! Right!" Cardillo says. "You had to bum a ride on the back of a Vespa!"

"From that big girl with the monster pigtails!"

"That wasn't part of the show?" the captain asks, and his cheeks are all flushed. "You roared through the crowd with a *huldre* on a Vespa right up to the stage! Everyone thought it was fantastic!"

"I wouldn't call it *roaring*," Marko tells him, and then Drew asks, "What's a *huldre*?" and after that, stories start flying and Troublemakers are laughing and Marissa and I just enjoy soaking it all in.

The captain did try to include Marissa and me in the conversation. The first time was when our appetizers were served. They came in fancy chilled shrimp cocktail glasses, but instead of shrimp, there were chunks of raw fish buried under a red sauce.

Fancy dish or not, it looked pretty gross to me.

Marissa was sort of playing with hers, too, and the captain took a break from his conversation about music to tell us, "Oh, try it. It's delicious!"

"What is it?" Marissa asks in a kind of squeaky voice.

"Herring!" he tells us. "A favorite in Norway!" Then he chuckles and says, "Go on. It won't bite."

And he's, you know, *watching* us, so we're pretty much forced to use our fancy little mini-forks and take bites of saucy red herring.

"See?" he says, like a happy little boy.

We smile and nod to be polite, but it's tangy and salty and cold.

And also . . . interesting.

So even though Marissa's had enough after one bite, I wind up trying another piece. And another. And pretty soon I have to admit I *like* it.

During the main course, he asks me, "So how do you like being the daughter of a rock star?"

I almost laugh and say, Well, it's been a weird couple of months, that's for sure! But when I glance over at Darren,

240

I don't know—it's like he's holding his breath. Like what I answer matters to him.

Or maybe he just doesn't want to get into how it was he didn't know he had a daughter until a couple of months ago.

Which I totally get.

So what winds up coming out of my mouth is, "You can have the rock star part, but the rest is good."

The captain does a kind of nod. Like, Ah. Only I can tell he's not really sure what I mean.

Darren, though, gives me a smile that's either grateful or relieved, or maybe both. Then, probably trying to switch subjects, he makes the mistake of asking what it takes to become a cruise ship captain, and for the next half hour we hear all about Captain Harald's childhood and his dream of becoming a mariner and his training in the fjords of Norway—including the *names* of all the fjords—and the extensive knowledge and skill required to become captain of a cruise ship.

I guess even he knew he'd been going on forever, because he finally looks around the table and says, "But enough about me. How do *you* like the cruise so far?"

Drew and Cardillo tell him that they basically just got there but that so far "everything looks rockin'," which seems to make the captain happy. And Marko and Darren make nice comments about the ship and how we'd had a great time snorkeling in Puerto Vallarta, which gets steady nodding and smiles from the captain.

But then he turns to Marissa and me and says, "How about you? Are you having a good time?"

Now, I was about to say, Yeah, and let him get on with conducting the conversation, but Marissa, *Marissa*, says, "It's been great except for the whole Kensington mess." She rolls her eyes. "That's taken up a *lot* of time."

"The Kensington mess?" he asks.

And that's when it finally hits me.

HOLY COW!

This is the CAPTAIN!

He knows EVERYTHING!

So I say, "You know—because Kate Kensington disappeared?"

"Who?" he asks.

One look at him and I can tell he really doesn't know who I'm talking about. So as calmly as I can, I ask him, "Noah hasn't talked to you about that?"

"About what?"

"His aunt's disappearance?"

"From *this* vessel?"

I nod. "She hasn't been seen since Sunday night."

He looks horrified. "You're referring to Noah Marlowe? Our cruise director?"

I nod again. "He said he was doing everything he could, but I didn't understand why we just kept going if someone went overboard."

"Overboard!"

"That's what her grandson thinks."

Marissa butts in with, "He's the reason we know any of this." And then Marissa, *Marissa*, says, "And *he* seems to be missing now, too."

"The grandson is?" The captain looks back and forth at us and finally says, "You're not just pulling my leg here?"

We shake our heads.

"Well, you did get that note," Darren says to me.

"Which I think someone else wrote," I tell him, then hand the note over for Captain Harald to see.

"What's this 6-6-6?" he says, and he sounds worried.

So I have to explain that it has nothing to do with the devil and about the coded notes and all of that. And when I'm done, he hands the paper back and says, "People use reunions on our ships for all sorts of purposes. Maybe this is like a dinner theater?"

I fold the paper up and put it away, saying, "Or maybe someone shoved a billionaire grandma overboard because they wanted to inherit a bunch of money."

He studies me. "I'll ask Mr. Marlowe about it. But I'm sure if it were serious, he would have reported it to me." And since our waiters have come to take away our dessert dishes and refill coffees, he uses that as an excuse to totally switch topics. "So," he says, turning to look at Drew and Cardillo, "are you two on board for the duration, then?"

"No," Drew tells him. "We're being flown out Friday morning."

"Apparently a ventriloquist is taking our place," Cardillo says with a grin.

And that's when something else hits me.

Hard.

I butt in with, "We're at sea the whole way back, right? No more ports?"

"That's right," the captain says.

I look at Cardillo. "So you're flying out on a helicopter?"

Cardillo nods. "That's what we've been told."

My heart starts beating faster and my head starts feeling like it's going to float away, 'cause I'm sure I've just figured it out.

I mean, if you've got a billion bucks and you've had a major fight with your family and you're stuck on a cruise ship with them and just want to get *away*, you don't need to jump overboard!

You can hire a helicopter to come fetch you!

So I ask the captain, "Were there any helicopter transports on Sunday or Monday?" and let me tell you, I am totally perked up in my seat.

"On this cruise ship?"

"Yes!" I pant, all eager-eyed and waggy-tailed.

And you know what he says?

He says, "No."

No!

Not "Not that I know of," or "Not on my watch," or "I'd have to check the heli-log."

Just no!

The perky in me starts to sag, but I'm still holding out hope. "Are you *sure*?"

He chuckles. "If a helicopter landed, I would know about it." He smiles at me. "It takes a coordination of efforts, you know."

I think about that and go, "Oh, right. The ship is moving."

He smiles at me. "Exactly."

But I still can't believe that I'm not onto something. I mean, it seems like the *perfect* explanation to everything!

Well . . . except for the coded notes.

And Kip disappearing.

Still. I can't let it go. So I ask, "Well, what if there was a medical emergency? What if someone flew out in the middle of the night? What if—"

He puts a hand up. "I would know about it."

"But . . . don't you have a co-captain or something? I mean, who's driving the boat right now? When do you sleep?"

His smile's not looking too smiley anymore. "It's a ship, young lady, not a boat. And yes, the staff captain and I work together to navigate the vessel. If there was a medical evacuation or another unexpected need for the heliport, I would absolutely know about it!"

I sit back with a little frown. "So there's no way Kate Kensington flew out of here without you knowing about it?"

"That is correct."

I take a deep breath and finally let it out. "Thanks."

He gives me a kind smile now and says, "Try to enjoy your family instead of worrying about theirs."

"That is very good advice!" Marissa tells him.

And I guess he thinks that's a good note to end things on, because he stands up and thanks us for joining him for dinner. "You're welcome to stay and enjoy your coffee," he says to the guys, "but I need to get back to the bridge."

So everyone says thanks and nice to meet you and all that jazz, and then off he goes.

"Sorry," I say, looking around the table, because it feels like I've messed up dinner with the captain.

"Are you kidding me?" Marko whispers. "If I hear the word *fjord* again, I think I'll fjart!"

"You'll fjart?" the other guys laugh.

"Yeah, and it won't be fjun. Not fjor anyone."

Darren tosses down his napkin. "So let's fjind something else to do."

"I'm hangin' with the Samster," Marko says as we all stand up.

My eyes pop. "The *Samster*? Sounds like *hamster*."

"The Samminator, then," Marko says.

"That's *way* more like it," Marissa tells him.

"So where're we goin'?" Darren asks, putting his arm around my shoulders as we walk away from the table.

I grin up at him. "Haven't got a clue."

He grins back. "Perfect."

TWENTY-FIVE

We wander out of the dining room and through the elevator area, and then Marissa starts making noise about going to the Poseidon Theater to see what show's playing tonight. "If I remember from the Cruzer, it's *Music Across the Ages*. That sounds like something we'd all like, right?"

Darren kids her with, "Our very own cruise director."

"Better than our real one," I grumble, because knowing that Noah never reported Kate's disappearance to the captain didn't just bother me, it kinda scared me. Especially after what had happened in the Royal Suite.

I'd been trying to come up with reasons why Noah hadn't told the captain. The obvious one was that he had something to do with Kate's disappearance. What better way to control the situation than convince everyone you had authority to get to the bottom of things and then do nothing?

But . . . he didn't seem to have any *motive* for getting rid of her.

So maybe he hadn't told the captain because the Kensingtons were his family and private people, and he thought he could handle everything himself.

Or maybe by the time they knew Kate was missing, it was too late to turn the ship around, so why tell the captain? And maybe other people in the family wanted to avoid a scandal. Or the press. Or whatever people with big bucks who don't want their image tarnished worry about.

But if he never reported it to the captain, then there was probably no Coast Guard on the lookout for rich old ladies flailing in the water, and no alerts sent out to other boats, or anything!

So when Noah told us that he had a lot of authority on the ship and was doing everything he could, what did that *mean*? He must have done *something*, because Lucas and the others had made it sound like they weren't allowed to leave the ship. But I hadn't seen anyone going around questioning Kensingtons. Kate couldn't be holed up in some bar drinking blue martinis for three days. Shouldn't there be an official investigation going on?

Or . . . maybe there was, but they'd kept it quiet, like Bradley had said.

And maybe Kip had been right when he'd said he thought Noah was acting the way he was because he didn't think Kip could handle the truth.

Or maybe Noah *did* have a motive and I just hadn't figured it out yet.

Like . . . maybe *Ginger* was in the will.

Maybe she was fed up with being her rich sister's side-kick and wanted to finally get her mitts on some money of her own!

And maybe Noah was helping cover things up! Maybe

he was sick of the whole lot of Kensingtons—especially since it was obvious they thought he was a doofus.

So yeah, my brain was whisking around ideas and they were getting pretty frothy. And really, all it did was make me worry about Kip. Where *was* he? If he trusted Noah, and Noah turned out to be in the middle of a desperate murder cover-up, maybe Kip *was* in danger. Maybe he'd figured out the code and . . .

And *what*?

What were those stupid codes about?

Who had slipped them under the doors?

And why *codes*?

The whole thing was maddening and stupid and didn't add up!

Then, somewhere in the froth in my mind, I hear Darren ask, "Thinking about Kensingtons?"

"Huh?" We're walking through the casino now, but I sure don't remember getting there. "Oh. Yeah." I try to smile. "Guilty as charged."

"Do me a favor," he says, studying me. "Stay away from that Noah character, would you?"

I avoid looking at him, because the way he said it was real . . . intuitive. Like he can tell something's up. I do nod—a serious I-get-you nod—but what I really want to do is blurt out what I'd done up in the Royal Suite. I don't, though, because a) I don't want him to worry, and b) I'm afraid he'll think I'm stupid.

Not to mention reckless and psycho.

So I just keep walking.

And then he says, "And maybe take the captain's advice?"

I nod again, and then a grin kinda steals my face and what comes out of my mouth is, "You mean, enjoy my fjamily?"

That makes him laugh really hard, which makes me laugh, too. And then, from behind us, Drew calls, "Hey, me and Cardillo are gonna hang in here for a while and play some slots."

"Let's have a band meeting over breakfast," Darren says. "The buffet's on Deck 11, way in the back."

"Noon?"

"Sounds good!"

So the two of them veer off and the four of us keep going, until Marko spots the casino bathroom and says, "I'll be quick!" and hurries through the door.

Five seconds later, he's back. And I'm thinking, How is that even possible? when he tells Darren, "Boozer with a bruiser," and now they *both* hurry inside the bathroom.

I look at Marissa and go, "Boozer with a bruiser?" and she shrugs and says, "Got me."

A few seconds later Darren and Marko come out of the bathroom dragging a man along the floor by his armpits. Marissa and I move in closer while Marko lays the guy down and snatches up a ship phone, which is mounted on the wall between the women's and men's bathrooms. "Holy smokes!" I gasp. "That's Bradley Kensington!"

"It is?" Darren asks, which is understandable, 'cause the body sprawled out on the floor is not looking too Kensington-esque, if you know what I mean.

I look closer and nod. "It sure is. What happened?"

"He looks passed-out drunk to me," Darren says. "Smells it, too."

"Is he breathing?"

"I wasn't interested in getting that close."

Bradley *is* looking really ripe, but still, I put my fingers up to his neck to check for a pulse, and when I feel it, I nod and go, "Tick tock."

Marko joins us. "A guy named Dr. Wadham is on his way," he says, then asks, "Did I hear you say that's Bradley Kensington?" And when I nod, he says, "For such a hoity-toity guy, he sure is wasted."

I'm about to stand up, but then I notice that there's a corner of a piece of paper sticking out of the pocket of Bradley's coat.

The paper's white.

With no lines.

And I'm sorry, but I just can't help it.

I pull it out.

It's a sheet of notepaper folded over once, and when I open it, what I see is a handwritten message.

Darlings, I'm sorry. I miss your father so. Go on and live your best lives. No tears, Mother.

I gasp and show it to Marissa, who gasps and shows it to Marko, who says, "Dude!" and shows it to Darren.

Trouble is, now I see the corner of another piece of paper sticking out of Bradley's pocket. And when I pull it out and unfold it, what I see is . . .

Darlings, I'm sorry. I miss your father so. Go on and live your best lives. No tears, Mother.

Only it's written about six times in a row.

I gasp and show it to Marissa, who gasps and shows it to Marko, who says, "Dude!" and shows it to Darren.

So now I *dig* through his pocket and discover a handwritten letter signed by Kate Kensington, plus Bradley's coded note, which is still clean—like he'd barely even looked at it, let alone tried to figure it out.

"Dude!" Marko says. "The worm was forging a suicide note from his own mother!"

I look over my shoulder and see a man carrying a Red Cross bag coming toward us. So real quick, I put the practice forgery note and Bradley's coded paper inside my purse, then jam the other papers back in Bradley's pocket.

Marko covers for me, intercepting the Red Cross–bag guy by sticking out his hand and going, "Dr. Wadham, I presume?"

I stand up in time to see the doctor give Marko a curious look before saying yes. Then he gets right to work, checking Bradley's heart and breathing. "He'll be fine," he says after a minute. "You related?"

"No," Marko tells him. "I'm just the lucky sucker who found him passed out in the bathroom."

Bradley starts groaning, which is our clue to hightail it out of there. "Thanks, doc," Marko tells him as we abandon ship, but the doctor doesn't seem to mind. "No, thank *you*," he says, then gets on his walkie-talkie.

"What are you going to do with those papers?" Marko whispers.

"I'm not sure," I tell him. And I'm not. But I know that talking about seeing forged notes and actually *having* them are two completely different things.

One's proof.

The other's just the fantasy of an annoying teenager.

And I can't deny it—something about having a copy of the coded note is making my brain feel . . . electric.

We're late to the show, so we're hustling to get there—I think partly because we all want to disappear for a little while. But as we're hurrying along, we pass by the Lute Lounge, where a jazz trio is playing an upright bass, a little sparkly drum kit, and an electric guitar. And suddenly Marko and Darren are craning their necks around like a couple of kids watching the ice cream truck go by.

"Dude!" Marko says. "That's a sixties Ludwig black pearl four-piece!"

Darren gasps, "And that looks like a bone-stock fifty-seven Les Paul!"

Now, I can tell they're dying to stay and watch the trio, but they don't even ask. They just follow along to the Poseidon Theater.

The theater is already packed because the show is about to begin, so it's hard to find four seats together and we wind up sitting two and two near the back.

Almost right away the lights come down and a woman bounds out onto the stage. "Good evening!" she says into a microphone. "I'm Christie, your assistant cruise director, and I want to know: Are you having a good time?"

Marissa and I look at each other, and while Christie's warming up the audience, I whisper, "So where's Noah?"

"Sometimes the assistant opens the show," Marissa whispers back. "Don't start reading stuff into it."

But I can't help thinking that maybe the captain is talking to Noah at that very moment. That maybe what I'd said has gotten him in trouble. And that if it *has*, I've definitely inked myself onto Noah's hit list.

Music Across the Ages turns out to be a stage show with pre-recorded music and a lot of dancing. And after we've survived the fabulous fifties and the psychedelic sixties, I look behind me at Marko and Darren and can tell that they're miserable.

"Let's go," I whisper to Marissa, and before she can argue, I'm excusing myself down the aisle, waving Darren and Marko along.

Marissa keeps whispering, "What? What?" like she has no idea why we're bailing.

Darren and Marko don't even question it. Marko just shakes his head when we're outside the theater and says, "Dude, we are gonna bomb tomorrow."

"Yup," Darren says, and he's looking really uncomfortable.

"Why?" Marissa asks. "And why did we leave?"

We all kind of stare at her. And finally I say, "Because Darren and Marko would rather be watching that jazz group—"

"Way!" Marko cries.

"And I'd rather be . . . anywhere else."

Marissa stares at us a minute, then says, "I thought there was an *emergency*."

Marko, Darren, and I look at each other, and at the same time we all say, "There was!" and then crack up.

Even though the Lute Lounge is a bar, no one kicks Marissa and me out. But while Darren and Marko are acting like they've died and gone to heaven, it doesn't take long for me to realize that I don't get jazz any more than I get dorky singing and dancing.

Plus, I can tell that Marissa is dying from boredom.

So finally I tell Darren, "You guys stay. Marissa and I are gonna head out."

"Where are you going?" he asks, like he can't believe I'm bailing on watching a guy noodle around on an old guitar.

"To message Casey and, I don't know—cruise around?"

"Tomorrow's kinda booked," he says with an apologetic little squint. "We've got the band meeting at noon, then we've got sound check and the two shows."

"We'll be fine," I tell him.

I can see him thinking. "How about we meet at the rooms at five tomorrow and regroup?"

"Sure."

So I start to take off, but he stands up and says, "Hey, hey, hey!"

"What?"

He puts his arms out.

"Seriously?"

"You're not getting out of here without one."

So I laugh and give him a hug, and he kisses the top of my head and tells me, "Have fun." And as we're leaving, Marko calls, "If you see the Kipster, tell him I've got sticks!" and waves with them.

When we're far enough away, Marissa gives me a big, gusting, "Thank you."

"Yeah, I didn't get it, either."

"So, first stop, the library?"

"Do you mind?"

"As long as you don't take forever!"

I laugh. "I just want to check in with Casey and tell him Darren thought my high-tops were cool."

"Promise?"

"Promise!"

Which, of course, turns out to be another promise I just can't keep.

TWENTY-SIX

Our walk up the stairs to the Lido Library is quiet until we reach the Deck 7 landing, where Marissa suddenly stops and goes, "That was *today?*"

I turn around to look at her. "What was today?"

"That we went snorkeling?"

I stop now, too, and rewind the day in my head. "Whoa."

"No wonder I'm so tired!" she says, catching up to me.

And she's right—all of a sudden, bed sounds really good.

"I hope the Puzzle Lady's not there," Marissa says as we go up the last flight.

"Me, too."

She eyes me. "Only because you were pretty rude to her before."

Which, ouch, I now can see is true. "Maaaaan."

She laughs. "If she's there, just tell her you're sorry."

Even thinking about doing that made me feel better. Plus, I was remembering that Marko had said he'd seen Teresa talking to her. It'd be nice to know if it had been about Kip, or if she had seen him since I'd wagged my flip-flops at her.

Anyway, by the time we reach the library door, I'm really hoping the Puzzle Lady *is* there, but it turns out she's not. And there's no Kipster in the corner sweating over codes, either.

"Rats," I grumble.

"You can apologize tomorrow," Marissa tells me, then waves me over to the puzzle table. "Check it out."

The puzzle's about three-quarters done and the picture hasn't gotten any less weird. There's the guy and the laughing skull in the tree, and under them are now two men digging up a treasure chest.

At least that's what it looks like to me. It's actually kind of hard to say, because the puzzle is like a faded photograph. You know—one of those black-and-white pictures that's turned a yellowy brown? And with all the little puzzle cuts, it really does look like a cracked and crinkled old photograph.

Then I notice that the rest of the pieces are nowhere. Not on the table, not in the table drawer, not in a box, nowhere.

"What are you looking for?" Marissa finally asks.

"The rest of the pieces! It's a whole section, so it's not like all of them can be missing."

"She probably took them with her, don't you think?"

"Why would she do that?"

"Maybe she doesn't want some upstart coming along and finishing it after she's done all the work?"

"Some upstart? Who would that be?"

Marissa shrugs. "Oh, anyone who might come to the library at, say, midnight when the rest of the world is either in bed or having actual fun somewhere."

I sit at a computer and log on. "Well, I think someone who spends their whole cruise working on an ugly puzzle that isn't even theirs and then hoards the pieces so no one else can work on it is missing more than a few pieces of her *brain*."

"Ah," Marissa says.

I whip around to look at her. "That was not funny."

"Was so," she giggles. "Actually, it was hilarious."

"Whatever," I grumble, and really, I don't want to think about the Puzzle Lady. I want to message Casey. So I send him a quick "Are you there?" and wait like a waggy little puppy at the back door. Trouble is, there's nobody home. And then I just sit there, staring at the screen, not knowing where to start.

"What's wrong?" Marissa asks when she notices that I'm not doing anything.

I shake my head. "I don't know what to say to him." And while I'm looking at her, it suddenly hits me that *she'll* be moving away soon. *Far* away. And if I'm having this feeling of a big gap with Casey after only four days, how in the world are Marissa and I going to stay connected over *years*?

How can we ever become the female version of Darren and Marko from across the country?

Marissa snaps me back into the here and now, saying, "You don't know what to say to him? What do you mean? You and Casey are *always* talking."

I look away. "You know how when someone asks how you are and you're miserable and a ton of stuff has happened and you don't know how to start, so you just say, 'I'm fine'?"

"Are you saying you're miserable?"

"No! I'm saying . . ."

And that's when it really sinks in that Darren's right—being there's important. There's no, you know, *substitute* for being there. You can tell a person all about where you've been and what you've done, but it's not the same thing as them being there during it. How could I explain about flip-flops and Fruity Island and *"¡Ándale!"* and snorkeling and dolphins and the symphony of nature? Or how I'd come to lock the cruise director and his mother out on a balcony? How could I explain about the fjishing I'd done while fjeasting with the captain? Or about finding forged notes in Bradley's pocket?

The whole day had been like looking for trolls in Norway.

You just had to be there.

"Sammy? Are you okay?"

I look at her, and I just feel like crying. "It's only been four days, and it already seems like there's this big . . . gap."

She leans in a little. "Between you and Casey?"

I nod.

"That's crazy!" She points to the keyboard. "Just start. Tell him about snorkeling. Tell him what Marko and Darren said about the shoes."

"But so much else happened today! And I have no idea what *he* did today."

"Yeah, and none of it really matters. What matters is you tell him that you miss him, stupid."

I can't help but laugh. "You have such a kind and gentle way with words."

"Start typing. I want to go to bed."

So I do and I wind up putting in plenty of mush 'cause, I don't know—I'm feeling plenty mushy. And when I'm all done and logged off, I look around for Marissa and see her over by one of the walls of books, her head cocked sideways as she reads the titles.

"You ready?" I ask her.

"You need to leave her a note," she says, not looking away from the books.

"Leave who a note?"

"The Puzzle Lady." She says it all matter-of-factly, then adds, "And none of this non-apology stuff. It needs to say *I'm* and *sorry*."

I let out a big ol' sigh, but I know she's right—a note is a good idea. Trouble is, when I go over to the printer station to get a piece of paper to write it on, the wastepaper basket catches my eye, and the next thing you know, I'm going through it.

"What *are* you doing?" Marissa asks when she figures out that I'm not doing any writing.

I keep looking through the pages from the top down. "I thought maybe there'd be a rough draft. Or maybe some evidence that Kip's been here today."

"A rough draft of what?"

"Of that *I'm OK* note."

She sits down nearby. "You really don't think Kip wrote it?"

"He's handwritten everything else, why would he suddenly type a note?" I get back to the papers, and I'm about to pass by one that looks like a whole lot of nothing—just a bunch of blue links and ads—but then the word *adoption* catches my eye.

"What's that?" Marissa asks, because I've taken it out to look over.

I check the footer. "It's page four of four."

"Of what?"

I look at the pages in the trash before and after it and say, "I'm not sure, but it's the last page of some article, and here under RELATED ARTICLES is a whole list of links about adoption."

"About adoption?"

"Yeah. Like, 'Costs of Adoption Lawyers,' 'Stepparent Adoptions,' 'Types of Adoptions' . . ."

"You're thinking Kip was here?"

"I'm thinking we should go to this site," I tell her, pointing to the tiny print in the footer.

So we go to the nearest computer, log on, and type in the URL of the site. And a split second later we're looking at a graphic of justice scales next to the name of the site—LegalAsk. And just below it, in bold black letters, is the title of the article that someone had taken the first three pages of: "Reversing an Adoption."

"Whoa!" Marissa whispers. Then she starts reading

the paragraph titles. "'Birth Parents Reversing an Adoption,' 'Adoptive Parents Reversing an Adoption,' 'Child/Adoptee Reversing an Adoption.'"

"Let's read that one," I whisper, pointing to the last one. And even though we're alone, my heart's whacking away, and whispering seems like the only way to talk.

So we both read the screen:

> Younger adoptees might wish to be emancipated from their adoptive parents. More commonly, though, adoptees wish to reverse their adoptions later in life due to failing personal relationships with their adoptive parents, or because they wish to inherit from their natural parents.

"Well, I don't think Kip would want to get unadopted for financial reasons," Marissa whispers. "It's more like he's hit the jackpot."

"Unless he hates being in that family so much, he's willing to give it all up to get out." I shake my head. "But I don't think Kip's the one who went here. I think it was Teresa."

"But . . . if she unadopts him, where would he go? Back to Kenya?"

I shake my head again and log off. "I have no idea how any of it works." Then I go back to the wastepaper basket, dig down to the bottom, and come up with . . . nothing.

"What *are* you looking for?" Marissa asks.

"At first I thought Teresa might have been here to print

out the *I'm OK* note, but there are no rough drafts in the trash."

"Sammy, who would need to practice writing *I'm OK*?"

"Well, sometimes you have an idea and then when you look at it, you come up with a better idea . . . you know."

She gives a little frown. "You're chasing wild geese again."

"The *point* is, there's nothing in the trash that has anything to do with the note, and there's also nothing with Kip's writing on it."

"So?"

"So I think Teresa was in here looking up information on reversing adoptions and had nothing to do with our note."

"So . . . you think it *was* Kip who left the note?"

I shake my head. "I think it was Noah. He has an office backstage, remember? It has to have a computer and printer in it."

She stares at me a minute, then says, "I don't like this."

I nod. "I don't, either."

We both sit there a minute until Marissa stands up and says, "Leave a note, and let's get out of here."

So I dig the pen out of my purse, rip a scrap from a sheet of mostly blank paper from the wastepaper basket, and write, *I'm sorry I was rude,* and sign it, *Sammy.*

"That's it?" Marissa says.

"It's got *I'm* and *sorry.* Meets all the requirements."

"How about *Dear Sue*? Or *Dear Ms. Taylor*?"

"Because she's *not* dear." I squint at her. "I can't believe you remember her name."

She gives a little shrug. "And I can't believe you remembered Kip's room number or parts of that crazy code." She gives me an exasperated sigh and says, "Just add it, would you?"

So I pout for a minute, and finally I write, *Hi, Ms. Puzzle Lady,* above what I've already written.

"'Ms. Puzzle Lady?'" Marissa cries. "You don't think that's rude?"

"No! I think it's . . . nice." I frown at her.

"Nice?"

"Yeah. Nice." I hold out the paper, studying it. "I don't see the word *crazy* anywhere on it." Then I add, "And if it's rude, why do you call her that?"

"Come on," she grumbles as she grabs me and drags me along. "I want to go to bed."

So I leave the note anchored under the puzzle, and when we get to our deck, I try to beat Marissa to the draw with the room key. And then remember.

"Rats!"

"What?"

"I forgot to switch keys with Marko!"

She swipes hers and laughs, "Guess you won't be sneaking out tonight."

Which should have been funny, but instead was like dropping a ton of bricks on me. "Oh, nooooooo!" I groan.

She turns around and sees that I'm serious. "What now?"

"Ms. Rothhammer's stupid work sheet."

Her eyes bug out at me. "No! I can't believe you're even thinking about it!"

"Marissa, I—"

"No! Just do it tomorrow. We're at sea all day. You'll have plenty of time. There's no way I'm letting you work on that tonight."

And then I remember something else—Darren still had my calculator. He'd put it in his coat pocket yesterday, and I'd never gotten it back from him.

But . . . he was wearing a different coat today.

And I *did* have their room key.

So I *could* go get it.

Marissa zeroes in on me. "What are you thinking?"

So I tell her.

"No!" she cries. "N-O, no!"

I know she's right. And letting myself into Marko and Darren's room seems really . . . wrong. Plus the idea of going back to the library in the middle of the night by myself was scary, so if I did my homework in the cabin, I'd be keeping Marissa awake. And I *was* really tired. I could tell because, homework aside, I didn't even want to look at Bradley's code sheet.

"I'm blocking the door," I tell Marissa, because I'm also remembering that Noah can get into anybody's room at any time.

"So . . . you're not arguing?"

I shake my head. "You're right—I'll catch up tomorrow."

"Thank you," she says, like a major miracle has just occurred.

We don't waste any time getting into bed. And when

my head hits the pillow, the whole cabin seems to spin a little—I am so, *so* tired.

But as I'm starting to drift off, I remember how the day had started, and a little giggle escapes me.

"What?" Marissa says through the dark.

"Why was six afraid of seven?" And before she can tell me to shut up and go to sleep, I giggle, "Because seven eight nine!"

"Go to sleep, Sammy."

"Night!"

And then I remember.

It was the *N* that had told the joke in my dream.

Noah.

TWENTY-SEVEN

After years of sleeping on a couch, I'm not used to sleeping in late. There's just not a whole lot of rolling over and stretching out and getting comfy on a couch. You hit the pillow and get in as many Z's as possible before you start feeling cramped, or wake up with your cat sleeping on your head because he couldn't find anyplace better to curl up.

Living at Hudson's now is better because I've got an actual *bed*, but I still wake up with Dorito suffocating me.

I don't think he quite knows what to do with himself yet.

Anyway, it turned out that having a bed to myself, no cat to suffocate me, and the Great Engine Lullaby humming through the night messed me all up. It probably also didn't help that the curtains were closed tight, making it pitch-black in the room, because when I woke up and saw the digital clock on the desk glowing 12:30, I thought, Wow, I've only been asleep for ten minutes?

And then it hit me that it had been twelve *hours*.

"Holy smokes. Marissa?"

"Hmm?" she groans.

I get up and go open the curtain. "It's after noon!"

"Close that," she snaps, then turns over and hikes up her covers. "Yesterday beat me up."

But it's really weird to be in the dark in the middle of the day, and it feels like shutting the curtains would be like sitting up in a coffin only to close the lid again.

Instead, I go over to the phone and punch in Darren's number, but all it does is ring and ring. "Rats," I grumble, putting down the phone.

Marissa sits up a little and glares at me. "Really?"

"Really, what?"

"The first thing you think about when you wake up is Kensingtons?"

"Who says I'm thinking about Kensingtons?"

"Who'd you just call?"

"Darren! I need my calculator."

"So the first thing you think about is *homework*?"

"Marissa! It's twelve-thirty! We have to meet Darren and Marko here at five! After that we've got the concerts. If I don't do my homework now—"

"You have all day tomorrow!"

"No! Stop that! I'm already behind schedule."

She flops back down and turns away from me. "Any schedule that has you doing homework on a cruise is a stupid schedule."

"Whatever. I'm going to go see if I can catch them at the buffet."

"Who?"

"Darren and Marko! They were having a band meeting up there at noon, remember? And if I don't catch them there, how will I find them? I need my calculator!"

So I get dressed as fast as I can, and I'm about to leave when Marissa groans, "Hang on. I'll go with you."

"Marissa, I'm in a hurry."

"I know, I know," she says, then pulls on a sweatshirt, shuffles into her flip-flops, and stumbles along after me in her ratty hair and sleep pants.

"You're going like that?"

She pulls her hair back into a ponytail. "You're complaining?"

"No. Fine. Come on, let's go."

So we hurry upstairs, and while she goes in one side of the Schooner Buffet U, I go in the other, and we meet up with each other in the middle.

"No luck?"

She just shakes her head.

And since I'm not too sure that she didn't just sleep-walk through her half of the search, I say, "Keep going and meet me at the front."

"By the elevators?"

"Yeah."

So I search the other half, but see no sign of trouble-makers of any kind, until I meet up with Marissa again and notice who's coming up the stairs.

"Uh-oh," I tell Marissa, and nod at JT and his parents.

Now, knowing Marissa, and considering how, uh, *ragged* she looks, I'm expecting her to either run and hide. Or freeze and be mortified. But instead she snarls and says, "Ask them about Kip."

"You're serious?" I whisper, 'cause that seems like a really gutsy—uh, make that *stupid*—thing to do.

But that's never stopped me before, and seeing how they're all of a sudden *right there,* I just smile at JT and say, "Hi. Hey, did you and your cousin patch things up?"

JT eyes Marissa with a sneer, then tells me, "Guess what. He's not actually my cousin."

"JT!" LuAnn says, practically biting off his head.

"Whatever," JT says, and keeps walking.

LuAnn and Lucas exchange looks, then hang back to smooth things over. "Sorry you girls have gotten caught in the middle of this," LuAnn says with a plasticky smile. "It's been a nightmare for all of us."

"So no word on Kate?"

Lucas shakes his head

"How about Kip?"

"Oh, I'm sure he's around here somewhere," Lucas says with a fake little laugh.

I tell him, "But nobody's seen him in, like, two days."

He does another fakey laugh. "As I said, I'm sure he's around here somewhere."

Something about LuAnn's plasticky smile and Lucas' fakey laughing and even the way they *look* is ticking me off. I mean, can you say spray-tan on rotten meat?

So before my brain can tell me, Whoa, girl, out of my mouth pops, "Or maybe knocking him off is just easier than unadopting him?"

Like a plastic bag thrown into a campfire, LuAnn's smile melts right off her face. "What are you talking about?"

But Lucas steps in with, "No, *why* did you just say that?" and he's not laughing anymore.

"You might want to ask Teresa," I tell him. "And while

you're at it, you might want to ask Bradley about faking suicide notes." I snap my fingers. "Or wait, maybe you all decided to do that together? It was your idea, right? Guess that's easier than waiting seven years for your inheritance or trying to figure out those coded notes."

The color is suddenly completely gone from Tan Man's face.

His wife's, too.

And LuAnn now looks like she's about to have a meltdown, so Lucas grabs her by the arm and tells me, "If you'll excuse us?" and hurries toward the buffet.

"By the way," I call after them, "Noah and Ginger know about the secret meeting in Teresa's room yesterday." Lucas whips around to look at me, so I give a little shrug. "Just sayin'."

Marissa zooms in on me as Lucas and LuAnn disappear inside the buffet, and, boy, is she looking wide awake. "Trying to get us killed once wasn't good enough for you? You have to go and do it *twice*?"

"Hey," I grumble. "Your idea."

"That was *not* my idea! My idea was to ask if they'd seen Kip, not to put them on the hot seat for murder!"

I take a deep breath. "Yeah, well, I got carried away."

"Again?!" And since I'm heading for the stairs, she grabs me and says, "Where are you going?"

"To find Marko and Darren?"

"But we don't know where they are!" She pinches her eyes closed and takes a deep breath. "Can we please get breakfast first?"

"You're serious?"

She sighs. "I'm starving."

Which didn't do much for my appetite, seeing how it made me remember what Kip had said about knowing what starving *really* meant. But I let her lead me back into the buffet, and as we pushed our trays around and hopped from island to island, all I picked up was an egg roll and a dish of Jell-O.

"That's all you're eating?" Marissa asks when we sit down.

"There is something just weird with that family."

Marissa smooths her napkin across her lap. "So quit worrying about them!"

I scan the room for Lucas and LuAnn. "And the notes. The notes make no sense."

"The coded notes or the *I'm OK* note or the non-apology note . . . ?"

"The coded notes. Why would someone leave notes that are impossible to decode? Why leave them at all?"

Marissa takes a whopping bite of eggs and says, "I think Kip left them."

I give her a little squint. "Why would he spend all day trying to decode a note he wrote?"

"To trick people into thinking he had nothing to do with them."

"I'm the only person who seems to care!"

Marissa swallows, swigs some lemonade, and says, "Well, notes are Kip's MO. Plus, he's sneaky and known for doing stuff like researching relatives on the Internet and then ratting on them. He can memorize people's pass codes and has probably snooped through their private accounts."

"Who says?"

"Kip practically confessed to it himself!"

Which was kinda true.

And very . . . unsettling.

"Still," I tell her. "Nobody would *kill* someone over that."

She frowns. "Unadopting did look pretty complicated."

"But . . . why would you look up how to unadopt someone if you'd already killed them?"

"Well, obviously, *she* didn't."

"But who besides Teresa would want to get rid of him? You don't throw someone overboard just because they annoy you or rat on you!"

"Sammy! Nobody's saying he's been thrown overboard but you!"

"Well, where is he, then?"

She heaves a sigh. "Avoiding other Kensingtons? Look, most of their inheritance has to go to building a hospital in Africa. Kip's from Africa. Kip and his grandfather were close. Everyone probably blames Kip for all of it."

"But that's not fair! Or rational!"

"Money makes people irrational," she says, spearing a sausage link with her fork. "Now eat, would you?"

So I ate. And the whole time I'm eating, I'm thinking about the stupid Kensingtons. Sorting things that had happened. Just like when Kate went missing, nobody seemed to be *doing* anything about Kip disappearing. It was like they didn't want to admit or have anyone else notice that he was gone.

Which got me wondering . . . what happens when a kid adopted from another country disappears?

Who's going to notice?

"Stop it," Marissa finally says. Then she sighs and says, "I can't believe I'm about to say this, but even doing homework is better than doing this."

"Yeah, let's go."

So we head back down to Deck 9, only I still don't have my room key, and I still don't have my calculator.

"Just let yourself in," Marissa says. "He's your *dad*. It's *okay*." She kind of scowls at me as she opens our door and leads me inside. "Besides, how many times have you *broken* in somewhere, huh?"

Which was true.

And not something I really wanted to think about.

"Sammy." She sighs and then just stands there, looking at me.

"What?"

"He won't be mad." She sits down on the bed. "He thinks you're awesome, can't you tell?" And since I'm still not budging, she goes, "Look. You're *family*. Family can take, you know, liberties."

"But . . . we're *barely* family." I look down. "It's like *I'm* adopted into this weird situation."

She studies me for the longest time, then finally says, "Maybe you and Kip were both surprises, but you and Darren are *nothing* like Kip and Teresa. Darren thinks having you as a daughter is awesome. Teresa . . . well, Teresa's obviously never been much of a mother." She shakes her head. "She should never have agreed to adopt him."

Her words seem to hang in the air.

Circle through the silence.

I blink at her and whisper, "Holy smokes."

"What?"

"Holy smokes!" I say louder.

"Holy smokes, what?"

Then my eyes practically pop out of my head and I jump off the bed. "HOLY SMOKES!"

If I was right, the Kensingtons *did* have a reason to want Kip gone.

A *big* one.

TWENTY-EIGHT

I explain what I'm thinking to Marissa, and she just sits there on the edge of her bed with her jaw dropped and her eyes popped. Finally, she says, "Whoa."

"Exactly. And now I really am worried about Kip."

"Take a deep breath," she tells me, taking a deep breath. So I do.

"What do we do with this information?" she asks.

"It's not information, it's a theory."

"What do we do about your theory?"

She's trying to be all calm and collected, but neither of us is feeling calm *or* collected. Especially not me.

"Okay," she says. "Telling Noah is out, would you agree?"

"Yes."

"And the captain is not your biggest fan."

I frown. "Neither is Ginger. And obviously the rest of them are out."

We think a minute, and then Marissa says, "Do you want to call guest relations?"

"Guest relations?"

"That's where you go if you have a problem."

"This isn't a *problem*. This is a possible *murder*."

"Which *is* a problem for Kip," she points out. "And Kate."

"Marissa!"

"What? I'm trying to think! What other choices do we have?"

My brain scrambles around for an answer. "Okay, if Teresa hasn't reported him missing—"

"Which, if your theory is right, she won't."

"And if there's no missing person reported by the parent, then there's no reason to investigate!" I shake my head. "And who's going to believe *us*?"

We both sit there, thinking some more, and then Marissa says, "And Saturday morning, when we walk off the ship, it'll be easy to cover everything up. All anyone will have to say is that he ran away from home."

We sit there some more, and finally Marissa says, "So what are we going to do?"

And that's when I know exactly what I want to do. "We're going to wait for Darren and Marko to get back," I tell her. "They'll help us."

"Wow," she says, studying me. "That is very . . . sensible."

There were a lot of other things she *could* have said, so *sensible* was actually a pretty big compliment. "Yeah, well, I'm fourteen now, right?"

She eyes me. "The shadow of thirteen has definitely been following you, though. Or maybe that's just you." Then, before I can say anything, she says, "We should stick together today. Especially after the way you mouthed off to JT's parents."

"Maaan," I moan. "What a mistake."

She pulls a face. "Usually is." Then she says, "But I sure don't want to be locked up in here until Darren and Marko get back, so how about we go to the library and I cruise the Internet while you do your homework?"

I blink at her and say, "You're serious?" 'cause, come on—I've pretty much ruined the cruise, and doing homework when we could be swimming or eating yogurt or rock climbing or doing *anything* else seems obsessive and unnecessary and stupid.

Even to me.

But she smiles at me and says, "Yeah, come on, let's go get your calculator."

I reach over and gave her a mondo hug, and promise myself that no matter how far apart we live, Marissa McKenze and I will stay friends forever.

I did call Darren's room again, and when there was no answer, I did think about trying to track him down. But in the end I did what Marissa said.

I let myself into his room.

"Hello?" I called, just in case, and when nobody answered, I stepped inside and checked the closet, which was right inside the doorway, like ours.

Trouble is, I didn't see the coat I remembered him wearing the night he'd taken the calculator from me, and I didn't want to just start pawing around. So I went over to the desk, thinking he might have taken it out and left it there.

Marissa follows me, and when I don't see the calculator, I tell her, "I am *not* going to start digging through drawers."

"So you'll do that in a stranger's place but not your own dad's?"

"Stop that! I don't think Darren and Marko are hiding bodies or people or . . . or are agents of foul play!"

She snickers. "Agents of foul play?"

"Stop it," I snap. "You're the one who started the whole foul-play thing!" And then I spot the coat Darren had been wearing. It's hung over the back of a small chair, in the corner by his guitar, and when I go over to it, I see Darren's empty Coke bottle from Cabo San Lucas propping up our cheesy say-cheese picture on his nightstand.

"Ohhhh," Marissa whispers when she sees me staring at it. "How sweet is that?" Then she spots an open notebook on the chair and whispers, "Is that a journal?"

"No snooping!" I tell her, but as I'm digging through the pockets of the coat, I can't help but notice that it's *not* a journal.

It's a lyrics book.

A lyrics book with chords and a lot of scribbles and scratched-out words and funny doodles.

And across the top of the page, in block letters, is *Nothing but Trouble*, which seems like a nice little song for a band named the Troublemakers.

So yeah, I'm feeling embarrassed and like a total nosy invader, but I do find the calculator and the paper I'd made notes on when I'd been brainstorming with Kip, so at least I feel justified in being there. "Got it!" I tell Marissa. "Now let's go!"

But on our way out, I decide I should leave Marko's sea-pass card and a note. So I use the notepad and pen on the desk, and I'm planning to just scrawl out something quick, starting with an apology for coming into the room, but the explaining and apologizing and promising that I hadn't snooped take forever, and then one thing leads to another and pretty soon I'm on my fifth page of the note-pad and Marissa's bored out of her mind, going, "What are you doing? Writing a book?" as she's trying on hats and sunglasses.

Finally, on the *seventh* page I tell him that we'll be in the Lido Library, or in our rooms . . . or maybe at the buffet . . . and that I have something important to tell him about Kip, so to please find us if they get back before five. *Then* I sign off, and we get out of there.

When we get back to our room, I stuff the calculator in my backpack, and after Marissa gets officially dressed, we head down to the library.

Now, normally when I'm all caught up in figuring something out, I do nothing but think about the situation. But this time I'm actually trying to keep my mind *off* Kip because I know that confronting the Kensingtons with my theory is a very bad idea. If I'm right, Kate going missing and Kip going missing are linked by one evil motive, and Marissa's right—mouthing off about it is going to get me nothing but killed.

It makes me feel safer that there are quite a few other

people in the library, and I'm secretly relieved that the Puzzle Lady's not one of them. "The note's still there," Marissa tells me as I scope out a place to work. "And the puzzle's the same as it was yesterday."

It flashes through my mind that it would be nice to be able to ask the Puzzle Lady what she and Teresa had talked about, and confirm that Teresa had used a computer, but I tell myself to get my mind off the Kensingtons until I can talk to Darren and figure out what to do.

So after I've logged Marissa on to Darren's account, I get situated at a table and force myself to focus on Ms. Rothhammer's work sheet.

It hadn't been that long since I'd done the first six problems, but the awful thing was that when I read the next one, I couldn't remember how to set it up, and I found myself getting frustrated all over again. What did I care what the molarity of 750 milliliters of a solution containing 25 grams of potassium bromide was?

What did *anybody* care?

I went back and tried walking through the work I'd shown on the problem before, and it *sort of* brought back how to do it, but it was still feeling kind of fuzzy, so I dug up Kip's notes.

Just seeing his writing made me feel bad. I didn't want to think about where he might be, or how he probably had no idea why everyone had turned on him.

Not that *I* knew for sure, but when something makes everything else make sense, it's probably true.

Anyway, I shook away those thoughts and focused on Kip's step-by-step notes. And pretty soon a kind of calm

Aaah swept over my brain. *That's right,* it murmured, *first find the atomic mass.*

So I took the periodic table and went hunting for potassium. Which turned out to be like hunting for gold—tricky. Instead of potassium's symbol being a P—which apparently phosphorus got dibs on first—it was a K.

That's right, a K.

Don't ask me.

Bromine was also tricky—first, because it was *bromine* and not *bromide* that I had to look up, and second, because although it did start with *B,* there were a lot of other elements that did, too. Like boron and beryllium and barium and bohrium and bismuth! And if you've ever seen the table you know that the elements aren't anywhere *close* to being in alphabetical order. They're just randomly scattered around.

Well, okay, they're grouped by *type* of element, but not knowing whether bromine was a gas or a metal or a *transition* metal or whatever made it really hard for me to find.

But eventually I did.

It's a halogen, by the way.

And a liquid.

Or just element 35 on your periodic table, in case you ever have Ms. Rothhammer.

Anyway, I followed Kip's notes and when I'd finished the first two problems, I was feeling better. So I tried to do the next one on my own. The problem had lithium sulfate in it, so this time the first thing I did was check Ms. Rothhammer's little chemical key for the formula, which turned out to be Li_2SO_4.

283

Lithium was easy to find because when I search for an element, I start at number 1, hydrogen, and read my way back and forth across the chart. And since lithium is the third element, I didn't have to read very far.

I already knew where oxygen was because I'd used it a lot, so that was a snap, and I spotted sulfur right under oxygen—no hunting required!

So I wrote out

$$Li = 6.94$$
$$O = 16.00$$
$$S = 32.07$$

And I was getting ready to multiply lithium's 6.94 by 2 and oxygen's 16.00 by 4, so I could add their products to sulfur's 32.07 and calculate the molecular weight of lithium sulfate, when a little *click* happens in my brain. And that little click starts what feels like an *earthquake* inside of me. At first it's a rumbling. A rolling of cells starting at my core, moving outward.

Then my body starts to tremble.

And my hands start to shake.

"Holy smokes!" I gasp, and then start scouring the periodic table.

Sure enough, there is no element L.

Only Li.

I write out *LIONN,* and above the *LI* I put lithium's atomic number: 3.

O is oxygen—element 8. So I write an 8 above the *O.* And N is nitrogen—element 7. So I write 7s above the *N*s.

Then I check the periodic table for any other possible combinations in *LIONN* that might stand for elements. Like Io or On or Nn.

There are none.

Using the periodic table as a decoder, the only possible translation is the number 3877.

My heart's whacking away because it feels like I've discovered the secret formula that will explain all the Kensington madness.

The real test is, will the number combinations translate into words?

TWENTY-NINE

When I'd returned Marissa's purse after our dinner with the captain, I'd stuffed Bradley's forgeries and the coded message paper into the little front pouch of my backpack for safekeeping.

So now I scramble to dig out the coded note and go straight for the first combination: 90 – 49 – 19.

90 on the periodic table is thorium, Th.

49 is indium, In.

And 19 is potassium, K.

My heart's going crazy, because what I've just decoded is definitely a word.

Think.

"Marissa!" I hiss across the room. "Pst! Marissa!"

"What?" she says, coming over.

I'm already busy on the next set of numbers: 4 – 39 – 8 – 60, and above each number I write the letters of the element it corresponds to.

Be – Y – O – Nd.

Beyond.

Marissa gasps. "You've got to be kidding me."

I've only got the next group of numbers translated to Mo and Ne when Marissa gets all excited and whispers, "Money!"

And she's right. The 39 is yttrium, which is Y.

She is totally excited now and whispers, "It's obvious, now that you've figured it out—they're chemists!"

"Well, the father was anyway."

"And Noah's into bad chemistry jokes."

I nod. "And Kip's a chemistry wiz."

She sits down next to me, all excited. "Let's do the rest!"

So we do, and in the end the message decodes to: *Think beyond money—kindness is essential. Find clarification in cabin 3877.*

"Wow," Marissa whispers, and after we both stare at it a minute, she says, "What does this *mean*?"

"It means we should go to cabin 3877."

"Us?" Her eyes get all big. "Sammy, this is not our mess! It's Bradley's and Teresa's and Lucas'!"

"Fine," I tell her as I pack up my stuff. "Let's have a convergence of Kensingtons."

"A convergence of—Sammy, no!"

But I'm already out in the elevator area, making a bee-line for the ship phone.

"Sammy, please, can we *think* about this?"

Which, yeah, probably would have been mature and, you know, *prudent,* but I was only three days into fourteen and not used to the responsibility yet. "I'm going to tell them to come here, okay? We'll stay in public."

She shakes her head like crazy as I punch in 9584 and wait as it rings.

"Rats," I say, putting down the phone.

"You can't expect them to be in their rooms."

"What else are they doing but hiding from each other and waiting for the cruise to be over so they can escape?" I think a minute and say, "Fore is minus two in cabin numbering, right?"

"What?"

But I'm sure it is, so I pick up the phone again and punch in 9582—Lucas and LuAnn's cabin number. And my heart is really jackhammering now because I'm remembering how I'd mouthed off at them this morning.

"Sammy," Marissa pleads, "we really need to wait for Darren and Marko."

There's no answer, which leaves Bradley's room. And there's no way I'm going near *that*—or the Royal Suite.

I look at Marissa. "How do you dial guest services?"

She looks relieved. "Dial zero and just ask."

So I do, and when there's someone on the line, I go, "Can you connect me to the Royal Suite?"

Marissa moans, "No!" but two rings after I'm transferred, the phone is snatched up.

"Ginger?" I ask, because there are loud voices in the background, but I didn't actually hear anyone say hello.

And then, even though I can tell there's a hand over the receiver, I hear Ginger's voice screech, "QUIET!" Then she comes on the line with, "Who's this?"

I twist the phone a little so Marissa can hear, too. "It's Sammy. We figured out the code."

There's dead silence for a minute and then over the receiver she calls, "Kip's friends figured out the code!"

"Who has?" I hear in the background. It's a man's voice. I think Lucas'. "Are you talking about those horrible girls?"

"Come over!!" Ginger says to me. "We're all here!"

Marissa shakes her head like crazy, and even burning with code-cracking fever, I know she's right. "There's no way I'm coming up there," I tell Ginger. "You guys need to come down to the Lido Library on Deck 8."

Then I hang up the phone.

Marissa covers her mouth with both hands. "I'm scared."

"As long as we're in public, we're okay," I tell her. Only we're all alone and already we hear feet pounding down the steps.

"No!" Marissa gasps, then yanks me toward the library door.

Only it's not a stampede of Kensingtons.

It's Darren and Marko. "Just got your note," Darren pants, and Marko's got his sticks together in one hand like a sword. "What's going on?"

"The Kensingtons are coming!" Marissa cries.

And there really is no time to explain, because now there *is* a stampede coming down the stairs, and Bradley's actually elbowing his brother back to get to us first. "What's the message?" Bradley demands, and he's looking like he never took a shower or even changed his clothes.

I kind of gulp, 'cause he's big and angry and ugly.

Like a pig-eyed, hungover, balding bull.

"I've got it right here," I tell him, trying to make my voice steady as I hold up his sheet. "But first you have to tell me where Kip is."

"Hey, that's mine!" he says, zeroing in on his name on the back of the paper. "How'd you get that?"

I pull it back a little. And since Darren and Marko are flanking me, I guess I'm feeling kind of brave, 'cause I tell him, "Guess you shouldn't pass out in public places. Stuff might fall out of your pockets. Like this and, oh, forged suicide notes."

Lucas and Teresa look at him with darts shooting from their eyes, and then Bradley comes at me like he's going to throttle me.

"Back off, buddy!" Marko says, jabbing him in the gut with his drumsticks, and Darren's fist is cocked and definitely not locked.

Bradley backs down but he's still pawing at the ground, and when I ask about Kip again, Lucas tells me, "It's a family matter," and Teresa has the nerve to say, "And your meddling is not appreciated!"

"Oh, really," I tell her. "Is that because you've deciphered the note yourself? Or is it because you're afraid I'll find out what happened to Kip?" I stare her down a minute, then decide to just go for it. "Because you know what? I figured it out—he's *not* your son. He's legally your brother. You wouldn't adopt him, so your father wound up doing it. Which means Kip gets a fourth of the inheritance. Which means the three of you have to share with a Kensington who doesn't look or sound or act like any of you."

"He's *not* a Kensington!" Lucas shouts.

"Tell it to the judge," I snap back. Then I add, "And if you guys have hurt him? We're gonna make sure you wind up paying."

And yeah, I'm totally shooting from the hip, and no, I don't know how we're gonna make sure they wind up paying, or *prove* anything, for that matter, but it doesn't seem to matter to Darren and Marko. They just stand there on either side of me, rock solid.

Then Marko growls, "So where's the Kipster?"

The Kensingtons give him a kind of blank look, and then Lucas says, "I have no idea."

"Neither do I," Bradley says.

So everyone turns to Teresa. "Me? I had nothing to do with it!" She looks at Bradley. "I thought *you* did."

Bradley looks at Lucas. "I thought *you* did."

"Did what?" Marko asks, then steps up with a stick in each hand. "If you idiots so much as laid a hand on him, I'm gonna do more than call the cops!"

"I didn't touch him!" they all cry, and although it's pretty clear that they all thought he was missing because one of the others had bumped him off and were just *fine* with that, none of them looks guilty.

"Now give me my paper!" Bradley bellows.

I squint at them. "Seriously?" And maybe I should have just told them to go look up a periodic table online and have at it, but suddenly I *got* that Marissa was right about the Puzzle Lady taking the last handful of pieces with her.

She'd done all the work.

She wanted to finish the job herself.

And then something else hits me. "Where's Ginger?"

The Kensingtons look back at the stairs, but if Ginger was coming, she would have been down ages ago.

My mind flashes to her being in the horde of people waiting for the elevator the morning we'd gone to Cabo San Lucas.

"Can she do stairs okay?" I ask.

"She does them *fine*," Teresa says, all full of disgust.

My mind goes back to that morning in Cabo San Lucas again.

Why would anyone wait an hour for an elevator to take them from the Schooner Buffet on Deck 11 to the Royal Suite on Deck 10? It's *down* one little flight of stairs.

And, like a tidal wave, it hits me.

She wasn't going to the Royal Suite.

"You know what?" I tell the lousy lot of them. "I know where she is."

"Where who is?" Lucas asks.

I head for the stairs. "Ginger! And your mother!"

"How can you know where our mother is?" Bradley asks, chasing after me.

"Maybe *she's* the one who made the codes!" Lucas cries.

"Or that damn kid put her up to it!" Teresa says. "I'd bet my last dollar he's behind *all* of this!"

"Who are you talking about?" I call up to her. "JT? Or your little brother?" Then I add, "And I don't think any of you have much of a last dollar to bet, do you? Trust funds all gone?"

"Shut up!" she screeches.

"Hey!" Marko yells, whipping around with his sticks. "Mind your measly manners."

I keep pounding down the stairs, my hands snugging my backpack straps tight so it won't bounce, while Marissa, Marko, and Darren form a protective U around me. "Where are we going?" Darren whispers.

"Down to Deck 3," I whisper back.

"Where are we going?" Bradley shouts, and he's already lagging about half a flight behind.

I ignore him and keep flying down the stairs.

"Answer me!" Bradley shouts. "Where are we going?"

Marko looks back up at him. "I know where *you're* goin', dude. Better get your heat suit on!"

Marissa snickers. "Get me a corn husker!"

"Hey, it was funny, didn't you think?" Marko whispers.

"It was right next to funny," Darren tells him.

"Sorta like the sidekick of funny," Marissa adds, and Darren and Marissa actually reach over my head and slap five on each other.

"I'm takin' that as an extreme compliment," Marko says. "'Cause sidekicks are always funnier than the main guy."

"It's true," I tell him over my shoulder. "And by the way, *I* thought it was funny."

"See?"

I grin at him. "You can be my sidekick anytime."

"I'm there!" he cries.

We're a whole deck ahead of the Kensingtons now, and Lucas yells, "You people are rude and crude and inconsiderate."

"And you're selfish and shallow and *slow*," I shout up to him, which for some reason makes Marko and Darren crack up.

And then there we are on Deck 3. I turn to Marissa and ask, "Where would cabin 3877 be?"

She thinks for a nanosecond and says, "Interior cabin, port side, aft."

"Lead on!"

So she does, and behind us I hear Lucas cry, "There they go!" as we disappear down a hallway.

"You realize we have no idea what you're doing, right?" Darren asks.

"I'm just glad you're with me," I tell him. And then there it is—cabin 3877.

Trouble is, there's a note taped to the door.

A note I was not expecting.

THIRTY

I'd have recognized the handwriting anywhere. And by the time I've peeled the note off the door, the Kensingtons are swarming around.

Lucas reads over my shoulder, " 'Go back to the Royal Suite'? What *is* this?!"

"A wild goose chase, obviously!" Bradley pants.

"Tell us what the note says!" Teresa demands.

So I shove Kip's note at her and say, "Here. See if you can manage to decode it." Then I push through all of them and head for the stairs.

"Not *this* note!" Teresa cries, like *I'm* the idiot.

Darren, Marissa, and Marko are right behind me, and as we charge back up the steps, Darren says, "Do we know why we're going back to the Royal Suite?"

"No," I tell him quietly. "I thought for sure Kate was down here, but that note was in Kip's handwriting."

When we make the first turn, I notice that the Trust Fund Trio are jabbing at the elevators.

At *all* the elevators.

Which means that the race is on, and with us having to go seven decks up, it's going to be close.

"I'm not sure I want to go back to the Royal Suite," Marissa says as we charge up the steps. "Not after what happened earlier!"

"What happened earlier?" Darren asks.

I look at Marissa like, Uh-oh, which Darren totally catches.

"Out with it," he pants. "What don't I know?"

"Uh . . . we were looking for Kip and things got kinda . . ."

"Kinda what?"

I pull a face. "Kinda out of control?"

"Now, *that's* an understatement," Marissa says.

"Marissa!"

"Well, it is!" Then she totally rats on me. "She locked Noah and Ginger out on the balcony so we could case the joint."

"We weren't casing the joint!" I tell him as I huff and puff along. "We were looking for Kip! And Kate! And any sign of . . . you know, foul play!"

"She locked Noah the Noose on a balcony?" Marko asks. "You're serious?"

"As a heart attack!" Marissa says. "Which is what he practically gave me when he appeared out of nowhere and grabbed me by the arm."

Darren looks at her, kind of wild-eyed. "How could he do that when he was locked out on the balcony?"

"He escaped," I tell him. "He must have gone under

the balcony divider, through Bradley's suite next door, and back in through the Royal Suite's front door."

"He was fast, too," Marissa pants. "Like, *poof*, there he was. It was scary!"

Darren's face seems to be frozen in some painful contortion as he asks me, "So how'd you get away?"

Again, Marissa blurts out the answer. "She hurled the urn through the air!"

"What urn?"

"The one with the grandfather's ashes in it!"

Darren's face is even more pained than it was before. "You hurled an urn of ashes into the air?"

"So Noah'd let go of Marissa to catch it!" I cry. "So we could escape! Which we did!"

We're now at the Deck 8 landing, and as we charge up the next flight of stairs, Darren mutters, "I'm starting to understand your grandmother better."

Which actually makes me feel terrible. "Look, I was just trying to find out what happened to Kip, okay?"

"Well, obviously, he's fine," Marissa says.

"Ginger must've called down there when the others raced to meet us at the library," I pant out. "How else could they have known we were coming?"

"They?" Darren asks.

My brain's racing as fast as my feet. "I'm thinking that Kate must've been down there, too, and that Kip figured out the code and found her."

"So you think the Diamond Dame is behind all this?" Marko asks.

"From what's in the message, I'd say she has to be."

"We haven't even seen the message, you know," Darren says, and he's sounding kinda disgruntled.

So I hand it over and tell him, "The periodic table turned out to be the decoder. I figured it out while I was doing my homework."

He reads it and frowns as he hands it over to Marko. "*You* figured it out. A family of chemists, and you're the one who decodes it for them?" He gives me a proud-papa look and says, "My child is a genius!"

I can feel my cheeks flush, and I'm about to say something about the Kensington "kids" not actually being chemists, when Marko hands the note back to me and I notice that while the rest of us are gasping for air, he's not breathing hard at all. He's just jogging along while we're all dying. And apparently he can read minds—or faces—because he grins at me and says, "I've basically run in place a couple of hours at a stretch several nights a week for my entire life. This is a nice little warm-up for tonight."

And that's when I remember.

They've got two shows to do!

"Have you even got time for this?" I ask Darren as we come to the Deck 10 landing.

"I haven't got time to miss this," he says back. And even though I'm not sure what that means, I like the way it sounds.

"The Troublemakers take it by a mile!" Marko announces, pumping a fist in the air when he sees that there are no Kensingtons in sight.

So we beeline for the Royal Suite door and ring the bell, and while we're waiting for the door to open, one of the elevators dings open, and over my shoulder I see Bradley step out, followed by Lucas and Teresa.

And then the Royal Suite door opens and I find myself face to face with a man.

A man I've never seen before.

And I'm about to say, "Who are *you*?" because all of a sudden *nothing* is making sense—only then it hits me that, yes, I *have* seen him before.

In the picture that was next to the urn.

And, *click,* using the periodic table of elements as a decoder now makes *total* sense.

"Dr. Kensington?" I gasp.

"Sammy," he says with a kind smile. "Kip has told me all about you."

Behind me I hear gasps and "It can't be," and "What *is* this?" and a breathy "Oh, no!" come out of the Kensington kids.

Now, maybe Dr. Kensington's not a young guy anymore, but his hearing must still be sharp, because he raises an eyebrow and says, "Oh, *yes*. And what this *is,* Bradley, is a test. Which you all failed miserably." Then he moves aside and tells his kids, "Your mother and brother are waiting. Get in here."

"Who's this guy?" Darren whispers to me as the Kensington kids file past us without a word.

"The dead dad," I whisper back.

When Darren realizes what we're actually dealing with, the cool rocker in him disappears. He locks eyes with

Dr. Kensington and says, "You faked your death? What kind of sick thing is that to do to your kids?"

Dr. Kensington's eyebrows both go for a stretch now. "They're grown adults," he tells him. "And desperate times call for desperate measures." Then he adds, "And they're clearly more upset to discover I'm alive than they were when they thought I was dead."

"And what does that say about *you*?" Darren says, totally not letting him off the hook. "My poor daughter here has been really worried about Kip. You're saying he's been with you this whole time? And your wife's just fine, too? What kind of sick game was this?"

I hold out Bradley's deciphered code to the Walking Dead Guy and tell him, "Yeah, I'm wondering whose idea the 'kindness is essential' part was? Because there's nothing nice about any of this."

"What are you doing with Bradley's copy?" he asks, taking it from me.

"It sorta fell out of his pocket when he was passed out drunk in the casino." I swing off my backpack and dig up the forged suicide note. "Along with this."

His face flushes red when he realizes what he's looking at.

Kate comes up behind him and says, "I'm so very sorry about all of this. Won't you come in?"

Dr. K. looks at her like, What? Are you crazy? And he actually says, "Kate, this is a family matter."

But she gives him a stern look and tells him, "Not anymore. Our children couldn't be bothered to figure out your message, but she did. She and Kip were the only ones who cared enough to even try." She reaches out and pulls me in while she keeps looking at her husband. "As hard as it was, and as much as I didn't want to, I went along with your charade. Now you're going to allow this. We owe her and her family an explanation."

"All of them?" he gasps.

"If you think we're letting her inside without us, you're certifiable," Marko tells him.

But then I realize that I don't want to go inside. I don't care about their stupid family feud. I don't want to hear them bicker and blame. Besides, Darren and Marko have a concert to put on!

So I tell Kate, "Thanks, but maybe it's better if we don't."

"But we owe you an explanation! And an apology!"

I step back outside. "Tomorrow's probably better."

"That's fine," she says with a smile. "Anytime that works for you. But promise me you'll come back."

I can see Kip sort of hovering a few steps behind Kate now. And although I probably should be mad at him, it hits me how the poor guy's really stuck in limbo. His best friend and mentor is a man who faked his death to teach his other kids a lesson, he'll never really be a real brother to the other Kensington kids, and they'll probably resent him forever for things that weren't his fault.

And since I don't really know what happened or completely understand the situation, it doesn't seem fair to snub him. So I give him a little wave, and when he gives me a grateful smile and a little wave back, I turn to Kate and ask, "Uh, does Kip have to be at your meeting?"

She sort of stares at me, and I can tell she's not sure how she should answer.

So I say, "I think after everything he's been through, you should let him go to a rock concert."

"A rock concert!" Dr. K. says, like it's the most absurd thing he's ever heard of.

But Kate puts an arm around Kip's shoulders and asks him, "Would you like to?" and when his head bobs, she says, "I think that's a fine idea." Then she asks him, "You're staying here, right? You've got your key?" and when he nods again, she tells him, "Well, have fun."

"Dude," Marko calls over to him, and holds up his sticks.

Dr. K. looks at his wife like she's lost her mind. "Dude?"

But Kip's already busting out of the Royal Suite with a total kid grin all over his face. "Awesome!"

"Awesome?" Dr. K. says, with his eyebrows all haywire.

"Come on, dear," Kate says, pulling her husband away from the door. "We're in for a long night and I think Kip's been locked up with us long enough. Besides, he already knows everything we're going to tell the others, so let him enjoy some time with his friends." Then she waves at me and calls, "Don't forget to come back tomorrow!"

So Kip escapes with us, and when we get to the stairs, I ask, "Is anyone else hungry?" because all of a sudden I'm starving.

Darren shakes his head. "Marko and I have to get ready for the show."

"Dude, we've got time," Marko tells him.

"No, dude, we don't." Then Darren turns to me and

says, "You'll be at the show, right?" like he's worried something else might happen.

"We'll be at both of them," I tell him. And since he's looking kinda doubtful, I laugh and say, "No sidetracks or falling overboard."

"Or locking crazy people on balconies?"

I laugh, "Promise."

Then Marissa puts on her best puppy-dog face and begs, "Can we pleeeeeease be backstage during the second show?"

Darren laughs, "Of course," which makes Marissa pump a fist and go, "Yes!"

So while Darren and Marko head down the stairs to Deck 9 so they can do their pre-show showering or rock star primping or whatever, the three of us go up to the Schooner Buffet. And this time, *boy,* I load up! I do the whole buffet line and hit all the islands, plus fill up two glasses of pink lemonade.

"So," I tell Kip when we're sitting down. "Start talking. Whose insane idea was all this?"

"Grandfather's," he says, and there's not even a hint of him acting like a secret-keeping Kensington. "Apparently the last time he and Grandmother were in Kenya on business, Bradley, Lucas, and Teresa all called him several times asking for money. He was in a very poor part of the country where there were starving kids and really bad conditions, and he decided his own kids were greedy and spoiled and didn't deserve another dollar. He wanted to cut them out of the will, but Grandmother argued against it. But then Grandfather got really sick with some virus and thought he was going to die in Africa. Nobody told me anything about it, but Grandmother told the rest of them, and instead of flying out to see him, they tried to get the lawyer to tell them what was in his will. When Grandfather heard about that, he got so disgusted that he came up with the idea of faking his own death to prove to Grandmother that all the three of them cared about was money."

"Looks like your grandfather was right," I tell him with a frown.

Kip sighs. "Yeah. It's pretty sad."

"So who all was in on this? And when did *you* find out?"

"At first it was just Grandmother, but after the big blowout over me being in line to inherit a quarter of the estate—which I had no idea about—she told Ginger, and Ginger got Noah involved."

I make a little face. "I think we got Noah in trouble with the captain."

Kip nods. "He's been 'relieved of his duties.' But now that everything's out, I'm sure Grandmother'll find a way to fix all that."

"So your grandfather was on board the whole time," I mutter.

He nods. "Down in cabin 3877."

"And Kate just couldn't take the way her kids were acting, so she went to hide out with him?"

"Right. Only they didn't stay locked in the cabin the whole time. They went out in disguises."

"They did?"

"Grandmother told me she *loved* going out in disguise and spying. You would never have recognized her, either.

She wore a black pantsuit with a black wig and had a gnarly mole on her lip—"

"That was *Kate*?" Marissa and I cry.

"You saw her?"

"She had a cane, right?" I ask. "And a big, ugly plastic necklace? And sunglasses?"

"Yes! That was her!"

I think a minute, then say, "That day we were trying to find Noah backstage . . . Ginger was getting Kate a disguise?"

He nods.

"Wow," I laugh. "Hiding in plain view, just like Darren and Marko."

"She and Grandfather eavesdropped on the others like crazy." He eyes me and says, "By the way, she called Kensington Clue 'eye-opening.'"

"She did?"

He nods. "She said that after she got over the shock of it, she thought it was funny, too." He takes a deep breath. "She also said that what you guys seem to have as family and friends is something money can't buy . . . but sure can destroy."

"Whoa. That's deep," Marissa murmurs, and I know she can relate—money's the thing that destroyed Marissa's family, and I'm pretty sure that no amount of it will ever patch it back together.

Anyway, Kip goes on to tell us how Ginger bribed the stewards to call the Royal Suite with news on Bradley's or Lucas' or Teresa's comings and goings. "Help is invisible to the three of them, so they never even noticed."

We're all quiet a minute, and then I tell Kip, "We were worried about you, you know."

He nods. "And I'm sorry. Noah said he put a note under your door."

"Yeah, but it was typed. I figured if it was from you, you'd write it by hand."

"I probably would have," he says, "but I was still sort of freaked out by . . . by . . ."

"By what?" I ask.

He sort of looks away. "You know that night I hung out with you guys?"

"The night you disappeared?"

He nods. "I woke up at three in the morning, and my mother—well, Teresa—was standing over me with this really scary look on her face. It looked like she wanted to *kill* me. So I grabbed some stuff and went up to Aunt Ginger's, and that's when she told me that I was really adopted by my grandfather and was in his will to get a fourth of everything. She also told me what was going on." He shakes his head. "I was mad and happy and scared for my life and hugely relieved. . . . It was a really weird night."

"So are you going to start living with your grandparents?"

Marissa adds, "Who are legally your parents?"

"I can't call them anything but Grandmother and Grandfather," he says. "The whole thing is just too strange." Then he takes a deep breath and says, "But yes. We talked a lot the last two days. It's going to be really good."

After that, he wants to know how I'd figured out the

code, so I tell him, and when I'm all done, he shakes his head and goes, "I don't know *why* I didn't think of it. Grandfather couldn't believe none of us thought of it, either. He said it should have been obvious to any Kensington."

"Obvious?" I cry. "Please."

"I know. He was pretty upset when he said that. But he also said he wanted to see them put an effort in—to really work at something. And Grandmother was hoping the three of them would come together to solve it."

I frown and shake my head a little. "I think the only thing they worked together on was planning a forged suicide note."

"A what?"

So I catch him up on that little find, and then have to answer a bunch of other questions—like how come we locked Ginger and Noah on the balcony and how we got Bradley's copy of the coded note and stuff like that. And we wind up talking about the details of everything until finally Marissa says, "I am *not* going to a rock concert looking like this." She eyes me. "And you are not hauling along that backpack."

I laugh, because it's not the first time someone's told me I can't bring a backpack to a concert. "Right." And then I see how late it is. "Oh, wow! Let's go!"

It was definitely time to rock 'n' roll!

THIRTY-ONE

There should have been a big warning sign outside the theater that said NOW ENTERING COUGARVILLE. "Where did all these women come from?" I whispered as we tried to find seats together. They were all wearing the cougar uniform, too—jeans with rhinestone detailing, skanky tops, and way too much eyeliner.

And you could just tell from the energy in the room—they were die-hard groupies.

"I'm kinda grossed out," I tell Marissa.

"He loves your mom," she whispers back. And for some weird reason, that makes me feel a whole lot better.

We actually get good seats about three rows from the stage by asking one person to move over one seat. And if it was even possible, I think Kip was more excited than Marissa. "I can't wait to see him play!" he kept whispering, and it took him saying it a few times for me to realize he was talking about Marko, not Darren.

And then something very un–rock 'n' roll happened.

The Troublemakers started on time.

Christie introduced them, the curtain went up, and

from the moment Marko whacked out the intro beat, the audience was on its feet.

Cougars everywhere danced.

And so did we!

Kip played air drums and whistled through his fingers and was so excited that, at one point, Marissa and I looked at each other like, Who *is* this guy?

But for me, it was watching Darren that was surreal. I knew his music before I knew him, but I hadn't actually seen him play before. The way he interacted with the audience and the band . . . the way he got caught up in the words of a song and made you really *feel* them . . . it was easy to see why people loved him.

He was *awesome*.

Anyway, about an hour into the concert, Darren starts telling the audience, "Hope you don't mind—we're gonna try out a new song on you. This one's for my daughter, Sammy." Then he looks out through the lights and goes, "Hey, you little troublemaker, where are you?"

I put up a hand like I'm not quite sure of an answer in Ms. Rothhammer's class. But Kip puts his fingers to his lips and lets out a whistle, and Marissa waves like crazy with one hand while she points at me with the other and shouts, "Right here!"

So great. Every cougar in the place turns her eyeliner on me. But then Darren goes, "Here's 'Nothing but Trouble,'" and launches into a song about a girl who's nothing but trouble, trouble, trouble.

"He wrote a song about you!" Marissa cries.

"Who says he wrote it about me?" I shout back. "He just said it's for me, not that it's *about* me."

"Listen, you idiot!"

And when he hits the chorus, which goes, "Brought down hard, brought down fast, by a girl full of trouble and her heart of glass," I tell Marissa, "I don't have a heart of glass!"

"For someone so smart, you sure are stupid!" she yells in my ear. "That just means he knows not to break it. That you've been hurt before. By your *other* parent."

"You cannot get all of that out of those three words."

"Sure you can!" she says. "If you know the situation." Then she pulls away from me and says, "Now shut up and listen!"

So I do.

And the truth is, I don't really hear much of the end of the concert after that song. I'm too dazed by the truth behind what Marissa had said, and the thought that somehow, despite everything I'd muddled through the past few years, I've wound up *here*, on a cruise ship of all places, teary-eyed over the words of a song.

A song written just for me.

Backstage on a cruise ship is small. And full of cables and cases and random *stuff*. But Marissa and Kip thought it was amazing. Kip, especially, since we were right near the drums during the second show and he could watch every little thing Marko did.

Darren didn't do "Nothing but Trouble" again, and I was glad. And after their *third* standing ovation, the curtain came down, and Christie told the crowds about everything they could still squeeze into their night and what was on the calendar for "tomorrow's exciting day at sea!"

Drew and Cardillo were happy to go check out the hot spots, and took off after their gear was packed away. But Marko made Kip sit at the drum kit for a basic lesson, and after he got a boom-*pow,* boom-boom-*pow* groove down, Darren played part of a Troublemakers song with him, and we all sang along at the tops of our lungs.

I don't think I've seen a happier boy in my entire life.

"I told you," Marko said with a grin after they were done. "All he needed was to beat on some drums."

After that, Marko and Darren were only interested in one thing:

Food!

They didn't want to go up to the buffet because they didn't want to deal with any rock star stuff, so the five of us holed up in a corner at Le Petit Café on Deck 5 and ate lots of little sandwiches.

We spent time talking about how awesome the concerts were, and then Darren asked me to fill in the holes of the whole Kensington mess.

"And no skippy-doodlin' around!" Marko tells us. "That whole situation is confusing enough without you skippy-doodlin' around!"

So we fill in the blanks the best we can, and when we're all done, Darren shakes his head and goes, "That is one bizarre story." Then he turns to Kip and says, "So what are you going to do, do you know?"

"Get some drums," he says, grinning at Marko. Then

he looks back at Darren and says, "But seriously? I'll be staying with my grandparents. It'll be okay." He checks the time and says, "Actually, I should get up there. Old people go to bed so early."

I laugh, 'cause it's not exactly *early*. And not long after he's gone, the rest of us decide to hit the hay, too.

"I am *not* talking Kensingtons tomorrow," Marissa says on our way up the stairs. "I'm going rock climbing and ice-skating and swimming and golfing and . . . and anything else I can squeeze into our one last day on this ship." She gives the rest of us a stern look. "And you're coming with me!"

We all laugh and say we will, but when we get to Deck 8, it hits me that I still have homework and haven't messaged Casey.

"No!" Marissa says, when I say something about it. "N-O! You can do your stupid chemistry on the ride home. You'll have *tons* of time in the car."

Which is actually true. And, since I now know how to do the problems, doable.

"Okay. But I'm going to message Casey. You guys go up without me. I'll be fine."

But they follow me in, and the first thing we notice is that the puzzle is done.

No Puzzle Lady, just the finished puzzle with a paperback book on top of it.

Marissa picks up the book and admires the puzzle. "No missing pieces," she says. Then she looks at the book and gasps, " 'Sue Taylor'?"

"What about her?"

She hands me the book, and there on the cover in big bold letters is her name. "'*A Bad Place to Die*'?" I say, reading the title. "She's a *writer*?"

"Hey, I've heard of her!" Marko says, taking the book. "She's a mystery writer!"

"Hmm," Marissa says, peeking around him at the book. "That would explain why she can't leave a puzzle alone until she's solved it!" She grins at me. "Kind of like somebody else I know . . ."

Marko snickers. "This whole time she's probably been taking notes for her next novel."

"What?!" Marissa and I cry, but Marko gives us a mischievous shrug and says, "I've heard that's what writers do. They sit around watching people, then stick them in their twisted tales!"

"Give that to me, man," Darren says, and takes the book. And after he's looked it over, he opens it to where there's a little paper-scrap bookmark.

"What?" I ask, because he's grinning.

"For you," he says, handing it over, and when I look at the page, I see:

For Sammy—

> *Stay feisty and fearless.*
> *And keep your shoes on.*

Sue Taylor

"Wow!" I gasp.

Marissa reads the inscription, then takes the book from

me. "You cannot be up all night reading this. One mystery per cruise is one mystery too many!"

But then I notice that there's a web address written on the scrap of paper. So I show it to Marissa. "I wonder what this is about."

She laughs, "Well, that one's pretty easy to solve."

So we go over to a computer and log on, and when I type in the address, what pops up is the same picture that's on the puzzle.

Only it's not a picture of a puzzle.

It's a picture of a book.

Darren's looking over my shoulder and reads, " '*The Gold Bug*, by Edgar Allan Poe.' "

"How cool is that?" Marko says. "A famous mystery writer solving a mysterious puzzle that turns out to be a mystery book by another famous mystery writer."

Marissa laughs, "Put me out of my mystery!" which makes Marko cry, "Get me a corn husker!" which makes all of us crack up.

After we're done laughing, I ask, "Do I have time to check in with Casey?" and when Darren says sure, I message him and get all happy because Casey *is* online. I know the others are waiting for me, though, so I pretty much just tell him that I miss him and can't wait to see him.

And then we just go to bed.

I was smart enough to leave the curtain a little bit open, so I wasn't all weirded out in the morning. And I didn't have any bizarre dreams about numbers and letters. I actually woke up feeling great. And happy. And ready to pack in some fun!

Trouble is, it didn't feel like I could really forget about everything and have fun until I'd gone up to see Kate, like I'd promised. Plus Marissa had mentioned that we should invite Kip to do her fun list, so the first order of business of the day?

Kensingtons.

Marissa was all for getting it over with, and after we showered and got ready, we decided to let Marko and Darren sleep in and zipped up to the Royal Suite without them.

It was only nine o'clock, but I rang the bell anyway, telling myself that old people get up early.

Which, it turns out, they do.

At least in this case.

Kate answered, and when she saw it was us, she gave us a mega-carat smile. "Darlings! Come in!" We trailed along behind her, and she said, "Kip is still sleeping and John is off filling his lungs with sea air. Can I offer you something to drink?"

Marissa and I had made a pact that we would keep the visit short, so I said, "No thanks."

Ginger was sitting on the white furniture, having a cup of tea. "Good morning, girls," she calls, like the Infamous Balcony Incident never even happened.

"I'm sorry," I tell her. "About . . . you know."

She chuckles. "Well, all's well that ends well, right?" Then she switches subjects. "You two are up early."

Marissa jumps in, saying, "Well, this whole cruise we've

been kind of preoccupied with the, uh, *Kensington* situation, so we really need to make up for lost time today. Do some rock climbing, golfing, ice-skating . . . that sort of thing."

I nod. "So we thought we'd come here first thing."

"Well, have a seat, won't you?" Kate asks. "I promise we won't keep you long."

Which turned out to be a total lie, 'cause after she apologized for her "deceitful ploy to resolve some family issues" and explained some of the stuff that Kip had already told us, she wanted to know every little detail of every little thing.

Then behind us we hear a door open, and Kip sticks a groggy head out. "Hey!"

"We're getting breakfast and going rock climbing," Marissa tells him. "You want to come?"

"I'll be there in a minute!" he says. "Don't leave without me."

And since we're stuck for a little while longer, I ask Kate, "So what's going to happen with the family now?"

She heaves a sigh. "A lot came out last night. I never knew how much the kids resented us for our absences." She shakes her head and looks away. "Building a business takes commitment . . . but so does building a real family. We certainly gave the kids everything they ever dreamed of, but when your children all tell you they felt neglected, well, you should probably stop defending and start listening."

"Tell them about the hospital," Ginger says.

Kate nods. "Clearly, money won't fix us. So John and I have given them a choice. Either take active roles in the building of the hospital in Africa or be disinherited."

My eyebrows go shooting up. "Wait—you really are going to build a hospital?"

"You can't imagine what it's like over there," she says quietly. "And John and I both feel it's a much more fitting legacy for the family than acquiring more assets. None of the kids are suited to take over the business, and we're ready to do something really meaningful with our wealth. So the kids can be part of it or go off in their own direction." She eyes me. "The first requirement is to move to Africa."

"You're serious?"

"I am. John and I were both poor growing up, and so we gave our children everything we never had. So they never experienced poverty or hunger or even the joy of pulling yourself up in this world." She frowns. "I'd like to believe it's not too late to redeem them, but it's going to require a radical change. So John and I have decided to force them into a situation that will open their eyes—living in Africa will certainly do that. I know they'll resent us for the first few months—"

Ginger says, "Oh, Kate, it's going to take longer than that."

"And that's okay," Kate says with a nod. "If being in that environment doesn't give them a sense of perspective, if building the hospital doesn't give them a sense of higher purpose, then nothing will."

"So are they going to do it?" Marissa asks.

Kate smiles. "Knowing my children? They'll do it for the money. I'm just praying they'll come away with something much more valuable."

Kip comes hurrying out of his room, saying, "Thanks for waiting!"

Marissa and I laugh, because he's acting so . . . excited. And I guess Kate likes the change in him, because when we stand to go, she gives Marissa and me hugs. And as she pulls away from me, she holds me at arm's length for a minute and says, "Kip told me how hard you tried to help. . . . How can I ever thank you?"

I pull a little face and look at Ginger. "I think we can call it even. I did lock your sister out on the balcony."

Kate laughs. "I'm guessing you thought you might be the next ones to disappear?"

"Yes!"

"And you ransacked the place looking for me? And Kip?"

"Yes!"

"So see? I do owe you," she says with a little smile. "Anything. I'm serious. Just name it."

I kind of eye her, because right before I fell asleep last night, there was something I was wishing for, but they definitely don't sell it on board, and asking seems crazy.

She studies me. "What are you thinking?"

I just shake my head.

"Tell me!"

So I do.

And I explain it.

And she says, "Done."

I laugh and say, "You can't be serious," and Kip goes, "Oh, you don't know my grandmother."

Kate gives me a smile. "I'll have the delivery made to

your room. Now run along! Go have some fun!" Then she tells Kip, "Just be back in time for formal night! Our family is starting over tonight!"

So we jet out of there, and I'm thinking we're going to go straight up to the buffet, but Kip stops at the stairs and asks, "What about Marko and Darren?"

"Kind of early for rock guys to climb rocks," I tell him.

But Marissa agrees with Kip. "It's our last day. They can sleep later."

So the three of us beat on their door, and when Marko opens with a sleepyheaded "We on fire?" we all laugh and tell him, "Get up! We've got rocks to climb!"

"And clubs to swing!"

"And pools to invade!"

Marko looks worried. "Can we eat first?"

We laugh again and tell him we'll meet him up at the Schooner Buffet. "And no dippy-dawdlin' around!" I call as the door swings closed.

Up at the buffet, we spot JT sitting with his parents. "Whoa, he does not look happy," I whisper. But from the way they're all talking so seriously and from the huge dark cloud over JT's head, I can tell that Kate's right—they're actually going to move to Africa. And it hits me how ironic it is that Kip's grandfather brought him here to save him from a life of hunger and poverty, and now his own children are being told to move there to save them from lives of selfishness and greed.

Marissa grabs me and drags me along. "We are not thinking about or talking to any Kensingtons except Kip, you got that?"

So we sit as far away from JT's family as we can, and in no time we're joined by a couple of men in mustaches, dorky hats, and glasses. "Wow, that was quick," I tell them.

"Don't want to be missin' out," Darren says.

Turns out they did *everything* with us. From rock climbing to golf to ice-skating—which, believe me, was pretty entertaining to watch them do—to basketball and a cutthroat game of water hoops, Darren and Marko were there for every second.

Even if their mustaches did come off in the pool.

After that, Kip said he needed to get back because he had to figure out how to get his clothes and stuff for formal night.

When he took off, I eyed Marissa, because I knew she had to be scheming ways to get us to go to formal night. But she just eyed me back and said, "The buffet's fine," which brought a round of cheers from the rest of us.

So we just lay there, not worrying about anything, soaking in the late-day sun.

Which felt so good.

And *relaxing*.

And I'd actually been lying there long enough to be almost asleep when I hear Darren say, "I've been thinking."

He's in the lounger right next to mine, and sure enough, he's talking to me. "Yeah?"

"About your mother."

And here I was having such a good time.

"I could be pretty angry at her," he tells me, "for keeping you from me all these years."

I nod, and all of a sudden I'm realizing that, yeah, I *really* missed out.

Actually, I was *robbed*.

"But here's the thing," he says. "I like the person you are, and you wouldn't be you without the experiences you've had. You wouldn't be you without your grandmother's influence or your mother's lack of attention the last few years, or if you'd grown up as a rocker's daughter. You would be somebody else." He gives a little shrug. "And the truth is, I'm almost positive that I wouldn't respect and admire and *love* that person the way I do you."

All of a sudden, there's a big ball of cement in my throat. And I can't really *say* anything, so what comes out is a grunt.

I can be so articulate.

He doesn't seem to mind, though. He smiles at me and says, "So I'm not going to dwell on what she did wrong. I'm just going to focus on how you turned out and be grateful that you've come into my life."

Hearing him say that, I'm reminded that even though I always knew I had a dad, he had no idea he had a daughter—*who* he was was a surprise to me, but *that* he was wasn't. And for some reason what comes out of my mouth is, "I used to carry your catcher's mitt around with me everywhere."

He sits up and flips up his sunglasses. "*You* have that?"

"I found it in Grams' closet. It's the only connection I had to you. So I kept it with me all the time."

"Marko!" he calls across the loungers. "*She's* got my mitt!"

"Dude, no, you're serious?" He looks at me. "You have no idea the mourning he's gone through."

"Why?" I ask Darren.

"Marko and I were the battery on our baseball team, senior year. He was the pitcher, I was the catcher."

"Dude, I told you to ask Lana if she had it! Remember that? I told you."

"Yeah, you said it was probably a hate crime."

"See? *See?*" Marko says, pointing. "You should listen to me more."

I laugh, "Well, you can't have it back, because I actually use it—Marissa was pitcher and I was catcher on our school's team."

"You're serious?" Darren asks.

So Marissa jumps in with stories about our softball adventures—and believe me, there are some *wild* ones—and when we've talked *that* completely out, we all agree on one thing:

It's time to eat!

So once again we hit the buffet for dinner, and once again Marissa makes us check out the show at the Poseidon Theater afterward. We actually stick around for the whole thing, too, because the ventriloquist/puppeteer guy is hilarious.

"Not as good as us," Marko says on the way out, "but definitely worth the price of admission."

And then it's time to pack. And say good night. And

roll our luggage out into the hallway, where Marissa assures us it will mysteriously vanish and then safely reappear in a warehouse onshore when we "disembark."

Walking into our room, I feel really . . . sad.

Like I'm waking up from an amazing dream and realizing it was just that.

A dream.

And then I see the box on my bed.

"No!" I gasp. But there's no mistaking this box.

It says CONVERSE right on it.

Marissa's jaw drops and she says, "Wow, money talks, huh?"

I laugh, "No kidding!" I zip across the room and flip the lid open, and not only is there a pair of size 11 high-tops inside, there's a multipack of Sharpies. "Holy smokes."

"Well, I guess I know what you're going to be doing tonight," Marissa says. "You want me to do one?"

I shake my head.

And after I've done all my packing and everything I'm *supposed* to do, I sit cross-legged on my bed with Darren's shoes in my lap and totally choke up.

I mean, where do I start?

How do I say what he's become to me?

How do I say, *I love you, Dad?*

I just sit there for the longest time.

Then finally I uncap a black pen and take a deep breath.

Let the adventure begin.

Don't miss the final Sammy Keyes mystery!

Turn the page for a sneak peek.

A WARNING FROM WENDELIN

Let me start by saying I'm sorry.

I know you were expecting Sammy.

I know you were looking forward to her telling you all about some madcap escapade that had her braving short-cuts or snooping through basements or ditching bad guys.

Or cops.

I know you're here to laugh and race along with her as she gets into scrapes and trouble and finally finds her way back home.

She would be here if she could, but . . . she can't. And since everyone else is either too busy trying to help or having too much trouble dealing to let you know what's going on, you're stuck with me.

I'm having a lot of trouble, too, believe me. But I thought you should know. As hard as it is to hear, as much as it hurts to tell, you deserve to know what's happened to Sammy Keyes.

1—WEDNESDAY NIGHT

Holly is the one who found her.

There was a lot of screaming.

And crying.

And as we all know, Holly is not a screamer. Or a crier. But afterward people said that her wails surely woke the dead.

Unfortunately, they did not wake Sammy Keyes.

Holly saw the whole thing—or, at least, parts of the whole thing—and when Sergeant Borsch found *that* out, he became relentless. (Or, as Sammy would have said, like a dog with a bone.)

"From the beginning," he commanded Holly, as he pulled her into a chair in the emergency room. "Every detail."

Despite his tough-cop exterior, Sergeant Gilbert Borsch was, at the moment, a gun-slinging puddle of misery, his face etched deep with a single burning question:

Who did this?

(Well, there were other questions forming lines among those already present from years on the force—questions like Why? and When? and Where? and How? But the deepest, most painful crease was caused by the fiery rage of Who?)

Holly wasn't focused on Sergeant Borsch or his topographic face. She stared instead at the door through which Sammy's stretcher had been wheeled, and whimpered, "Is she going to be all right?"

Sergeant Borsch sucked on a tooth (an infamous habit cultivated before his doctor had suggested he quit with the pastrami and take up with turkey). Then he gruffed, "I'm not a doctor," which was cop code for No, or Probably not, or Don't get your hopes up—the latter being something Sergeant Borsch had learned was safer for his heart than optimism.

Or, regrettably, pastrami.

But suddenly Holly's adoptive mother, Meg Talbrook, was blasting through the door, wrapping Holly in her arms as she panted out incoherent phrases and fragmented clauses and hopelessly dangling modifiers.

And since Meg was a dog groomer, which was just *thiiiis* far away from being a veterinarian, which (as everyone suspects but won't actually say) is just *thiiiis* far away from being a doctor, and since there were, at that time, no doctors in attendance, Holly looked at her mother with desperate puppy-dog eyes and begged, "Tell me she's going to be all right."

The fragmented clauses suddenly ceased, Meg's shoulders squared back, and her solid frame jelled into a protective barrier between her daughter and reality. Then she held her daughter's face in her hands and lied with the unwavering conviction only a parent in crisis can muster. "She's going to be fine."

"It's bad, Mom. There was a lot of blood. She wouldn't wake up. She wouldn't . . . she was just . . ."

"Who are we dealing with here, *hmm*?" Meg asked, sitting beside her. "Have you ever known anyone to get the better of Sammy?" She lifted Holly's chin. "She was breathing, right? Her heart was beating, right?"

"I don't know! They put a mask on her and stuck tubes in her and told me to stay back."

Meg cast a wary eye on Sergeant Borsch, silently asking what he might know of the situation, but the best the Borschman could seem to do was, "She wasn't under a white sheet, that's all I know."

"Don't you have connections?" Meg whispered. "Can't you find out?"

"They'll come out when they know something. That's how this works. Me demanding information is gonna get us nothin' but stonewalled. What I need to find out, ma'am, is who did this. That's *my* job, and I really need your daughter's cooperation."

Meg turned to Holly, who looked down to collect her thoughts, but instead got caught up thinking about her shoes.

They were high-tops, just like Sammy's.

It used to be just Sammy who wore high-tops, but now a lot of kids at William Rose Junior High did. Even (to the administration's chagrin) some of the teachers. It was just one of those *things*. Something Sammy had started, not by trying, but by just standing up and *being*.

"Holly?" Sergeant Borsch rasped. "Holly, please."

But instead of coming out with who, what, where, when, or why, what Holly said was, "She saved my life, you know. That time at the riverbed? When that creep was coming after me? She took him down with her umbrella."

"That big black thing?" Meg asked. "You never told me that!"

"Please," Sergeant Borsch said again, desperate for them to discuss the past in the *future,* not now, when he was trying to deal with the present.

Holly took a deep, choppy breath, held it for a moment, then said, "She was on her way home."

"Home?" Sergeant Borsch asked. "But that makes no sense! This happened at the Highrise!"

As you're probably aware, Sergeant Borsch is not known for his tact or his patience. And although he *is* a more tactful and patient man now than he was as a street-beat officer when Sammy first met him, these characteristics would need major work should he ever aspire to reach the rank of lieutenant. Or captain. Or (pray for the City of Santa Martina) chief.

So it came as no surprise to Holly that after just one short sentence Sergeant Borsch had already interrupted her, but Meg was not so accustomed to the lawman's brusque ways. "The girls had been studying for exams," she began.

"At the Pup Parlor?" Sergeant Borsch interjected, again interrupting after a single sentence.

"At our apartment above the business," Meg said. "It

was after nine and dark outside. I was heading off to take a shower before bed and told Sammy she should get home before her grandmother began to worry."

"But her grandmother no longer lives in the Highrise!"

Despite his propensity for interruptions, Sergeant Borsch's confusion was actually understandable. Not so long ago Sammy had lived illegally with her grandmother on the fifth floor of Santa Martina's only government-subsidized housing for seniors—the Senior Highrise (clearly named in a moment of unrivaled creative genius).

And although the secret of Sammy's residence had never been openly discussed, the Borschman had figured it out and immediately wished he hadn't. How could he let this girl continue to sneak up and down the fire escape and sleep on her grandmother's couch when doing so was clearly against the law?

It was the first time in his career that Officer Borsch had consciously looked the other way, convincing himself that there were bigger wrongs in this world than a kid sleeping on an old lady's couch.

Still, no one was more relieved than Gil Borsch when Sammy's grandmother married the straight-shooting Hudson Graham, and the lawbreakers and their cat took up legal residence with him on Cypress Street.

But that move had occurred months earlier, which is why (despite his abrasive demeanor and propensity for interruption) it was legitimate for an investigating officer to ask, "What was Sammy doing at the Highrise?" and ask it he did.

Holly's head quivered side to side. "She said something about the Nightie-Napper."

The creases in Sergeant Borsch's face deepened. Especially the ones above and between his eyebrows. Entire rivers could have coursed through them without hazarding overflow. "The Nightie-Napper?"

Holly nodded. "It bugged her that she never figured out who the Nightie-Napper was."

"So this . . . this *Nightie-Napper* did this to her?"

"No!" Holly's head quivering resumed. "At least I don't think so!"

Again, it was Meg who came to the rescue. "Holly, sweetheart," she said with a soothing voice, "we don't understand what you're talking about. Explain what a nightie-napper is."

"The Nightie-Napper has been stealing stuff out of the dryers in the basement at the Highrise. They've been doing it for a long time."

"Stuff?" Meg prompted. "Like . . . nightgowns?"

Holly shrugged. "And muumuus."

"Muumuus," Sergeant Borsch moaned. "What has this—"

Because Meg was a woman of both internal and external substance, it took a simple STOP hand signal for her to shut him down. Then she continued coaxing information from her obviously traumatized daughter. "Is the Nightie-Napper someone you think might try to kill a fourteen-year-old girl?"

Holly's eyes pinched closed. "The Nightie-Napper doesn't have anything to do with this!"

Sergeant Borsch's hands flew skyward. "Then why are you—"

STOP went Meg's hand again. And like a Rottweiler warning off an intruder, her eyes locked with his and her lips peeled back ever so slightly as she growled, "She'll get to it."

And after a little head bobbing and recollecting and sorting and thinking, Holly did indeed get to it. "Sammy talked about the Nightie-Napper. She also wondered if her gum was still in the fire-escape doorjamb. She was trying to picture what the new neighbor was like. Her name's Violet, and Sammy thought that was strange."

"Why strange?" Meg asked, but then with a laugh she got it. "Oh! First Daisy, then Rose, now Violet!"

"Exactly." Holly took a deep breath, then continued. "It seemed like she missed the place. I told her she should take me there someday, because I'd never been inside, and after all the stories she'd told, I really wanted to sneak up the fire escape and peek down the hallway and hide out in the basement and maybe catch the Nightie-Napper red-handed."

Now, an ordinary parent might have filed this particular conversation away in her mental To Be Discussed folder, but Meg was no ordinary parent. She had taken the runaway Holly in, saving her from a life of homelessness, and no sleuthing adventure through a seniors building would (or could) come close to the dangers Holly had already faced.

Besides, this wasn't about going places you shouldn't. This was about Sammy.

So Meg simply waited for Holly to continue, needing to employ only one STOP signal to quell Sergeant Borsch's questions before Holly's focus returned.

"After she left, I watched her through the window. She rode her skateboard up to Main Street and crossed Broadway, only when she got to the other side she didn't cross again and go toward Hudson's the way she always does. She just stood looking over at the Highrise for a little while. Then she rode down Main and disappeared into the bushes like she used to when she lived at the Highrise."

Meg asked her daughter a question that Gil Borsch would never in a million years have thought to ask: "Did that upset you?"

Holly's head bobbed. "Yes! I'd *just* talked to her about wanting to go there with her—why couldn't she wait for sometime when I could go, too?"

"So you watched to see if she really was going up the fire escape?"

"Yes! And she did! And at first I was really mad!"

"But then?"

"But then I saw someone start up the stairs after her."

"And . . . ?"

"And . . . and they were moving fast. Like they were chasing her. I called her cell phone to warn her, but her phone started ringing in our kitchen! So I opened the window and yelled for her to watch out, but that was hopeless because of the traffic. And then there was a big struggle and I saw Sammy fall off the fire escape." Her eyes welled with tears. "It was the third floor, Mom. Nobody can survive that."

"There were bushes," Meg assured her.

Even in that moment Holly recognized the irony of Meg's statement. Bushes had been a big part of Sammy's duck-and-cover routine. Bushes had concealed her from foes and cops alike. Bushes had been her primary spy spot, and once again, she had landed in them.

Only this wasn't funny.

Not funny at all.

But pondering the irony of bushes provided a silence and, consequently, a long-awaited entry into the conversation for Sergeant Borsch. "How would you describe this person who followed Sammy up the stairs?" he asked. "Tall? Short? Thin? Hefty?"

Holly thought a moment, then shook her head. "Kind of medium."

If there's one answer Sergeant Borsch has been known to ridicule, it's "kind of medium." But this time it didn't seem to even register on his finely calibrated annoyance meter, and he just went on. "Man? Woman?"

Holly hesitated. "I figured it was a man, but . . . but . . . I guess it *could* have been a woman."

"Hair? Clothing?"

"It was dark! I don't know!"

"Where did the assailant go? Up? Down?"

"I don't know! I saw Sammy fall and I screamed and called 911!"

"How'd you know it was Sammy falling and not the other person?"

"Her backpack! She was wearing her backpack!"

The three of them sat there, Holly in tears, Meg trying to comfort her, and Sergeant Borsch numbed to the core.

He had nothing.

Nothing to work with.

Not a single clue.

2—THE SWINGING DOOR
OF (MAYBE) DEATH

News travels fast in the digital age, and not long after Holly smacked Sergeant Borsch with the one-two punch of Don't Know and Not Sure, teenagers started coming through the emergency-room door.

The first one on the scene was Heather Acosta.

"Where is she?" she panted, looking around wildly as if Sammy were her best friend, instead of the girl she'd tortured and *wished* dead for well over a year.

Holly groaned at the sight of her. She was not (and would likely never be) convinced that Heather was sincere in her newfound enthusiasm for Sammy. And despite Sammy's willingness to let bygones be bygones, Holly was not one to forget Heather Acosta's long history of deceit and revenge (not to mention brazen backstabbing). It was hard for her to believe that three "shell-shocking" days in Las Vegas had really changed Heather.

But there Heather was, panting and gushing concern, her red hair flashing like a squad-car light as she spun around, searching for Sammy. "She's not . . . ," she said, her voice trailing off as she cast her wide eyes on Holly, Meg, and Sergeant Borsch.

And since Holly, Meg, and Sergeant Borsch each held similar suspicions about Heather, none of them jumped up with assurances that Sammy would be all right. They simply stared.

What this lack of assurance triggered in Heather was a crumpling at the knees and a scream so fierce and pathetic and *loud* that emergency-room personnel began appearing to see if anyone was being stabbed in the waiting room (something that was, unfortunately, not unheard of at Santa Martina's Community Hospital).

"Stop it!" Holly shouted at Heather. "We don't know anything yet!"

But Heather was folded into herself on the floor, so deafened by her own primal wailing that she didn't hear what Holly was saying.

And then Casey Acosta came blasting in and saw (and heard) his sister wailing on the floor, which immediately set him falling into the same pit of despair as his life with Sammy flashed before his eyes.

The tortured look on his face could have broken the heart of Death himself. If Death was around. Which nobody really knew at that point. (Although in the emergency room the odds were alarmingly high.)

What Casey's reaction *did* do was kick Holly into gear. "No one's said she's dead yet!" Holly shouted, jumping out of her seat. "They're still working on her!"

This did a nice job of shutting Heather up, but it didn't happen fast enough for Nurse Cathy Abbey, who came ramming through the main interior door, shouting, "You need to SHUT UP out here!" Her jeans were a tired blue, her shoes a scuffed white, and the geometric designs on her smock were a telling sign of her impersonal approach to patient care.

"Is there any news?" Holly asked.

"When there's news, we'll tell ya!" Nurse Abbey snapped, then withdrew through the emergency room's swinging door of fate.

"So she's not . . . ," Heather asked, looking up from her crumpled position on the floor.

"We don't know!" Holly snapped, and then to her enormous relief, Marissa McKenze rushed in from outside, followed almost immediately by Billy Pratt.

Marissa and Billy were tried-and-true friends. Maybe not with each other, seeing how Marissa had dumped Billy for the smooth-talking Danny Urbanski, breaking Billy's heart for at least a week. But Billy and Marissa had been through the thick of things with Sammy, and that's what mattered now.

"What's *she* doing here?" Marissa seethed after Holly had given all of them a quick recap. Like Holly, Marissa trusted Heather about as far as she could throw a tiger. "And who is she texting?"

"She's not just texting," Holly said, craning a little to see better. "She's posting."

"What? No! Tell her to stop! We don't want a bunch of people here!"

But the reality was, neither Holly nor Marissa knew how to tell Heather to stop. The only person who seemed to be able to reason with Heather was Sammy . . . and sometimes Casey.

But Casey was fighting back tears as he whispered with Billy, and Marissa didn't have the heart to interrupt their conversation to ask him to deal with something she could do herself. Even though she couldn't.

Meg had noted Heather's flurry of phone activity, too, and saw a different sort of downside. She leaned over and asked Sergeant Borsch, "Does Sammy's grandmother know what's happened?" The question was met with the blank look of a man in shock, so she added, "Rita's the guardian—I'm sure they'll need her here. And someone really should tell her before the rumor mill does." Then, since the lawman still seemed too stunned to take action, she offered, "If you have her number, I could call her."

Gil Borsch did, in fact, have the number, but even through the daze of his despair he knew this was not the sort of thing he should break to Rita over the phone. So he pulled himself together and stood, saying, "I'll tell her in person." Then he gave his cell number to Meg so she could call him if there were any developments and hauled his heavy heart outside.

On the short ride over to Cypress Street, it occurred to Sergeant Borsch that he was the very worst person for this job. Since the facts were sketchy and the outcome uncertain, he didn't know what to say. The situation was a gray on gray, and Gil Borsch worked best when things were black on white.

So he called his wife. However, instead of acknowledging that he really needed to talk to somebody, he convinced himself he was doing it because she would want to know. After all, Deb was a huge fan of Sammy's. She'd even asked Sammy to be a bridesmaid in their wedding! Never mind that Sammy had almost *ruined* the wedding with one of her daredevil escapades—that was beside the point. Deb loved her and would want to know.

Plus, he could try this breaking-the-news thing out on her.

Unfortunately, it did not go well.

Not due to Deb's reaction.

Due to his.

Besides breaking down while breaking the news, Gil Borsch also broke the hands-free law while making the call—something he'd been quick to ticket other drivers for doing.

So after hanging up he felt both broken up *and* dirty—worse off by far than he'd been before he'd made the call.

But as awful as he felt (and as raw and red as his eyes now looked), he was already at the Cypress Street residence, and really, there was no turning back from duty. Especially since Rita and Hudson were both sitting on the porch, presumably waiting for Sammy's postcurfew return.

Sergeant Borsch appearing at the Cypress Street residence (either via squad car or in his personal vehicle, which he now drove) was not, in and of itself, cause for concern for Hudson or Rita. The two had grown to know (and even like) the lawman, especially since he seemed to keep a weather eye out for Sammy and had delivered her home safely from one tangle or another more often than they cared to recall.

This time, however, neither the front nor back passenger door of Gil Borsch's car swung open.

This time, no skateboard or backpack or high-tops emerged.

This time, Hudson was the first to realize, something was wrong.

"Sergeant?" he called, hurrying down the porch steps as Rita followed closely behind.

So, with a fumbling of words and barely checked emotions, Sergeant Borsch managed to convey the crucial points:

Sammy was hurt.

Badly hurt.

They needed to get to the hospital.

Now.

Old people are not known for their quick movements. But these two seniors became instant Olympic contenders, dashing and leaping and propelling into the house and out again, as they snatched up keys and cash and insurance cards and dived into the Borschman's car without invitation.

Gil Borsch just went with it. He jumped in behind the wheel, slapped his portable spinning light onto the roof, and gunned it back to the hospital.

The car was still rolling when Rita and Hudson (apparently still vying for slots in the Olympics) bolted out and dashed for the emergency-room door, leaving Sergeant Borsch to find legal parking on his own.

Once through the door, Rita and Hudson skidded to a halt.

It was as though William Rose Junior High School were conducting an assembly in the waiting room.

Only there was no presenter.

Just chaos.

"QUIET!" a voice across the room bellowed, and when Rita looked for who had made the sound, she saw a bullish woman with bulging eyes. "WHERE'S THE LEGAL GUARDIAN FOR SAMANTHA KEYES?" Nurse Abbey shouted.

"Right here!" Rita called, holding up her hand.

The flash mob of teens turned to face her. And while they didn't break into a spontaneous rendition of Queen's "Bohemian Rhapsody," they were clearly in a Bohemian Rhapsody state of mind, parting to let this older woman through as they wondered, *Is this the real life? Is this just fantasy? Caught in a landslide, no escape from reality . . .*

Then they watched the guardian and the nurse disappear behind the Swinging Door of (Maybe) Death.